EARLY PRAISE

"Congratulations on *The Menu*. I wish you all the best with it. Continue to use your gifts to glorify God!"

— Matthew West, Christian Singer/Songwriter, *Mended*

"Steven Manchester's *The Menu* is an inspirational tale that proves love can come in many different forms. Poignant and heartfelt, *The Menu* teaches us that the heart often sees clearer than the eyes. I highly recommended it!"

— Betty J. Eadie, #1 *NYT* & International Bestselling Author, *Embraced by the Light*

"Why are we here on earth? What happens when we die? And where is God? These are humankind's most important and enduring questions. *The Menu* brings a fresh and exciting perspective to these ancient questions. Consistent with what I've found in my near-death experience research, this book presents very real and powerfully inspiring messages about human life and the glorious afterlife. This outstanding book is well written and enthusiastically recommended."

— Dr. Jeffrey Long, *NYT* Bestselling Author, *Evidence of the Afterlife: The Science of Near-Death Experiences*

"*The Menu* is a tender parable of love, loss, faith, skepticism, and the results of getting what we ask for. In the masterful hands of Steven Manchester, the story soars with inspiration, while remaining beautifully rooted in the fierce challenges of everyday life. *The Menu* is the perfect book to share with a friend. Bravo!"

— Anne Hillerman, *NYT* Bestselling Author, *Cave of Bones*

"Steven Manchester wields the pen of a poet. With vivid scene settings and believable dialogue spoken from unforgettable characters that jump right off the page, *The Menu* is a page-turner that kept me up late into the night!"

> – Dannion Brinkley, *NYT* & International Bestselling Author,
> *Saved by the Light* and *Peace in the Light*

"In *The Menu*, Steve Manchester writes a personal development book disguised as a novel. In it, he gives us the keys to love, happiness, and life purpose. Steve grabs your attention in the first chapter and draws you in, as he both eloquently and effortlessly teaches his readers about love and struggle through the lives of Phinn and Maddie. I want ALL my friends and loved ones to read *The Menu*."

> – Bearj Jehanian, Author of *Break Down the Walls to Success* and
> *America's #1 Transformational Speaker and Trainer*

"Steven Manchester writes like Nicholas Sparks on steroids *The Menu* serves up a unique, uplifting tale of both first and second chances and the role fate plays in all of our lives. Manchester pulls out all the stops in taking us on a spiritual journey that proves anything is possible when love is involved. In *The Menu*, he has crafted a book that resonates in the soul as well as the mind, its powerful message lingering long after you turn the final page. This is storytelling of the highest order, as eye-opening as it is mind-bending."

> – Jon Land, *USA Today* Bestselling Author, *Murder,*
> *She Wrote* series

"*The Menu* addresses some of life's biggest concerns from a very thoughtful and creative perspective."

> – Brian Fox, Renowned Artist – *www.brianfoxstudios.com*

"I loved *The Menu*. This beautifully written book about life's challenges, love and soulmates is a real gem. Guaranteed to evoke many emotions, it will make you smile and make you cry, but it will also uplift you with its deep spiritual wisdom. *The Menu* is a truly beautiful story, and Steven Manchester is a very gifted author."

> – Dr. Penny Sartori, International Bestselling Author, *The Wisdom of Near-Death Experiences*

"Steve Manchester has given us an intriguing glimpse into the unknowable, exploring heavenly mysteries in a down-to-earth fashion. Some very tasty things are on *The Menu!*"

> – Rick Beyer, *NYT* Bestselling Author, *The Greatest Stories Never Told*

"Steven Manchester is a gifted storyteller who knows exactly how to pull at the heartstrings. Typical of his life-changing journeys of self-discovery, his devoted fans will find much to love in his new novel."

> – Julianne MacLean, *USA Today* Bestselling Author, *The Color of Heaven*

"In *The Menu*, Steven Manchester takes us on a journey we have not likely travelled before. There are surprises all along the way, as his protagonist, Phinneas Reed, forges his path through life. Becoming the man he was destined to be, Phinn must examine not only the hearts of those around him—but his own. He finds that the deepest mysteries lie within himself. Manchester finishes his story with a suspenseful ending that will not only satisfy the reader but might make him or her take a deeper look into their own heart."

> – Donna Foley Mabry, *NYT* Bestselling Author, *The Cabin*

"As a seasoned hospice professional, I've had the honor of being present for countless existential conversations among patients and families, and I can affirm that spiritual awareness is never more present than at the end of life. Steven Manchester uniquely intertwines eternal life, love, and faith with purpose-filled earthly missions through the endearing characters' own triumphs and heartaches. The characters spiritual journeys—before, during, and after life on earth—are sure to spark some very timely and hopeful existential discussions, something good for all of our souls."

     – Catherine Dehlin, RN, BSN, CHPN, CHCM, *Fazzi Associates*

"Steven Manchester's *The Menu* reminds us of the importance of having faith and living life to the fullest. This lovely story will resonate deep within your soul."

     – Linda Pynaker, Renowned Psychic Medium and Author,
     www.lindapynaker.com

"Steve Manchester's *The Menu* is a story of transcendental inspiration. It is a legacy to his heirs and a lesson to all humankind. In *The Menu*, Manchester eloquently shows us that life is a balance sheet, a yin and a yang, and that if we are to live a life well-lived, we must balance our own personal life's ledgers. And we must leave this world a better place than we found it. A truly thought-provoking story of love, faith, and one man's greater power."

     – Sue Nedar, Founder & President, *Footlights Repertory Co.*

"The Norman Rockwell of Literature, Steven Manchester has bared his soul in the intense story, *The Menu*. Extraordinary in its inspiration, it is heartening, exalting, and above all, thought-provoking. *The Menu* is a gift of uplifting hope but more importantly, unwavering love."

     – Shannon Gonzalez, Book Blogger, *Literarily Illumined*

"Steven Manchester plumbs the depth of his emotional core with his latest release, *The Menu*. He paints an imaginative personal journey for his protagonist, Phinn Reed, which is both painful and glorious. Manchester explores the true nature of love, faith, trust, and man's emotional relationship with God. His depiction of heaven is beautiful, comforting, and creative; but make sure you have a full box of Kleenex at hand. If you liked *The Shack*, then *The Menu* is a must read. Steven Manchester does not disappoint."

– John Lansing, Bestselling Author, *The Fourth Gunman*

"Steve Manchester's book, *The Menu*, has had a marked influence on my life. His poetic emphasis that we are never alone is profound. If wit and wisdom, style and spiritual insights are the foundation to a great book, then Mr. Manchester has created a masterpiece. For anyone trying to expand their spiritual journey but find that your intellect is getting in the way, this may be the door opener you are looking for; *The Menu* is a gateway to embracing the infinite love of God, who is always there for us—before, during, and after our lives on earth."

– Claude Tetreault, Hospice Companionship Volunteer,
Tetreault Advertising – www.tetreaultagency.com

"Steven Manchester has done it again with *The Menu*! This author always draws me in. I can never read one of his books quickly enough to find out how it's going to end. Then when I do get to the end, I want the story to just keep going."

– Nancy Jones, Book Blogger, *Sunny Island Breezes*

"Steven Manchester's work will make you laugh and cry, and flip through descriptive pages deep into the night."

– Robert Dugoni, *NYT* and #1 Amazon Bestselling Author,
My Sister's Grave

"*The Menu* by Steven Manchester is a brilliant, spiritual story that brought tears to my eyes. Its storyline is filled with memorable moments that touched my soul. Once again, Mr. Manchester has proven that he is a master at writing thought-provoking, wholesome stories that you are always sorry to see end."

— Diane Moyle, Book Blogger, *Book Bug Blog*

"*The Menu* is a captivating take on life, love, and what it means to truly have faith. Author Steven Manchester delivers a story that will move the most devout or loosely attributed amongst us, taking us through all stages of the human condition with his trademark humor and heart. With passages that will move you from laughter through tears, and a message that not only assures us everything will be alright, but that even in our darkest hours, we're never really alone, this is another great addition to this author's body of work and a must-have on your bookshelf."

— Gina Reba, Book Blogger, *Satisfaction for Insatiable Readers*

"*The Menu* has it all—love, loss, intrigue, suspense, redemption, and a satisfying ending after having our hearts crushed. I was brought to tears at several points throughout. But while it reads like an adventure—and such a good one—the over-arcing theme is more elevated than that. While this is crafted as fiction—and crafted well, I must add—there is a core of truth that weaves through this novel from beginning to end. It is a story that will stay with you long after you are finished reading it and have you thinking, 'Okay, it's a story, but I think our relationship with God is actually *like* that.' I thought about this book long after I finished reading it. That is a sign of a good story and this is certainly true of *The Menu*."

— Dr. Laurin Bellg, Bestselling Author, *Near Death in the ICU*

"*The Menu* by Steven Manchester is a beautiful tale of love, of faith in living, and of choosing to embrace our choices to the fullest. It is a love story we can all identify with—with its ups, downs, pain, and the greatest rewards of all. Manchester's characters are simple and human; and one can feel the love they are desperate to share. A powerful, yet simply-told romance of faith restored, love grown, and lives shared."

    – Dianne Bylo, Book Blogger, *Tome Tender*

"*The Menu* has taken Steven Manchester's storytelling to a new level; his gift of words has a way of reminding us of our humanity and how each decision we make not only affects us—but affects those around us and those that come after us. What a fantastic book, making me catch my breath with each page turned. *The Menu* should not only be on the top of your to-read list, but in your hands!"

    – Donna McBroom-Theriot, Book Blogger, *My Life – One Story at a Time*

"What is most beautiful in *The Menu* is that this life account is one of credible sincerity, truth, compassion, recognition of frailties and strengths, and acceptance of whatever comes. Loving honesty seems the integral quality that makes this novel an intimate, endearing, and engaging story every reader will love. Fine, fine writing!"

    – Viviane Crystal, Book Blogger, *Crystal Book Reviews*

"Steven Manchester has hit another home run. I absolutely loved *The Menu*."

    – Robert Denson, Editor, *Sunpiper Press Book Review*

"*The Menu* exudes a powerful message that opens the mind to the true meaning and gift of life."

    – Deborah Beauvais, Radio Personality, *Love by Intuition, Dreamvisions 7 Radio*

"*The Menu* gives us a new look at life and how we live it. It really comes down to choices—choices made before we even come to earth. Steven Manchester provides us with so much wisdom and clues to surviving life's disappointments and sorrows. What we survive now will make us stronger and make us appreciate what we finally achieve. Faith will help in our successes. *The Menu* is filled with true emotion that will have you cheering and crying along with Phinn. Another one not to be missed; pick up *The Menu*. Read it and savor it—then read it again."
  – Debby Guyette, Book Blogger, *Single Titles*

"*The Menu* is an amazingly inspirational story that simply stirred my soul. All of Steven Manchester's books have touched me in one way or another, but there is something about this story that had me experiencing the full gamut of emotions. *The Menu* will stay with me for a very long time."
  – Kathleen Anderson, Book Blogger, *Jersey Girl Book Reviews*

"*The Menu* is a beautiful story that takes us on a poetic journey through the circle of life, death, and love. An inspiring read."
  – Andrea Hurst, Bestselling Author, *The Guestbook*

"In *The Menu*, Steven Manchester has gifted us with a fresh expression of the possible relationship with God, free will, and a fear-free perspective on death available to all people. Through the sweet voyage of a couple finding eternal love, we realize life doesn't end, love doesn't end—death does not possess the power to eradicate either."
  – Melissa Corliss DeLorenzo, Author, *The Mosquito Hours* and *Talking Underwater*

"Steven Manchester is a gifted storyteller. *The Menu* is an awesome read."
— Joyce Hart, Inspirational Literary Agent, *Hartline Literary Agency*

"*The Menu* by Steven Manchester presents an honest and at times overtly personal exposition of faith, beliefs, choices, judgement and emotions at the purest of levels."
— L.P. King, Publisher, *Mountain Mist Productions, Australia*

"I loved *The Menu*. Steven Manchester's tongue-in-cheek sense of humor is wonderful!"
— Martha Bolton, Award-Winning Author, *The Home Game*

"Steven Manchester has delivered once again; this time, in *The Menu*, a fabulous story that teaches us that love and death aren't to be feared, but to be treasured. Manchester's books are always so well written, but this one takes his skills to a whole new level—causing us to wonder about our own lives and beliefs."
— Paula Mitchell, Book Blogger, *Community Bookstop*

"*The Menu* is absolutely amazing, capturing the essence of the human soul. I felt so connected to every word in this book and believe anyone who reads it will feel the way. Life is meaningless without love. God has truly gifted Steve Manchester."
— Laura Ferreira Washington, Radio Personality & Author, *A Sickness You Can't See*

The Menu

by

Steven Manchester

For my grandchildren, whom I've yet to meet

ACKNOWLEDGMENTS

First and forever, Jesus Christ—my Lord and Savior. With Him, all things are possible.

Paula, my beautiful wife, for loving me and being the amazing woman she is.

My children—Evan, Jacob, Isabella and Carissa—for inspiring me.

Dad, Mom, Billy, Julie, Caroline, Caleb, Randy, Kathy, Philip, the Baker girls, Darlene, Jeremy, Baker, Aurora, Jen, Jason, Jack, Lucas, the DeSousa's, Laura—my beloved family.

My talented and generous BETA Team: Dan & Sue Aguiar, Darlene Ballard, Sue Bishop, Stephanie Borden Brown, Jason & Jen Fazzina, Brian Fox, Bella Manchester, Evan Manchester, Jacob Manchester, Paula Manchester, Russ McCarthy, Sue Nedar, Brandt Swanson, Claude Tetreault, Hen Zannini.

Lou Aronica, my mentor and friend.

My life has been richly blessed for having known each one of you.

AUTHOR'S NOTE

The Menu has been a labor of love for me, sharing an intimate expression of my faith journey through all its bumps, warts, and exhilarations.

Like my grandfather before me, I am a storyteller—period. With *The Menu*, I'm not looking to challenge anyone's spiritual belief system, nor am I attempting to rewrite dogma. Instead, I'm simply telling a story that has the passionate potential to connect each and every one of us at a very basic level—melding the spiritual and human aspects of our core existence. "None of us are ever alone." I believe this truth in every fiber of my being. For me, few things are more tragic than a fellow human being who is feeling alone. Hence, *The Menu.*

The spiritual journey is a personal one for me; I am not only a believer but a follower. That said, I did not write *The Menu* to recruit. I penned *The Menu* to connect, while also sharing my vision of "going home" and how the miracle of death should be no more feared than the blessing of birth.

My ultimate hope is that the sharing of this message will bring comfort to you, all our children and, hopefully, their children too.

Wm. Paul Young, author of the soul-awakening novel, *The Shack*, recently told me, "Grace to you on your adventure…and the constant sense of relentless affection."

I sincerely wish the same for you.

Enjoy the journey!

Steve Manchester

"You are never alone—not ever.
Nothing could be more impossible."
                                    – God

According to the Meriam-Webster Dictionary, the definition of *menu* is *(a) a list of the dishes that may be ordered (as in a restaurant) or that are to be served (as at a banquet); (b) comparable list or assortment of offerings.*

What the definition fails to reveal is that Merriam-Webster was inspired by a higher power.

The Menu

ENTRÉE	PRICE
LOVE	APATHY
HONOR	DISGRACE
JOY	SORROW
COURAGE	COWARDICE
HOPE	DESPAIR
FAITH	DISBELIEF
HUMILITY	ARROGANCE
SERENITY	FEAR
TRUST	CORRUPTION
CONFIDENCE	DOUBT
PEACE	CHAOS
FRIENDSHIP	ANIMOSITY
DIGNITY	LOW SELF-ESTEEM
HONESTY	IMMORALITY
COMPASSION	FRIGIDITY
KINDNESS	CRUELTY
CONSIDERATION	INCONSIDERATION
LOYALTY	DISLOYALTY
RESPECT	DISRESPECT
GOOD HEALTH	ILLNESS
WEALTH	POVERTY
INTELLIGENCE	IGNORANCE
STRENGTH	WEAKNESS
BEAUTY	*MARKET VALUE*

CHAPTER 1

It was eternal dawn. Two silhouettes stood in the soft light of a cloud. Through the veil of fog, the taller shadow handed the other a thin book and patted him on the shoulder. The gold embossed, burgundy cover was the approximate size of a menu. Amid the faint sound of birds chirping and a whistling wind, the silhouettes remained faceless.

Gently and lovingly, God wrapped his arm around Phinn's shoulder. "This is your life. Order whatever you wish, but keep in mind—whatever you choose to taste, you have to finish," He told Phinn before sending him into the world.

Nodding anxiously, Phinn started flipping through the menu. As he read, God continued in a serious whisper, "And you should also know that others have made their own choices." There was a pause. "Choices that are different from those you'll pick."

"I understand," Phinn replied, though there was no way he ever could. As he scanned all of the possibilities within the giant menu, his excitement took over. "Whatever I wish?" he asked.

The tall silhouette nodded. "Yes."

"I want the love of family and friends," Phinn read from the menu.

"That's fine," God interrupted, "but first your gender."

"Huh? I don't follow you."

"The spirit has no gender, but on earth you must be either a man or a woman. Which will it be?"

"A man," Phinn quickly announced. "I want to be a good man."
He nodded in confirmation.

"A good man," God echoed, returning the nod. "That's a wonderful start."

"I love poetry," Phinn hurried, "and I'd also like to create or design things, you know?"

God smiled. "I've always loved the act of creation myself."

"And it's important that I know compassion," Phinn added.

"It's yours, but not before experiencing pain and suffering," God answered.

Glancing up at his Father, Phinn gave it some thought. "Sure, I'll accept pain and suffering for compassion."

God nodded.

"I also wish to have commitment and wisdom and…"

"Good choices, Phinn, but not before conquering trials and tribulations."

Phinn looked up from the menu again. "And courage?" he asked.

"After overcoming fear."

"Honor?"

"Once you have faced shame."

"Success?" Phinn asked.

"Much failure," God answered.

Phinn stared at his master before closing the book and handing it back. "I can't have any of the good without the bad, can I?"

"Sure, it's called love; and no matter what you do, I'll always love you," God promised. "Pretty clever design, don't you think?"

Phinn nodded.

God squeezed Phinn's shoulder with His great hand. "You're given one life, Phinn, and as my child you inherit all things. Everything is yours." He smiled. "Don't you want to experience all that I've created, and experience everything that you'll create yourself?"

"I do," Phinn responded, robustly.

"Very well then, you will taste it all. But before your journey begins, you must tell me your purpose."

"I don't understand," Phinn said.

"What will be the reason for your human experience?" God asked, patiently.

There was a dramatic pause. "More than anything," he answered with great joy and confidence, "I want to find my soul mate."

Smiling wide, God embraced Phinn and then kissed him on the cheek. "Excellent," He said, handing Phinn a book. "This is yours."

Phinn lifted the book to eye level. "What am I supposed to do with this?"

"It is your life's ledger." God explained, removing His arm from Phinn's shoulder. "Your accounting."

"Forgive me, Father, but I don't understand."

"Your life is the greatest gift you'll ever receive. And the greatest sin you can ever commit is to squander that gift. Along with your life, I am also giving you free will to make your own choices." He raised one eyebrow. "Kindness or cruelty, integrity or corruption—each decision will be yours alone to make. But free will also carries accountability." He gestured toward the book. "This is your ledger. Every single thing you think, say, and do will be documented; and when you return home to me, we'll review it together. Do you understand?"

"Yeh…yes," Phinn nervously stammered. "But…but how do we pay for our sins?" he asked, nervously.

"Most people receive a conscience."

"*Most* people?" Phinn repeated, surprised. "Not everyone has a conscience?"

God shook his head. "It's on the menu—page three, I believe—but there are those who avoid it."

"And for those who don't have a conscience, how do they...?"

"Trust me, they'll also experience the impact of their thoughts, words, and deeds on earth." God nodded. "You know that saying—this is going to hurt me more than it hurts you? Where do you think that comes from? I'm the king of clichés." He shook his head. "I love clichés," He said, smiling. "I created them early on."

Phinn stared at him in anticipation.

"I digress," God said, looking into Phinn's eyes. "When I watch one of my children make the wrong choice or some detrimental decision," He explained, "believe me when I tell you that it pains me to sit back and do nothing. But what else can I do?" He half shrugged. "Otherwise, you would all be puppets, and I never wanted that." His smile returned, portraying a joy brighter than the sun. "I've always thought that puppet shows are overrated."

Phinn chuckled.

"But understand that free will requires no interaction on my part," God said.

"There's no way to change that?" Phinn asked.

"Of course there is," God said. "It's called prayer."

Phinn pondered this idea.

"It has to be the will of many for me—the universe, as some folks like to say—to intervene," God explained.

"Well, at least I'll be getting a conscience," Phinn thought aloud, shuffling his feet. "You'll be with me, right?" he asked, his voice sounding sheepish.

God draped his warm arm around Phinn's shoulder again. "Always," He promised. "I will be with you in your most joyous moments and unspeakable pains."

"Unspeakable pains?" Phinn squeaked.

"Your life on earth is barely a fraction of your existence, Phinn. The pain you'll experience is so temporary that it's actually insignificant in the grand scheme of things. The lessons learned, however, are invaluable because they will last for all eternity." God gestured toward a river of light. "Learn to live within the rhythm and flow of life's river. There will be smooth stretches and dangerous currents to navigate along the way, but your faith will be your vessel. You can either build a sturdy ship or a leaky raft—as always, it's your choice."

"Okay," Phinn said, "faith." The confidence and excitement he'd felt at the start of their conversation had all but left him.

"I know you're afraid, Phinn, but you must learn to embrace the fear. That's where growth can be found. As I said, there's a rhythm to life—a balance. Rain and sun. Good and evil." God laughed heartily. "So take chances. Make mistakes. Ride the big waves and squeeze every last drop out of the life I'm giving you." He peered into Phinn's eyes. "Stay humble and kind, and be generous with your bounty, trusting that it will be replenished. And whatever you do, don't return home to me with any regrets." He nodded. "Love hard. Play hard. Work hard. And be sure to relish the ride. I promise, it'll be remarkable."

"Love hard," Phinn repeated, making another mental note.

"Well, it is the reason," God said, giving Phinn's shoulder another gentle squeeze.

"The reason for what?"

"Love is the reason for everything," God said, matter-of-factly,

"…for life." He then gestured with His mighty hand. "Savor the feast and remember in your heart that I am always by your side."

Phinn moved forward before looking back. "Will I remember… you know." He pointed around the cloud. "Any of this?"

God offered a loving nod. "For a short time, yes, but the memories of home fade with the progressive measurement of time on earth. You won't remember any of this until you return to me. No one does."

"And what about death?" Phinn asked, the nervousness in his voice apparent.

God shook his head. "The idea doesn't exist except in the imagination of mortal man. Once your purpose has been met and you've lived out your life on earth, you'll simply return home to me—to eternal, unconditional love." God pointed down. "Now go experience it all, as I, too, will experience it through you."

Phinn bowed his head.

"And don't be so serious, Phinn," God said, chuckling, "it's only life."

One deep breath later, Phinn stepped out of the cloud and into the river of light.

• • •

It was like heaven, Phinn remembered, *or at least as close to heaven as I could have ever imagined. Life was so simple back then and unbelievably kind. My space had plenty of privacy, and not a soul bothered me. I basically kept to myself for that period of my life. I suppose some people would say it was a time to find myself. For me, it was actually just a wonderful phase of personal growth.*

Each night the soothing sounds of waves lapping nearby rocks gently lulled Phinn to sleep. It was warm, like a summer eve after a much-needed rain shower. *And I can't remember feeling the thirst or hunger pangs that I've felt since,* Phinn thought. At times, from somewhere beyond the hissing surf, he could hear the faint Irish tongue of a woman singing the sweetest notes he'd ever heard. *That was my favorite,* he thought, *she had such a lovely voice.* There were many nights when those soft melodies put him to sleep. *She must have been shy because I never saw her face.* Even so, Phinn knew she was some kind of angel and quickly came to rely on her to quell his smallest worries. *It really was a heavenly time.*

And then it happened, he thought, his pulse quickening. *I can only hope that time will erase the memory from my mind.*

Phinn was waking from one of his afternoon naps, when his sweet dreams suddenly turned into a horrifying nightmare. *All at once, the walls felt like they were closing in around me,* he thought. *I couldn't decide whether it was my imagination or a bad dream—something I wasn't ready to face—when I heard a wet, sucking sound. I listened closely. The waves that usually brought on serenity began to rage out ferociously. Instinctively, I closed my eyes, while my head began to throb. As if my skull had been placed in some invisible vice, the pressure was so great that it made me want to vomit. For whatever reason, my peaceful world had abruptly turned to chaos. Although I had no idea what was going on, I sensed it wasn't going to be good. For the first time in my life, I was paralyzed with fear.*

An incredible force pulled at Phinn's tense, quivering body, drawing him in one set direction. At first he fought desperately to go back. *And then I saw it,* he thought. *I was being drawn toward a bright light that came from a door I never even knew existed.* To Phinn's own surprise and bewilderment, he was strongly attracted to the light and found himself fighting to reach it. *My heart felt like it might beat completely out of my chest.* Still, he forged on.

Searching for that gentle voice that had always calmed him, instead Phinn heard the most horrid screams coming from the other side of the door. *It's my bashful friend!* Just then, his whole world began to shake and tremble. *And I knew I wasn't the only one in trouble,* he recalled. *There was pain everywhere—in my body, my mind, my heart. And the screams outside the door were far worse than anything I'd ever heard. That, alone, scared me close to death.* Still, some powerful force pushed and pulled, compelling him forward. *There was so much pain,* he remembered, *that I knew there was no way I was dreaming. And, without knowing why, I went with it.* The half of him that never wanted to go eventually gave way to the braver half. *Call it curiosity, fate—whatever,* he thought, *but something beckoned everything inside of me to go. So I did.*

What a mistake! he thought. *No sooner did I have my head outside the door than I knew it was a mistake. The light that had attracted me so strongly just moments before was now the most intense, obnoxious glare. It burned into my pupils and made my sweating head pound harder. I also remember the cold,* he thought. *No, not cold—it was freezing.*

Finally managing a squint, Phinn spotted the faces of strangers who didn't look at all friendly. Some poked him, others prodded; and then he looked down and saw it. *It was blood!* There were puddles of blood everywhere. *Oh God,* he thought; but it was too late. *Someone lifted me in the air, turned me sideways, and slapped me. I howled at the top of my lungs. What injustice!* he thought. *I hadn't done anything wrong.*

And then Phinn heard her. It was that gentle Irish voice that had always rocked him to sleep. She was back; and at a whimper, she announced, "It's a boy, Patrick, and he's so beautiful. Light hair, blue eyes, ten fingers, ten toes..." She trailed off. She was crying, and it made Phinn feel horrible. *And then she pulled me to her,* Phinn recalled, *and at that moment, no matter what madness we'd just gone through, I somehow knew that everything would be okay.*

As if breathing for the first time, Phinn was laboring for air, when he heard another familiar voice. This one was deeper and not nearly as gentle, but he still knew it. *That's when I shifted on the freckle-faced woman's chest to listen.*

"He looks like either a Michael or a Phinn to me," the man said.

The pretty lady began crying again. "Then Phinneas Michael Reed it is," she whimpered.

And the rest, as they say, was history in the making. My journey had begun.

CHAPTER 2

It was a Saturday, just after noon—three weeks from Phinn's twenty-fifth birthday—when there was a knock on his apartment door.

"Come in," he called out, making his way through the sparsely decorated kitchen.

Tina opened the apartment door, making Phinn smile. His petite girlfriend was a stunning beauty, with caramel-colored skin and dark eyes that betrayed her Asian heritage. Although Phinn had been seeing her for two years, they rarely went out. Instead they spent most of their time at his place. "Hey, babe," he said, happy to see his love.

Tina just stood there, never stepping inside. "I…I feel sick, Phinn," she stammered.

Phinn rolled his eyes. "You should feel sick," he said, smiling. He approached her for a hug, "I think you drank more than I did last night. What were you thinking, mixing wine with martinis?"

"No," Tina whispered, "you…you don't understand. I should have told you sooner but…"

"What is it?" he asked, stopping short.

She paused, her face making his stomach flop sideways.

"I'm pregnant, Phinn," she blurted.

He froze. "You're…wh…what?" he stuttered.

She nodded, both her eyes and body language signaling that she was in a state of torment. "I'm pregnant," she repeated, sounding like she'd just announced a terminal illness. "I've taken three home pregnancy tests, and they all came back positive."

"But…but we were safe," he said. "We were safe, right?"

She shrugged. "I thought so."

"You *thought* so?"

"Don't put this on me," she snapped.

"But you were drinking last night. If you think you're pregnant, then why would you..."

"I know...I know," she interrupted, throwing in a pathetic shrug. "I need to stop that. It's just that I've been so stressed out lately and..." She shrugged again.

Swallowing hard, Phinn tried to form a rational thought inside his buzzing brain. "We're having a baby," he said softly, finally pulling her into his arms. "We're having a baby."

She returned the hug, but it was cold, devoid of emotion, except maybe fear.

"It's definitely not the way I planned on becoming a father, but..."

"Do you think I wanted to become a mother like this?" Tina asked, her tone harsh and unkind.

He leaned back to peer into her eyes. They were leaking tears. "Whoa, whoa... this could be the best thing that's ever happened to us, babe," he said, suddenly having the gut feeling that only a fraction of the picture was being portrayed.

"Do you think so?" she asked.

"I do," he said, "I've finished college and I'm finally working as an architect or an apprentice, anyway. We could..." He stopped, his heart filling with terror as her sniffles turned to full-blown sobs.

When she finally composed herself enough to speak, Tina mumbled, "Maybe I should just go take a nap?"

"Good idea," Phinn said, instinctively placing his hand on her abdomen. "Get some rest."

Although he was still in shock, Phinn ran out to the closest Babies-R-Us. Walking aimlessly up one aisle and down the next, he looked at cribs, strollers, and a dozen different styles of car seats. The entire tour felt surreal. *How on earth can I be having a baby at this point in my life?* he wondered; he wasn't sure of how it should make him feel, but he knew that something didn't feel right.

His thoughts then entered a darker room, where he questioned the possible reasons for Tina's dread. *But we've been exclusive,* he told himself, *at least from my end.* He pictured that dead look in his girlfriend's once-sparkling eyes, *Is it because she isn't telling me the complete story?* He shook his head. *Don't even think that way, man,* he scolded himself. *She's been faithful.* He sighed heavily. *Right?*

Phinn wandered into the diaper aisle, where a hundred cases were stacked to the ceiling. He scanned up to the rafters. *I wonder how many diapers a baby can go through?* He grinned. *I'm having a baby,* he thought, like it had just dawned on him. *I'm having a baby with the woman I love.* His chest went warm and his eyes filled. *Will it be a boy?* he wondered. *A girl?* He shook his head and chuckled; it was more of a giggle. *Who cares, as long as it's healthy.* He was feeling giddy, absolutely overwhelmed with joy at the realization of being an expectant father. "I'm going to be a daddy," he said aloud, grabbing a pair of yellow baby booties off the rack; it was the first of a million things he looked forward to giving his child. *And I'm going to be the best daddy ever,* he silently vowed, walking on air all the way to the checkout line.

Although the small token was hardly wrapped by a professional hand, Phinn was excited to see Tina's face when she opened it.

After a long yawn, she peeled off the wrapping paper and stared down at the tiny pair of booties. "Oh Phinn," Tina said, "they're…"

He handed her a piece of paper. "This is the real gift," he said, excitedly. "It's a poem." He smiled. "The first one for our child."

"You wrote a poem?" Slowly—almost reluctantly—she accepted the paper. "Unborn Child," she read, already choked with emotion.

"Unborn child, my future friend
into the womb this vow I send:
Upon your birth I'll take your hand
and carry you until you stand.

"Unborn child, I've seen your face
within my dreams; a kinder place,
and fell in love with angel's eyes
like winking stars of twilight skies.

"Unborn child; a gift from God,
I must admit that life is hard,
but you shall smile each day you live
for love and time is what I'll give.

"Unborn child, I've heard your voice;
a heartbeat in life's hectic noise.
It whispers that I'm not alone
for in a while you will be home.

"Unborn child, my boy or girl;
a blessing sent to change my world.
I cannot wait to finally meet…"

She stopped, her face awash in tears.

Phinn was pleased that she was so moved by the poem. He studied her face a moment longer. His joy turned to fear again.

"...for on that day," she finished, "I'll be complete." She quickly handed the paper back to him.

Oh God, he thought.

She burst into tears—mournful tears.

"What is it?" he asked, a bolt of panic zig-zagging across his chest.

Tina leaned in to kiss him.

Instinctively, he pushed her away. "Talk to me, Tina," he pleaded. "I know you're freaked out, but this baby could be the best thing that's ever happened to us. I love you and you love me, and we could finally..."

"I don't know if I can do this, Phinn," she blurted, backing away.

"What do you mean, you don't know if you can..."

"I'm sorry," she said, "but I'm not sure that..." She stopped herself, her eyes now wide. "My...my family," she added, lowering her tone. "I...I just can't deal with this right now. I need to go." She hurried for the door.

"Tina, wait," he said, starting after her. But she was already out of the apartment and halfway down the stairs. "Don't leave like this," he yelled after her. "We really need to talk."

The entryway door slammed shut.

He hurried to the window and looked down to the street. Tina was ducking her head into the car when she looked up. Their eyes locked; although only a moment, it was long enough for Phinn to see the pain and sorrow that ached in her heart. *You need to get used to the idea, babe*, he told her in his head, watching as she slid into the driver's seat and steered away from the curb, *because this baby's coming whether we're ready or not.* At that moment, the sickest feeling came over him.

Phinn called her. It went straight to voicemail. He left a message. He then called her again—every other hour—leaving messages and texts for the next two days. Each one went unanswered. *It's like she's disappeared,* he thought, fighting off a growing sense of panic.

Phinn went to her parents' house, but they claimed they hadn't seen her. "We thought she was with you," her father said in a tone that didn't infer his approval.

Phinn returned to his car and called her again. "Tina, please," he said, "call me as soon as you get this. I know you're scared. I am too. But you're going to be a great mom. And I promise you that I'll be the best father I can be. We can do this, babe. We really can. I love you, and like I said, this baby's going to be the best thing that's ever happened to either of us. I can feel it in my heart." He paused. "Call me back, please."

She never did, leaving him stranded on the battlefield of his mind.

The weekend finally arrived. Phinn's phone rang. "Thank God," he said aloud. *It's Tina,* he presumed, answering the call. "Hello?"

"Phinn, it's Pete."

"Oh, hey," Phinn said, unable to disguise his disappointment. "What's up?" Pete was a mutual friend who'd introduced Phinn and Tina.

"Hey, listen bro, I hate to be the one to..." He stopped.

"What is it?" Phinn asked, an inexplicable horror growing in him.

"Have you talked to Tina?" he asked.

"Not for a few days. She won't answer my calls. Why?" The sick feeling in his stomach was beginning to climb into his esophagus.

"I just spoke to Kristy. She told me that she gave Tina a ride to the clinic yesterday and..."

"Clinic?" Phinn repeated; he'd always despised Kristy, Tina's party-girl friend.

"Yeah," Pete said, his voice getting eerily low, "Planned Parenthood."

"Wh...what?" Phinn stuttered, the swelling panic breaking on him like a wave in full force.

"I'm sorry," Pete said, barely audible, "but Tina had an abortion, bro."

Swallowing his vomit, Phinn juggled with his phone, almost dropping it. "I...I need to go, Pete," he managed, his world spinning out of control, "I need to talk to Tina."

"I'm so sorry, buddy," Pete reiterated, "but I thought you should know."

"Yeah...yeah, thanks," Phinn said, feeling anything but gratitude.

Phinn dumped one call and immediately jumped on another. With trembling hands, he punched in the last few numbers. *It can't be true*, he thought. *She would have told me first. We would have talked about it. There's no way...* The call rang once and went straight to voicemail. *She's screening my call.* Phinn's heart drummed like a rabbit's foot inside his throat. "You need to pick up, Tina," he said after the beep. "We need to talk. I just got off the phone with...it doesn't matter. I just heard..." He paused, the horrid words wedged behind the thumping rabbit. "I...I just heard that you and Kristy went to..."

There was a beep, his message reaching its maximum length. *Ugh!* He called back. One ring later, he was sent to voicemail again. "An abortion?" Phinn blurted at the beep. "You had an abortion, Tina? Please tell me that's not true. My God, I hope not. But…" He was struggling to hold back the tears. "You've been avoiding my calls and texts and you won't call me back, so what am I supposed to think? I can't…" There was a beep, his message reaching its maximum length again. *Oh, come on!*

Hyperventilating from a drowning rage, he called again and was sent to voicemail. "Do you realize what you've taken from us—from me?" he hissed, unable to contain his anger any longer. "And you didn't even give me an opportunity to discuss it with you. I realize it's your body, I do, but this was my baby too. It doesn't make sense. I love you and…" Tears streamed down his face. "I should have had the chance to…" There was a beep, Phinn's message reaching its maximum length. He rifled the phone onto the floor.

For the next five minutes—or five hours, he couldn't tell—Phinn cried so hard that he could feel capillaries bursting by the dozen in his face. Pulling the poem *Unborn Child* out of his pocket, he shredded it into confetti. *If she didn't want our baby, then I could have raised it,* he thought, unsure of how he would have done that. *But if our child had walked the earth, abandoned by its mother, then Tina would have never lived it down,* he thought, recognizing the past tense and suffering for it. *She'd be labeled and have to pay the price for it.* He shook his sorrowful head. *Getting rid of the baby was the only way to relieve her of that lifetime burden.*

As his heart hemorrhaged, Phinn called Tina one last time. It rang once and went straight to voicemail. "You'll pay for this," he began. Although his words remained angry, his tone betrayed a cleanly broken heart. "And I hope you do," he added, fighting off his body's need to sob. "What you've done can never be taken back, Tina, do you realize that?" As his voice began to quiver, he rushed to finish his final message. "It's between you and God now," he whimpered, "and best of luck with that." He hung up before the sadistic beep, feeling dizzy from not taking a single breath since the start of the call.

CHAPTER 3

Days of deep mourning turned into weeks of abysmal depression. It was the strangest thing; Phinn had never met the baby, yet he missed the child something awful—as if knowing in the deepest recesses of his soul that the permanence of Tina's decision had changed the course of time. *At least in my life,* he thought. Inspired by a guilt he couldn't shake, he recognized and accepted that he'd been a sinner. *I impregnated a woman out of wedlock*, he thought, *and we weren't even committed to each other—not really.* In his opinion, being committed was even more important than some piece of paper. *Sure, I was willing to do the right thing and start a family*, he thought, *but somewhere along the way, I wandered off my path.* Giving it some serious consideration, he sighed heavily. *But even if I am being punished for all of the wrong I've done, Tina ending the pregnancy doesn't fit my crimes.* He felt like the victim of the worst kind of betrayal. *This punishment is beyond cruel.* He'd lost an irreplaceable opportunity to continue his bloodline; a link in his legacy had been broken forever. *And I didn't even have a say in it,* he thought. *I know it's Tina's body, but...* He started to weep. *I can't wait for Mother's Day,* he thought, filled with enough contempt to choke on the toxin, *so I can send her a card.* He wiped the bitter tears from his face. *And then I'll send her a card every Mother's Day after that.*

Phinn lay in bed, staring up at the ceiling. The best he could hope for was that the sharp, piercing pains in his chest would eventually dissolve into aching throbs. *How could God have done this to me?* he wondered, his eyes heavy from too many hours of lost sleep. *If there even is a God*, he thought, yawning.

The world went black, as he slipped into a deep sleep.

• • •

Phinn recognized the veiled silhouette of God standing in a cloud.

"Folks make me laugh when they claim they don't believe I exist," God said, laughing at the ridiculousness of it. "That's like looking in the mirror and not believing in yourself." As He shook his head, His eyes turned to angry slits.

Phinn's mind immediately went blank, all of the blinding rage and seething hatred that was poisoning him now gone.

"How dare Phinn squander the greatest gift in the universe!" God roared. "That's it. I've seen enough." He took a deep breath. "Death, where are you?" He summoned.

Phinn shuddered with fear, realizing he was invisible, watching the scene unfold as if he were looking through a window.

Death appeared. "Wherever you need me to be, Boss. It's my sole purpose to serve you." He wrung his hands and grinned. "And you know I love my work."

God pointed down. "Bring Phinneas Reed to me. He's done."

Eyes wide, Phinn stopped breathing.

"Done?" Death asked, looking down and shrugging. "Already?"

"He's had more time than he's deserved," God said, shaking His head like a disappointed father. "I want him home. He needs to pay for his sins."

Death scurried away.

From on high, God shook His head in disgust, the light surrounding Him fading until everything went pitch black.

A moment later, the terrifying sounds of a car crash echoed into the darkness, twisted steel and broken glass—immediately followed by the sound of a heart monitor flat lining.

• • •

Panting, Phinn awoke and popped up to a seated position. Covered in a film of cold sweat, he struggled to get his bearings. *It was only a dream*, he told himself before scrambling to remember every detail he could. But it was all so hazy. *It's like I could have had the nightmare years ago.* Still pondering the heart-thumping experience, he thought, *One thing I do know is that I'm going to pay for my sins. Lust, greed…I'm going to answer for all of it.* Confirming the long-held fear with a nod, he decided, *There's no avoiding it. It's the price owed for my life on earth.* It took a while before he could bring his breathing back to normal. *And I need to start wearing my seat belt.*

• • •

Although Phinn believed that *the great sin* was between Tina and God, he also felt some responsibility for it and could no longer shoulder the unbearable weight. To him, abortion was a crime against humanity. *It throws off the entire cycle,* he thought, *the grander scheme.*

Arriving at St. John's Church, Phinn climbed a set of steep granite stairs that hadn't felt his step in years.

The smell of incense permeated his senses. With the exception of several wall sconces, the only light in the long building came from the flickering glow of a hundred small glass candles, offerings of prayers for desperately needed help, or the souls of deceased loved ones. It took a few moments for Phinn's eyes to adjust. In that brief time, he could hear his heart banging in his chest. *I've never felt so much weight before.*

Sick with grief, he walked a dozen steps to the last pew where he fell to his knees. Clasping his hands together, he scanned the darkened room. Statues of saints lined the walls just beneath colorful stained-glass windows, each one casting their eyes toward the heavens. *The awful things they must have heard here,* he thought, preparing to offer his own difficult confession.

On trembling knees, Phinn closed his eyes and began to pray for forgiveness as hard as he'd ever prayed. After mentally reciting The Lord's Prayer, he thought, *Forgive me, Father, for I have sinned…for many years now.* He closed his eyes tighter. *I realize that I've lived a less-than-wholesome lifestyle, and Tina aborting our baby feels like I'm being punished for all of that now.* His eyes stung with tears. Opening them, he stared at the giant crucifix that hung over the darkened altar. *I've been lustful and selfish, I know that. And I also know that I've been lost and must find my way back, but…* He began to weep mournfully. *But why did my baby have to pay for my sins? I…I don't understand. You could have done anything to me. But not this. This is too much, Lord. And…and it's just not fair. I didn't even know that Tina was going to…* He stopped, knowing that it did no good to cast blame during a confession of his own sins. *Please forgive me, Father. I have brought this upon myself. I know that in my heart. But I promise that I'll change. You have my word.* He began to bless himself, when he paused the motion. *Please take good care of my child for me. And let him or her know that I'm so sorry.* He began to sob heavily again. "I'm so sorry," he wailed aloud, his pain echoing off the cold stone walls and returning to him as a stinging slap across the face.

Phinn finished blessing himself and stood. As he started out of the church and made his way to the top of the granite stairs, he still felt the full weight of the burden he'd carried in. *Not the slightest hint of relief,* he realized, bracing himself for another punishing bout with grief.

More disheartened than he'd ever remembered feeling—and hoping to walk off some of his funk—Phinn drove to Brayton Point Park on the banks of the Taunton River. Fortunately, the place was desolate, the usual screams of children playing on the big slide absent.

With his eyes focused on the empty baby swing, he dragged himself toward the bluestone path and was just beginning his walk when he bumped into someone. "Oh, sorry," he said, looking up to see Arthur Tetreault, an older man Phinn hadn't seen since he was a foolish adolescent, standing before him. *Wow,* Phinn thought, *I haven't seen Mr. Tetreault since…* He thought quickly. *Since I almost got my head kicked in at that biker bar and he drove me home.* His mind immediately went back.

• • •

It was a hole-in-the-wall bar, located just a few towns over. The lighting was dim, the cocktails were cheap, and the tattooed bartender couldn't have cared less about something as trivial as underage drinking. Being talented pool players, Phinn and his high school buddy, Doug, decided it was a bright idea to hustle some of the locals. As several pairs lined up awaiting their turn, Doug announced, "Losers buy the drinks."

Within a half hour, the dynamic duo had enough booze sitting in front of them for a month.

"What do you boys say about upping the ante?" a bearded local suggested.

"Sure," Phinn said, chalking up his cue, "what were you thinking?"

"How 'bout twenty bucks a game?" The toothless man smiled. "Unless that's a little too rich for your blood?"

Phinn snickered. "I was hoping you were going to say fifty," he said, breaking the rack and scattering the colored balls to all four corners of the green-felted table.

Several games later, a short stack of twenties sat on the table's scarred edge, with Phinn and Doug exchanging excited grins.

"Next!" Doug called out.

Within minutes, Phinn announced, "Eight ball, corner pocket." With a gentle touch, he kissed the cue ball with his stick, dropping the black eight ball straight into its designated hole. "Good game, gentlemen," he said, fighting off a smirk.

"Yeah, good game," one of the bikers echoed, as he grabbed the stack of twenties and stuffed them into his jeans pocket.

"What the…" Phinn started to complain when he felt two burly men grab him and begin dragging him toward the door.

"We're gonna teach you boys a lesson," one of the men growled.

Phinn instinctively collapsed to the filthy floor, only to be immediately lifted into the air.

"And beat ya senseless," another voice chimed in.

Phinn squirmed for his life, but to no avail. Amidst the blurry chaos, he saw Doug being carried out ahead of him, his panicked friend kicking and screaming the whole way. *Oh God, please…* Phinn thought, still struggling against the inevitable.

The mob was just beyond the front door and into the parking lot when Phinn's pounding heart felt like it might shatter his eardrums. *Oh God,* he repeated in his buzzing head, *not this.* He closed his eyes.

"Stop!" a different man yelled out, his voice deep and firm.

Phinn opened one eye to see an older gentleman hurrying toward them.

"You lay a hand on those two kids, and I'm calling the cops," the man barked, his voice getting closer, stronger. "And I'm guessing that none of you need the trouble."

Without hesitation, the bikers dropped Phinn onto the pavement.

"You're one lucky boy," the scraggly-haired local hissed; he was close enough for his putrid breath to leave a lasting impression in Phinn's whirling mind.

"Get up, boys," the good Samaritan ordered. "I'll take you both home."

Still dazed, Phinn scrambled to his unsure feet.

The older man extended his hand. "I'm Mr. Tetreault."

Phinn grabbed it for a shake. "I'm Phinn and this is Doug." He gestured toward his grimacing friend. "We can't thank you enough, sir. We were just…"

"Save it for the ride, son," Mr. Tetreault said. "We need to get out of here before those animals change their minds." He started for an adjacent parking lot, with the boys in tow.

"What about my car?" Doug asked.

"You can come back and pick it up in the morning."

"And the money we won shooting pool?" Doug asked.

Tetreault stopped in his tracks to study Doug. "Do you have a death wish or something?"

"Whatever," Doug said, jumping into the back seat of the man's faded blue Jeep.

Without another word spoken, Mr. Tetreault dropped Doug home first.

On the final leg of the ride, Phinn struggled to sober up. "We definitely screwed up, Mr. Tetreault," he admitted, breaking the silence, "but…"

"Save the confession for your mother," Mr. Tetreault said, dryly.

As they walked to the front door—Phinn drawing in deep breaths with each crooked step—Mr. Tetreault grabbed him by the arm. "Just be honest, son," he said, ringing the doorbell. "It's the only path."

Phinn's mom answered the door, her face instantly etched in worry.

After introducing himself, Mr. Tetreault explained, "Mrs. Reed, your son and his buddy were drinking at a pretty rough bar a couple of towns over. Evidently, they were hustling some of the unsavory clientele at pool, men who didn't appreciate being swindled." He looked sideways at Phinn. "I'm just glad I was there to stop what was about to be a vicious beating."

"Me too," Phinn muttered. "Thank you."

"Oh, my God," Phinn's mom gasped. She looked at her boy. "What on earth were you thinking?"

"My guess is he wasn't thinking, ma'am," Mr. Tetreault quipped before turning to Phinn. "Can I leave you with some advice?"

"Of course," Phinn said.

"You might want to steer clear of your friend, Doug. Trust me, he's a bad seed, and more often than not, we become the company we keep."

Phinn thought about it. "How do you know he's the bad seed," he asked, shrugging, "and that it's not me?"

"Phinn!" his mom snapped, grabbing his forearm in a death grip.

"No," Mr. Tetreault said, grinning, "it's a fair question." He locked eyes with Phinn. "Let's just say that I have a strong sense for these kinds of things." After nodding at Phinn's mom, he turned to walk away.

"Thanks again for your help tonight," Phinn called after him.

"You're welcome." The kind man looked over his shoulder and grinned. "Don't be in such a hurry to grow up, Phinn. It'll happen fast enough, believe me." He walked off into the dark night.

With his mother's hot breath on his neck, Phinn stumbled into the house.

"What were you thinking?" she asked again, more worried than angry.

"It was nothing, Ma."

"But it could have been really bad, right?"

He shrugged.

"Don't ever do that again," she said, pulling him to her for a tight hug. "If anything ever happened to you, I don't know what I would…"

"I'm fine," Phinn repeated.

She pushed away to look at him. "You've been drinking hard liquor. I can smell it on your breath."

"Ma, I…"

"That Mr. Tetreault's right. Doug is bad news, and I knew it from the first time I laid eyes on him. " She shook her head. "You're done with him, Phinn. That I can promise you."

"I'm sorry, Ma, I didn't…"

"Shhhh," she said, "we'll discuss your consequences in the morning. For now, get to bed and sleep it off."

"Okay, Ma." He shook his head. "But I am sorry."

She hugged him again. "We'll talk in the morning," she repeated. "For now, I just thank God you're okay."

• • •

Phinn returned to the present and looked up, almost surprised that the man was still standing before him. "Hi, Mr. Tetreault, how are you?"

"I'm well, Phinn, thanks," the grinning man said, his gruff voice betraying that he'd once been a smoker. "It's nice to finally bump into you again. Are you still shooting pool?"

Phinn laughed, politely. "No, sir, those days are done."

Mr. Tetreault nodded. "Good to hear. So how are you?"

"I'm good," Phinn lied, "thanks."

The older man studied his face. "Actually, it looks like that might not be true."

Phinn shrugged; it wasn't the most convincing gesture. "I'm fine," he said, his voice sounding broken.

"Really?"

Phinn offered a second, even more pathetic shrug. "I haven't seen you in years, Mr. Tetreault. I don't want to burden you with my troubles."

The man looked around the deserted park. "It's hardly a burden, Phinn. It's just you and me, kid. So let's hear it; what's eating at you?"

Phinn started to walk, with Mr. Tetreault matching each step.

"I…I've been seeing this girl, Tina, for a couple of years—or I was seeing her, anyway."

"Okay," Mr. Tetreault said, waiting for him to go on.

"Well, she recently told me that she was pregnant."

Mr. Tetreault nodded, remaining silent.

"She…I…" Phinn stopped to force back the asphyxiating lump in his throat. "A few days ago, I learned that she went behind my back and had an…" He stopped again, sucking in as much air as he could. "She had an abortion."

Mr. Tetreault cringed. It was slight, but it was there. "Behind your back?" he confirmed, the three words triggering a memory that had been locked away in some hidden compartment in Phinn's mind.

• • •

Tina might be cheating on me, Phinn thought, something deep in his gut telling him to open his eyes. *She's been acting even stranger than usual…more distant*. Without any explanation, Tina was never home. *She isn't even picking up her phone or returning my messages*. For all intents and purposes, she'd vanished.

With his suspicions peaked, Phinn followed her one night to a high-rise condo where John—her "friend from work"—lived. The rest transpired in some sadistic blur.

Nearly frothing at the mouth, Phinn leaned into the intercom and pressed the button. "John," he said, trying to keep his voice even, "this is Phinn Reed, Tina's…the girl you're screwing around with… I'm her boyfriend. Anyway, why don't you come out to the parking lot so we can discuss this like men?"

There was no response.

Phinn laid on the button again. "John," he taunted him, "it's best that we settle this right now." He felt high on an overload of oxygen. "Because if you don't come out here, I promise you that I'm going to..."

The sound of the front door's buzzer echoed through the empty parking lot. Phinn's head snapped up to see Tina descending the stairs. Her face was set like granite, as she met him face-to-face.

Beating back the bile in his throat, Phinn roared, "How long has it been going on? How long have you been screwing around on me?" He gagged on the words.

"You know, I really don't feel like arguing right now," Tina muttered, turning to walk away.

Phinn was on her heels. "I just asked you a question!" he screamed, his hot spittle spraying the back of her neck.

Her cell phone rang. She started to answer it when Phinn shot her a look that could have sent her straight to the pearly gates. She let the call go to voicemail. "As much as you think my life rotates around only you, Phinn," she said, speaking slowly, "I..."

"That's it, we're done!" he screamed and stomped away, putting an end to their relationship. *I finally let myself fall in love,* he thought, sobbing to each step, *and this is what I get for it.*

The following Christmas, Phinn took ill with the measles. Although he never understood how she'd found out, Tina showed up at his apartment.

"I made a terrible mistake," she said, more humbled than he'd ever thought possible for her. "Please forgive me, Phinn. I love you, and I was so stupid. It was the worst mistake of my life." And for the next few minutes, she begged his forgiveness.

Right then and there, Phinn knew that he cared more for her than his own pride or dignity. "Fine, we can get back together," he finally surrendered, "but that'll be the last time you ever betray me."

"Of course," she purred, flicking her tongue just under his ear to start his engine, "it'll never happen again. I swear it."

I can forgive, he thought, his mind dizzy from lust, *but I'll never forget.* He struggled to finish his thought with Tina's wet tongue wagging inside his ticklish ear. *Forgetting what you did to me would make me a fool.*

• • •

Phinn emerged from the stomach-churning memory and looked into Mr. Tetreault's eyes. "Yeah, behind my back," he repeated, his voice now gravelly, "I admit that I'm not ready to become a dad at this point in my life, but…" He took a few deep breaths. "But I didn't want this." He shook his head. "I didn't want this at all."

"I'm so sorry, Phinn," Mr. Tetreault said softly.

Phinn nodded his appreciation. "Tina broke my heart, for sure, but it's more than that." He looked at the silver-haired man. "She took something from me—no, from the universe—that she had no right to take."

Mr. Tetreault maintained his silence.

"And I need to make it right," Phinn said, nodding with conviction.

"How do you mean?" the older man asked.

"I mean that I obviously had something to do with it. If I'd lived the right way…" He paused. "Maybe I should go make a formal confession?"

Mr. Tetreault smiled, without a single hint of judgment in his intelligent eyes. "Seems to me that you just did, Phinn." Sighing heavily, he looked out onto the horizon beyond the river before them. "Some things in this world are out of our hands, my friend. All you can do is be honest with yourself and with God, and do your best to walk that truth every day." He nodded. "You're going to stumble, Phinn. We all do. But have some faith that you're not alone in your walk."

"Thanks," Phinn said, instantly feeling the tide of relief wash away some of the guilt; it was exactly what he'd hoped to receive at church.

"Of course," Mr. Tetreault said, grinning. "that's what I'm here for."

Phinn chuckled politely again.

"If you ever need to talk," the kind man said, "I'm at the park a lot, walking." Looking back toward the river, he inhaled deeply. "It's the perfect place to find peace."

"Thank you, Mr. Tetreault," Phinn said, shaking his hand, "I'll remember that." As he turned to walk away, he thought, *What luck to run into Mr. Tetreault again.*

Phinn continued on the winding path through the park. On his third lap, he offered a silent prayer to God. "Forgive me, Father," he began, speaking truthfully from his heart. "I've never felt sorrier about anything in my life. If you ever allow me to have a child in this lifetime, I swear I'll be the best dad I can be. You have my word. Whatever that child is destined to experience, joy or pain, I'll be right there by his or her side." He took a few deep breaths and looked out onto the river. "Please bless my unborn child, Father," he said, his eyes welling up, "and let him or her know that I'm so sorry for what happened." Even more weight lifted from Phinn, helping him to square his slumping shoulders for the first time in weeks.

• • •

A few weeks passed when Phinn rushed out of his apartment, eating the breakfast of a neglected child: a Yoohoo and half of a toaster pastry. While his stomach began to creak and complain, he ran into Mr. Tetreault again at Brayton Point Park. They shook hands, and without a word, began to walk together, side by side.

"So how have you been?" the older man finally asked, breaking the silence.

"Better," Phinn admitted, "not healed, but better."

"Better is good, right?"

Phinn nodded. "It is," he said, "but this isn't a simple breakup. Tina aborted my child, and I still can't understand how she…"

"You feel strongly against abortion?"

"I never really gave it much thought until recently," Phinn said, shrugging. "Never had to."

"And now?" Mr. Tetreault asked.

Phinn stopped walking. "Well, I'd never want someone to have power over my body and what I choose to do with it."

One of Mr. Tetreault's eyebrows stood up straight.

"But personally, I don't believe in abortion," Phinn explained, "for me, that is."

"Well, isn't that what Tina did," the man said, treading lightly, "took power over her own body and made a choice?"

Phinn began walking again. "Sure, but she should have included the baby's father in that decision," he quickly answered. "That's the thing, she never even discussed it with me. I was never allowed to state my case." He shook his head. "And this wasn't just any woman, Mr. Tetreault," he struggled to explain, "this was the woman who was pregnant with *my* child. Don't you think I had the right to weigh in?"

"Whoa," Mr. Tetreault said, "I'm the one asking the questions here."

Phinn smiled; although he couldn't give more than that, he smiled.

The two men finished their walk along the river in silence.

• • •

It had been a long time since Phinn had been alone. *I can't remember the last time I didn't have a girlfriend,* he realized. *I've actually forgotten what it's like to feel comfortable in my own skin.* Thinking further on it, he wasn't sure he'd ever been. *And that's obviously a problem,* he decided. *I need to be okay being by myself.* He sighed heavily. *If I can't be comfortable with me, it only makes sense that no one else will.* As a first step, he decided to dine out alone at a restaurant.

Watching couple after couple—who'd arrived after him—get escorted to tables, he finally questioned it. "Is there a reason I can't get a table?"

"Oh, I'm so sorry," the hostess said. "I thought your party hadn't arrived yet." She grabbed one menu and quickly seated him.

Phinn reviewed the drink menu and was ready to order a cocktail for quite some time before having to flag down one of the waitresses. "Any chance I'll be able to order sometime tonight?" he asked.

"You aren't waiting for someone to join you?" she asked, surprised.

"Someday, I hope," he joked.

She didn't smile.

"I'll be dining alone tonight," he said.

She nodded. "What can I get you to drink?"

"Let me get the melon marguerita, please."

"Okay," she said, writing it down. "Are you ready to order your meal?"

He shook his head. "Give me a few more minutes with the menu, please."

She snapped her pleather-bound order book shut and walked away.

Someone's all business, he thought, returning to the menu.

In what seemed like seconds, the stone-faced waitress reappeared and placed the phosphorene green drink in front of Phinn. "What will you be having?" she asked, her order book already open and pen in position.

Phinn's mind scrambled. "Ummm...let me start with the Caesar salad. And...ummm..."

She sighed.

"The fettuccini Alfredo with grilled chicken," he concluded, closing the menu.

"Just so you know, that dish is enough to feed two."

"It looks like I'll be taking some home then, huh?"

Void of any emotion in her face, she reached out to take the menu.

"I'd like to hold onto it, if you don't mind," he said.

Sighing again, she scurried away.

Wow, she's working on a great tip, he thought. As Phinn sat alone, he observed the surrounding tables; a symphony of different conversations was going on all around him, with most people laughing. A mother and a young boy were sitting in the corner, clearly engaged in a serious conversation. Phinn's mind immediately drifted off to a different place and time.

• • •

Phinn and his mom sat across from each other in a well-lit booth. "He's not coming back, is he, Ma?" young Phinn asked, struggling to beat back the tears that swelled in his eyes.

"I really don't know, sweetheart," she answered honestly.

The first tear broke free and traveled the length of Phinn's cheek. "How could Dad have just…"

"But I'm here, Phinn," she quickly interrupted, "and I'm not going anywhere."

"Promise?" he asked, surprised by the blurt.

She reached across the table and grabbed his hand. "You're my life, sweetheart. The one thing you need to understand is this—there is no me without you."

He ran his face across his shirt sleeve. "Okay," he muttered.

"Do you believe me?"

"I do."

"And we're going to be fine, okay?"

"Okay," he repeated, feeling the first hint of relief since his father had moved out.

• • •

Emerging from his daydream, Phinn thought, *What I wouldn't do to still have you here with me, Ma.* He checked his phone. *No text messages or emails.* He then watched as his crass waitress spent extra time with her other customers, showing more patience and consideration to her bigger parties. *She's hedging her tips,* he realized and snickered, *but she'll get exactly what she deserves from me.* He checked his phone again. *No messages.* As he sat there, sipping his bittersweet cocktail, he waited an eternity. *This sucks,* he thought, feeling lost and alone in a room full of happy people.

When his food finally arrived, he found the portion big enough to feed one person with a normal appetite. *Just as I thought.* As he tore through his meal, he tried unsuccessfully to block out everything around him. *Just eat and get out of here,* he told himself.

No more than fifteen minutes passed before he called the waitress over with the same level of respect she'd shown him. "The check, please."

"No dessert?" she asked, flashing the first smile of the night.

Too late for that, lady, he thought. "Just the check."

Paying the bill, along with an unusually modest tip, he stepped out of the restaurant and into the dark night. *I think I'll go with takeout from now on.*

• • •

The weekend before Mother's Day, Phinn was at the local pharmacy picking up his thyroid medication. As he walked down the aisle, he considered grabbing a Mother's Day card and sending it to Tina. *Nah,* he decided after reading through a few of the sappy messages, *she's not worth the trouble.* Stepping further down the aisle, he realized he no longer felt the mind-numbing anger and contempt for her that he once did. The months had already ground down the edges until they could no longer slice into his heart. The loss of his child, however, remained a dull ache in his soul. He couldn't shake it; something valued beyond explanation had been stripped from him. *And I didn't even have a say,* he repeated in his head for the millionth time.

Even still, he decided not to mail her the cruel reminder. *Tina's just not worth the trouble,* he repeated to himself. *Besides, it's between her and God.* He reflected even deeper. *And it's about time I find a way to get on with my own life.*

CHAPTER 4

Phinn reported to Luna Bella Architectural Group early. He was the only one there, already designing plans for a new commercial building on his giant drafting board, a solitary light shining above his workstation.

Gia, the firm's secretary, turned on the rest of the lights. "Mornin', Phinn," she yelled across the floor.

Phinn offered a half-hearted wave, his eyes barely leaving his work.

Minutes later, the boss, Steve Nichols, arrived with his briefcase in hand. As he walked toward his office, he stopped and spent a moment over Phinn's shoulder, admiring the work. "Are we ever going to get you out of the dark ages and onto a computer?" he teased. "CAD would save you so much time."

Phinn looked up. "Designing anything on a computer is like challenging a five-year-old to a game of chess," he explained, grinning. "It's just plain cheating." He looked back at his work and the grin widened. "This is art, and I love the creative process too much to cheat."

Chuckling, Steve patted Phinn on the shoulder and headed for his office. "At the pace you work, Michelangelo," he said, "I have no complaints."

Just then, Karl Kawa walked through the door. Steve spotted him. "If only everyone produced half the quality," he said, raising his voice.

Karl took a quick left into the coffee station. Steve shook his head. Watching the entire situation unfold, Phinn laughed before returning to his work, his focus intentionally drowning out the rest of the world.

At the end of the day when most employees had already gone home, Phinn was still laboring away on his project, his progress clearly visible.

Karl sauntered over in his carefree manner. "Are you thinking about putting in another eighteen-hour day," he asked, peeking over Phinn's shoulder, "or do you want to head out for a cold one?"

Phinn emerged from his haze, straining to register his friend's face for a few strange seconds. "No," he yawned, stretching out his back, "to both." He thought about it. "I need to go walk off some stress. I'm hoping to get in a few miles at Brayton Point."

"You okay?" Karl whispered.

"I'm fine," Phinn said, looking back at his work. "Just need to stay busy."

"Maybe you need to stop moping around and move on, man," Karl said. "It's been…"

"You have no idea what I've been through," Phinn snapped back in a volume louder than intended. "No one does!" It was true. *Everyone assumes it was just a simple breakup with Tina*, he thought. No one knew there was a third—much more innocent—party involved.

Ignoring the passionate outburst, Karl softened his approach. "You wouldn't have time for a full-time girl anyway."

Phinn gave it some thought. *No matter how great sex can be, and it can be pretty mind-blowing*, he thought, *I'm not so sure it's worth the torment.* He shook his head, fully aware that his raging hormones would not agree for long. "If it was the right girl, I'd make the time,"

Phinn shot back, surprised to hear those words come out of his own mouth. "And speaking of time, where are you on that DeSousa Project? Steve wants to know if you're prepared to…"

Karl checked his watch. "All righty then," he said, "I guess I'll see you tomorrow." He rushed toward the door. "Bright and early," he added over his shoulder, and was gone.

Smirking, Phinn returned to his building design. *Just a few finishing touches*, he told himself.

• • •

That weekend, Phinn stepped into the local pub to find Katie Fleet, an old school friend who was now a middle school teacher, sitting at the end of the bar. He hurried to give her a hug, thinking, *She looks exactly the same, with her chestnut hair and toffy-colored eyes.*

"This is so crazy, Phinn," she said. "I was just thinking about you."

"You were?" he said, one eyebrow bouncing to the beat of the house music. *What I wouldn't have given to hear that from you when we were in school,* he thought, his mind racing back to those early days.

• • •

Phinn was nearly fifteen when he stood with the other male wallflowers at a school dance. He stared at Katie, his longtime crush, who was wearing a pretty paisley dress. *I'd give anything to be with her,* he thought. But she was completely unaware, continuing to dance with another boy. As Phinn watched, the young couple kissed. *Oh no,*

Phinn thought, unable to take his sad eyes off her.

While one wallflower after the other summoned the courage to ask different girls to dance, Phinn stood alone. *It's either Katie, or no one,* he decided. Though other girls showed interest in Phinn, he couldn't have cared less. *Katie is sensitive and kind, the perfect catch,* he thought, hypnotized by her every move.

Catching a ride home, Phinn—frustrated and confused—tried slipping past his mother and head to his bedroom.

"How was the dance?" she asked, waiting for him at the kitchen table. "Did you find your wife there?"

"I think I did," Phinn sadly admitted, unable to hold it in, "although she didn't even know I was there."

His mom grabbed the remote control and clicked off the small flickering television on the counter. "Let's hear it," she said, patting the chair beside her.

Phinn collapsed into the worn seat. "There's this girl, Katie, at school. I've liked her since I can remember. She's a dancer who's really into musical theatre and..." He paused. "And she likes me, too—or at least I thought she did until tonight." He shook his head. "I was going to tell her how I feel, but..." He stopped.

"But?"

"But she was dancing with another guy, and then they started kissing." He shook his head, trying to clear the visual from his mind.

"Oh Phinn," his mother said, sighing. "Don't you remember what I told you about the opposite sex?"

He nodded, thinking, *Please God, not that same spiel again!*

"Some things just aren't going to make sense until you're older."

"That fine, Ma, I get it," he muttered. "But that doesn't make me feel any better right now."

She placed her hand on his knee. "I know, sweetheart. Having feelings for someone who doesn't feel the same can hurt. But remember—you're not the first to experience it."

"You mean, you and Dad?"

"No, not me and Dad," she said, shaking her head. "I'm talking about you right now."

But Dad left you, Ma, Phinn thought, *he left us.*

"You also need to remember who you are," his mom continued, "that you're sweet and…well, very handsome, if I do say so myself." She smiled. "And someday, Phinn, the woman you're meant to be with will see all of that as clearly as I do."

"Sure, Ma."

"I mean it, sweetheart. You have so many great things ahead of you—you have no idea."

"I hope so," he mumbled under his breath.

"I know so," she said, pausing. "Unfortunately, you're also going to feel your share of pain along the way. We all do." She smiled wider. "But have faith that you're never alone."

"I know that, Ma."

"Do you?" she asked, peering hard into the windows to his soul.

"I do," he said, smirking. "I have you, right?"

"Always," she whispered.

Turning in for the night, Phinn knelt at his bedside and prayed, *Forgive me for my sins, Father, and please bless my mom. She's such a great person.* After blessing himself, he added, *And I wouldn't mind it all that much if you sent Dad back to live with us again. I miss him.* Blessing himself again, he pushed a pile of dirty laundry onto the floor and turned in for the night.

• • •

Katie slapped Phinn's arm, jarring him enough to yank his mind back into the pub. "I wasn't thinking about you in that way," she said, laughing. "I have this boy in my class who reminds me a lot of you." She smiled. "He's a great kid."

"Of course he is," Phinn said, joking.

"But he's also a bit troubled."

"Gee, thanks."

"His name's Micah. He's smart and sweet, but he's also a little too self-absorbed for his own good."

"Conceited?" Phinn asked.

She nodded. "A narcissist in the making."

Ouch, Phinn thought, knowing Katie had always been more honest and forthcoming than anyone he'd ever known. "And he reminds you of me?"

Katie merely smiled. "Micah's being raised by his mom," she said. "No dad in the picture; and I worry that if he doesn't get the right male guidance, he could easily wander off in the wrong direction."

"And you want me to talk to him?"

She maintained her smile. "Although you've always tried to hide it, we both know that your emotional IQ is through the roof."

Phinn placed his index finger to his puckered lips. "Shhhh," he whispered, "no one's supposed to know."

"And you don't think that writing poetry is a dead giveaway that you're a sensitive guy?"

He placed his finger back to his grinning lips. "Shhhh …"

"I think you and Micah would really hit it off," she said. "In fact, I think you'd actually be good for each other."

Phinn laughed. "Katie, if I wanted to be a volunteer in the Big Brother program, then I would be."

"But you're a little too self-absorbed at the moment, is that it?"

"Ouch!" This time, he said it aloud. "How 'bout I buy you a drink while you give me some time to think about it?"

She grinned. "I'll take that drink," she said, "and I'll also let Micah know that you'll be in sometime next week to talk to him."

"Well, I guess there's nothing to think about then," Phinn said.

Katie laughed. "It'll be good for your soul, Phinn." She leaned in toward him until he could smell the body lotion on her. "Seriously, you can make a huge impact in this kid's life with a simple conversation. I just know it."

"Then I'm happy to do it, Katie."

She kissed his cheek. "I knew I asked the right person."

I hope you're right, Phinn thought, suddenly worried that he might screw the kid up even more than he already was.

They'd just ordered drinks when Phinn asked, "So what should I say to Micah when I meet him?"

"I'd start with hi," Katie said, grinning.

"But..."

"All you need to do is talk to him and you'll know exactly what he needs, Phinn." She winked. "And I'm buying this round."

Phinn sat for a second before he started to laugh.

"What?" she asked.

"You always were persistent," he said. "Remember that time you were dancing and fell over some stairs. You broke your arm, right?"

"I did," she said, joining in on the laughter, "and I wanted to finish the number, even though my arm was dangling and I was in some real serious pain."

Phinn continued to laugh. "You haven't changed one bit, my friend."

...

Micah was a platinum-haired twelve-year-old with a smile that demanded a second look.

This kid's going to do well with the ladies, Phinn thought. "How are you?" he asked.

The boy grinned. "I'm good, dude."

"My name's Phinn." He extended his hand.

The pre-teen grabbed it. "Micah," he said, giving it a firm shake.

"So you're in the eighth grade, huh?"

"Yeah. It sucks."

"Really?" Phinn said. "I liked eighth grade."

"You must have gone to a different school."

Phinn laughed. "Actually, I didn't. I went to your school."

Micah nodded, dismissing it. "There are a few hotties, but..."

"Hotties?" Phinn repeated, knowing instantly why Katie had recruited his assistance. *Solely driven by libido*, he assessed.

"Girls," the kid explained.

"So you have a girlfriend?"

Micah smiled, showing off his pearly whites. "At least one a week," he said.

Oh boy, Phinn thought, taking a deep breath. "So you're that guy, huh?"

The smile disappeared. "What do you mean, *that guy*?" Micah asked, defensively.

Phinn took a seat, contemplating whether it made more sense

to ease into this talk. *I just met this kid*, he thought. Shrugging to himself, he decided to dive right into it. "The guy who builds such a bad reputation in middle school, by the time he gets to high school, nobody—guys or girls—wants anything to do with him."

Micah opened his mouth to speak, but nothing came out. He was clearly confused, resembling a dog that had just been shown a card trick.

"Listen Micah, you're obviously a gifted kid. You may have the brains, the looks—all of it—but that's only going to get you so far in life, believe me." He nodded. "People want to be respected and treated well; and the older they get, the more they expect it. The cute little games you're playing with girls right now and getting away with…those won't last much longer."

"Wow," Micah said, "that's harsh."

"It sure is," Phinn said, "and it's also the truth." He cleared his throat loudly to refocus the boy's avoiding eyes. "You don't want me to lie to you, do you?"

"I guess not," he said.

"It's easy, Micah. Just treat people the way you want to be treated, and you'll do great in life." He nodded. "Just be kind."

"Cool," Micah said, concealing any emotion from his face.

They talked for a few minutes more before Micah politely excused himself.

Maybe I laid it on a bit too thick? Phinn pondered, giving it some thought. *I doubt he'll ever want to talk to me again.*

A few days passed when Phinn's phone rang. "Hello?" he answered.

"Hi handsome."

"Oh, hey Katie."

"Listen, I don't know what you said to Micah, but I can already see a difference in him."

Phinn was pleasantly surprised. "Really? He's not a tool anymore?"

Katie paused. "Well, let's just say he's not as sharp a tool."

Phinn laughed.

"And he's asking if you're going to come around again. He wants to shoot hoops with you."

"You're kidding me," Phinn said, even more shocked.

"You wouldn't want me to lie to you, would you?" she said, revealing that the boy had shared some of their conversation. "So what do you say?"

"Of course," Phinn said, a warm sensation passing through him, "I'd love to visit with him again." *This is awesome*, he thought, enjoying the role of mentor more than he would have ever guessed. Feeling an unusual sense of purpose, he decided to take a victory lap down at Brayton Point and share the good news with his own mentor, Mr. Tetreault.

• • •

In the months that distanced Phinn from his great heartache, he helped two couples move into their new homes, attended three weddings and a baptism—each event a stark reminder of everything he was yet to attain in life. *The clock's ticking away, and I'm way behind*, he thought, beating back the stomach acid in his throat. Being single in his mid-twenties felt like a harsh punishment for a lifetime of poor judgment and bad decisions. *I feel like I'm serving jail time*, he thought, *and I've wasted too much sand in that hourglass already.*

Ready to emerge from his self-imposed isolation, Phinn called a few friends until he reached old faithful—Karl. "You want to head out and get some dinner tonight, maybe catch a movie?" he asked.

"On a Saturday night?"

"Yeah, why?"

"It's date night, bro," Karl said.

"Oh yeah," Phinn said, remembering. "So you have plans already?"

"Everybody has plans already." There was a pause. "Do you want to join us?"

"I appreciate it, but there's nothing more pathetic than playing the third wheel."

Karl laughed. "I was hoping you'd say that."

"Where are you going to eat?" Phinn asked.

"The T.A. Restaurant over on South Main. They make the best Portuguese steak."

"Yeah, I love that place. I used to go there all the time with..." Phinn stopped. "I haven't been there in a while."

"So what are you going to do tonight?" Karl asked, changing the subject.

"Like I said, I'm going get some dinner and catch a movie. Maybe I'll see you guys at the cinema?"

Karl snickered. "Oh man," he said, "I think you just found something more pathetic than playing the third wheel."

"Whatever," Phinn said, "I'm done staying home on a Saturday night. Besides, I've actually learned to like being by myself."

"Why don't you just ask someone out?"

"I'm done with that too," Phinn said.

"Any word on what Tina's been up to?" Karl asked, displaying his signature lack of sensitivity.

"From what I hear, she's hooked up with some new sucker."

"Wow," Karl said, whistling, "at this point, so many people have seen her *privates,* they could legally be considered *publics.*"

Phinn laughed—for the first time since his unborn child had been taken from him—and realized that the healing process was well underway. "You are completely out of your mind, Karl," he said, grateful for the chuckle.

"No argument here," Karl said, laughing. "Well, have a good time tonight, lone wolf."

"You, too, knucklehead."

• • •

The autumn leaves had turned a magical palette of red, yellow, and orange, already starting to fall to the ground to provide nourishment for the next season. Amid the shedding oaks and maples, Phinn pulled up to Brayton Point Park and shut off the ignition. Dressed in old sweat pants and a light running jacket, he stepped out of his car and inhaled deeply. It was mild out, the lingering salt from the river making him lick his lips. *Maybe I should ditch the jacket?*

In the playground beneath the big red slide, a father and his three children were playing loudly, talking about burying some bottle cap as a treasure. "Some guys have all the luck," Phinn muttered under his breath. In the grass, two boys kicked a soccer ball back-and-forth, while a pair of women sat on a nearby bench, watching.

With the exception of these two happy families, Mr. Tetreault was the only other person in the park. As had become a routine in recent months, Phinn visited with his old friend before starting his walk. "Good afternoon, Mr. Tetreault," he called out, approaching his mentor.

Mr. Tetreault looked out toward the horizon. The sun was just setting, and the dusk was warm with light. "It is in California, I suppose." He grinned. "So how are you?" he asked. The question had also become part of their ritual.

"Better," Phinn answered, as usual.

Mr. Tetreault smiled. "Healed?"

Phinn gave the question the thought it deserved. "I'm close, I think."

"Good to hear."

"I still feel down at times," Phinn admitted, "but it's a different sorrow now."

"How so?"

"I feel lonely," he said, surprising himself even more than his confidant.

Mr. Tetreault's smile expanded. "For companionship?"

Trying to conceal his grin, Phinn nodded.

"Sounds to me like you're healed, my friend," Mr. Tetreault said.

Phinn nodded again. "It's clear to me now that Tina wasn't the one for me," he said, "but I'm starting to wonder whether I'll ever find her."

"Her?"

"The right one."

"How do you know *the right one* isn't out there looking for you right now?" Mr. Tetreault asked, his raised eyebrow expecting a response.

Phinn felt a sudden rush of heat. "I don't, I guess," he said, grinning at the possibility of it.

"Have you been out and about, making yourself available?" the sage asked.

"No," Phinn admitted, considering all the hours he'd spent hunkered over his drafting board.

"Well, *the right one* is probably not going to find you at work," Mr. Tetreault said, as if reading Phinn's mind.

"Or maybe it's my fate to be alone," Phinn suggested, still not through feeling sorry for himself.

Tilting his head, Mr. Tetreault raised his probing eyebrow again; neither gesture suggested agreement.

"You don't believe in fate?" Phinn asked.

"I believe that the good Lord gives us the perfect conditions to experience anything we ask for," Mr. Tetreault answered. "It really becomes just a matter of choice on our part."

Phinn was confused.

Mr. Tetreault smiled. "It's simple, Phinn. We ask. God delivers." Shaking his head, he sighed. "The complicated part is that we either don't recognize the prayer when it's answered, or we complain about the outcome of the very thing we asked." He stared at Phinn, who felt increasingly uncomfortable with the extended eye contact. "What is it that you want, Phinn?"

"To find my soul mate," Phinn blurted, taken aback for the second time. Although it was the truth, the phrasing felt foreign to him.

"Then go out into the world, make yourself available and find your soul mate," Mr. Tetreault said, matter-of-factly.

"If only I were so lucky," Phinn said under his breath.

"Lucky?" the man snapped back, his firm tone surprising Phinn. "It's your life, son, so own it," Mr. Tetreault said before softening his approach. "Phinn, if you can't imagine it, then it can't be. We call our own shots." He looked toward the horizon and nodded. "I've always believed that we create our own experiences and everything that makes up who we are." He looked back at Phinn with soul-penetrating eyes. "If it were different, there would be no such thing as free will, right?"

"Right," Phinn agreed, knowing it was going to take days—maybe even weeks—to process the impromptu lesson.

The generous guru grinned. "You know what, I think we might need a simpler perspective." He nodded. "Let me introduce you to a good friend of mine. He's as smart as they come and, if anyone can offer you some valuable insight, he's the guy."

"Ummm, okay…"

Phinn followed, while Mr. Tetreault approached the two young boys playing soccer.

Very funny, Phinn thought.

"Hi, Mason," Mr. Tetreault said, "this is my friend, Phinn."

The boy couldn't have been two minutes past six years-old, his brown hair matching a pair of eyes that were wise beyond their time. He was wearing a tank top.

That's strange for this time of year, Phinn thought.

"Hi, I'm Mason Sterne," he said, extending his small hand for a shake. He grinned. "Sun's out, guns out," he added, gesturing toward his bare arms.

Phinn laughed. "I'm Phinn Reed," he said, giving the boy's hand a squeeze.

Mason pointed to his friend. "That's Evan, my best friend." His eyes shifted toward the green bench, where the two ladies were laughing. "And that's Amy and Carol, my mom and grandma."

This kid's a trip, Phinn thought, amused.

"Mason," Mr. Tetreault said, "Phinn's having trouble with something and I was hoping you could help."

With a single nod, the boy waited to hear more.

Phinn involuntarily snickered.

"Phinn's looking for something he can't seem to find right now," Mr. Tetreault explained, ignoring the snicker.

Mason's eyes drifted off for a moment. "Stop looking," he said bluntly, his attention returning directly to Phinn. "Whenever I lose something—like one of my toys—I look for a little while and then I stop."

"O…okay," Phinn stammered.

"The toy knows I'm looking for it," Mason explained, shrugging, "so it'll just come to me when it's ready."

"And that works?" Phinn asked, stunned.

Mason's smile made his chocolate eyes twinkle. "Every time."

Mr. Tetreault snickered; it sounded different, though—victorious.

From the mouths of babes, Phinn thought, smiling.

"Thank you, young man," Mr. Tetreault told the boy, "we appreciate the help."

"You're welcome," Mason said, looking back at Phinn and smiling.

"Thanks Mason," Phinn said, "it was nice meeting you."

"You too, Phinn," he said, flexing his dimples.

As the boys resumed their play, Mr. Tetreault turned to Phinn. "Some answers can only come from an expert." He began walking. "Children are the wisest people I know. No distractions. No judgment. Just truth."

Phinn thought about it. *Stop looking,* he repeated in his head, considering the advice, *it'll come to me.*

"Just remember that gratitude is the only attitude that works in making dreams come true," Mr. Tetreault added, yanking Phinn from his thoughts, "the *only* one."

"O…okay," Phinn said, his mind scrambling to take it all in.

Mr. Tetreault chuckled. "Don't be so serious, Phinn," he said, "it's only life."

While goosebumps ran the length of both forearms, the hair on the back of Phinn's neck stood at attention. *Where have I heard that before?* he asked himself, scanning an empty file cabinet in his mind. There was nothing, no recollection. *Well, I've definitely heard it somewhere,* he thought.

As he started his solo walk, Phinn considered that it had already been nearly a year since his breakup with Tina. *In that time, I haven't dated anyone,* he realized, *or given it any real thought until now.*

CHAPTER 5

Phinn had always considered online dating to be somewhat embarrassing, but he realized with passing each year that the local dating pool shrunk exponentially. He hated pubs and nightclubs. And he could only fake it for so long at church socials. He also knew several happy couples who'd been successful and found love over the Internet. *It's the way now*, he decided, *or at least one of them.* Reservations aside, he decided to play the online love lotto. *I'll start looking and then stop*, he decided, remembering Mason's counsel, *and let her come to me when she's ready.* After paying his fees, he completed a fairly detailed profile.

I'm an architect by trade who loves to write. I enjoy good movies and books, as well as trying new foods and traveling. I'd prefer to stay out of the tourist traps, and instead rub elbows with the locals to experience their culture. I enjoy helping people—and this is not a pitch. I'm involved in the community and drawn to children's causes. I love going out into the world and experiencing life, but I also love coming home and chilling out in the comfortable space I've created for myself. Animal lover—check. Nonsmoker—check. And sorry, but I enjoy my occasional beer. As far as music, I enjoy all types, though I'm not overly fond of rap. I'm a one-woman kind of man who believes that no one should try to change another person. I'm not very religious, but I am a man of great faith. I'm an optimist, but also a realist. I'm not perfect, not even close, but I try every day to be the best man I can be. Essentially, I'm a work in progress looking for another work in progress, who I can grow with and experience everything.

He read it over a few times, snickering at his own words each time. *It's important to be truthful, I guess, It seems foolish otherwise,* he thought, *as any embellishments or fabrications will eventually be sniffed out anyway.* "I'm not opposed to long walks on the beach or the sound of rain on the roof," he said aloud, "but I'm not sure I should call them out, either." He chuckled to himself.

• • •

At first, it was exciting. When privacy allowed, he'd log onto the dating site and check his account. He could see how many views he'd gotten or when someone waved at him. He studied their photos, figuring many had to be outdated by a decade. He then read their profiles. *There are a lot of fiction writers out there searching for a partner,* he surmised, shaking his head. *There's no way these women can be that perfect,* he thought before realizing he was sitting in judgment of them. *Which means they're judging me too.* He didn't like it. Still, he forged on through this peculiar modern-day mixer.

One girl, *Madelyn Renaud,* immediately jumped out at him. She seemed more plain than many of the other women. *More real,* he thought, *maybe even normal.* Her smiling head shot teetered between cute and beautiful; she was on the plus size, with brown hair and dark eyes that shone through the laptop screen.

I'm new to the area, she'd written, *and don't know many people yet. But it's important to know that I wasn't born yesterday, either.* Phinn smiled at that one. *I'm a photographer who loves to cook—and eat. I also love to be cooked for—and eat.* He smiled again. *Unfortunately, I'm in a never-ending battle with calories.* "Now that's what I call being honest," he said aloud, finding it refreshing. *I love good movies and better books, especially poetry.* He slid to the edge of his seat. *I'm a nonsmoker and a social drinker, and I'm a dog lover who—until recently—lived with the four-legged love of my life. I enjoy travelling, though I don't do nearly enough of it. I'm looking for a friend to spend some time with and to show me around, but I'm also open to see where it might lead. Basically, I'm a work in progress.* Phinn lost his breath.

After reading the ideal profile three more times, he sent her a wave and then waited for her response—more nervous than he could remember being with the opposite sex. *And that's if she even exists,* he thought. *With my luck, I'll end up falling for some middle-aged cat fisher who hasn't left his mother's basement in twenty years.*

Within the hour, Madelyn returned his wave, adding the note, *Hello, Work in Progress.*

Hello, Work in Progress, he replied, *can I call you?*

She offered her email address instead.

Good girl, he thought, *she's cautious.* He quickly dropped her a line. *Hi Madelyn, I love your profile and would really like to have dinner with you some night. Are you up for it? Phinn.*

As he awaited a response, he read his brief email a few times, scolding himself for not easing up to the invitation. *Maybe I should have taken my time and not been so direct?*

Phinn received her response. *Nice to meet you, Phinn. And please call me Maddie. Only my grandmother called me Madelyn. I'd love to meet you for dinner. Does Friday work for you?*

Phinn couldn't remember feeling more excited. *Absolutely,* he wrote, *how does seven o'clock sound, out in front of Adolfo's? That is, if you like Italian? Phinn.*

I love Italian, she wrote.

I can pick you up, if you'd prefer, he suggested.

More than a few minutes passed before he received her reply. *Please don't be insulted, Phinn, but I don't know you. I'd rather we just meet there.*

I understand, he wrote, sorry that the world had come to this.

Phinn, I'll see you in front of Adolfo's at seven o'clock on Friday. Looking forward to it. Maddie. She included a picture that looked very similar to her profile photo.

Thank God she's real, he thought, already anxious to get to the end of the week.

• • •

Trying not to pace, Phinn waited at the front door of Adolfo's Restaurant. "Maddie," he said, as she approached. *She looks just like her profile picture,* he thought, feeling thrilled.

"Hi Phinn," she said, a real excitement in her voice. The dark-haired, full-figured beauty moved toward him like they hadn't seen each other in years. She gave him a hug.

She smells like sugar cookies, he thought. Lightheaded from a few shallow breaths, Phinn handed her a colorful bouquet of freshly cut flowers. "These are for you."

Her chestnut-colored eyes lit up. "Oh, they're beautiful. Lilacs are my favorite." Bringing the bouquet up to her nose, she inhaled deeply. "Thank you."

You're beautiful, he thought, feeling his face blush. He opened the heavy wooden door for her. "After you."

She looked at him. "A true gentleman, huh?" she whispered, smiling.

While his heart skipped a beat—or three—he shrugged. "The

world has definitely changed," he said, "but as long as I'm around, chivalry remains alive and well." He cringed as soon as the lame line passed his lips. *As long as I'm around*, he repeated in his head, *what an idiot!*

Her smile widened. "I'm glad to hear it."

Frosted globes hung from twenty-foot vaulted ceilings of stamped tin, pouring soft light upon the building's welcoming interior. Beige Tuscan stucco walls were adorned with terracotta pots, dripping with green ivy. A young raven-haired hostess stood at her mahogany station.

Phinn approached. "Reservation for Reed," he said.

She checked her large blotter before looking up. "Of course, Mr. Reed," she confirmed with a smile. "We have you down for two this evening."

Nodding, he looked sideways to see Maddie staring at him— and smiling. His heart skipped again.

"Right this way," the hostess suggested, tucking two long burgundy-colored menus under her arm. After escorting the grinning couple to a small round table in the corner of the large room, she turned to them. "Will this do?" the Mediterranean beauty asked.

Phinn looked at Maddie.

"Perfect," she confirmed, never leaving his stare.

"Yeh...yes," Phinn stuttered, pulling out Maddie's chair and waiting for her to take her seat before he claimed his own. *Relax,* he told himself. *Don't you dare screw this up.*

Placing the menus in front of them, the hostess concluded, "Your server will be right with you."

"Nice place," Maddie said, her scanning eyes taking in the warm details that surrounded them. "I'm new to the area, so…"

"I know," Phinn interrupted. "I'm happy I picked it."

"You've never been here?" she asked.

"Not without you," he said, his attempt at flirting sounding pathetic to his own ears.

She laughed. "Excellent. So this is *our* place then."

He swallowed hard. "That's what I'm thinking," he managed.

She giggled again before picking up her menu. "So you're an architect who loves to write?" she said, never opening the menu.

He smiled. "I am. I've always been a word guy."

She nodded.

"And you're a photographer?" he confirmed.

She picked up her phone and took a picture of him. "Always been a picture girl," she teased.

He laughed. "It's a good thing I'm not in the witness protection program anymore."

Her smile disappeared.

"I'm joking," he quickly added, "I'm joking."

The smile returned. "So you enjoy trying new foods and traveling, huh?"

He nodded. "I do." He grinned. "And you love to cook?"

"And eat," she added, gesturing toward her plump torso. "Don't forget that part."

"Well, you'd never know it," he said.

She blushed at his kindness. "Should I take that as a compliment?"

"Absolutely."

"Then you don't mind a woman with a little meat on her bones?"

"I think you're beautiful," he blurted.

She smiled, thanking him with her eyes. "And I think you're very handsome."

"Thank you."

She placed her menu down and lingered in his eyes. "So we both love good books and movies. We're nonsmokers and social drinkers. And we both love music."

"Except rap," he interrupted.

She nodded. "Right, except rap." She began counting on her fingers. "Let's see, we're also animal lovers and doers of good deeds and…" She paused to smile. "Am I missing anything from our perfectly packaged profiles?"

He half-shrugged. "Nope, I think that tongue twister's pretty much captured it." He nodded. "We're both works-in-progress."

"Works-in-progress," she repeated, her eyes twinkling at the phrase, "I love that."

A handsome waiter approached the table, placing two glasses of water, as well as a basket of toasted crusts of bread and some dipping oil, into the middle. "Hello, I'm Jonah. I'll be serving you this evening."

Both Phinn and Maddie acknowledged him with a nod.

"Can I start you both off with a drink?" he asked.

Phinn gestured for Maddie to order first.

"I'll have a glass of the house chianti, please."

Phinn looked at Jonah. "Can you make that a carafe with two glasses, please? Thanks."

As Jonah stepped away, Maddie's hypnotic smile returned. "Now where were we?"

"We were reviewing our online profiles," Phinn said, trying not to sound giddy.

"Oh, that's right, and I was just getting ready to start the question and answer portion of our program."

He laughed. "Oh good, my favorite," he said, leaning back in his chair. "Go ahead, shoot."

Leaning in toward him, she folded her hands on the table. "I get the part that you're an optimist, as well as a realist. In fact, I love that."

"Good," he said, unsure whether he should have been so transparent.

"But what did you mean when you wrote that you're not very religious but are a man of great faith?"

"Oh man," he said, trying not to smile.

Her face instantly changed. "I'm sorry, Phinn. If I'm being too forward then…"

He grabbed her hand. "Stop," he said, rolling his eyes, "I was just hoping you were going to stump me."

Her smile slowly returned, though not nearly as slow as the time it took for Phinn to remove his hand from hers. "I'm more interested in having a relationship with God than worrying about what some corrupt church and its antiquated rules think of me," he explained. "I'm a Christian, not a salesman. My faith is very personal to me."

"I understand," she said, "believe me, I do." This time, she placed her hand on his and left it there. "So how strong is your faith?"

"Strong enough to get me through some pretty rough stretches of road," he answered, honestly.

She nodded. "That's great," she said, concluding her interview.

Jonah returned with the wine. "Have you decided on any appetizers?" he asked, pouring out two half glasses.

Phinn shook his head apologetically. "I'm sorry," he said, "but we haven't even looked at the menus yet."

Jonah nodded. "Just signal me when you're ready."

"It may be a while," Maddie said in jest.

"I figured," Jonah said, smiling. "Take your time. I'm here when you need me." He stepped away.

Phinn looked at Maddie. "It may be a while?" he repeated.

They both laughed.

"I like your honesty," he admitted, raising his glass. "What should we toast to?"

Maddie lifted her glass to meet his. "To *us*, of course."

"Of course," Phinn said past the lump in his throat, "to *us*."

As the kissing glasses rang out, Phinn couldn't remember ever feeling more excited—or filled with hope. He took a sip of wine.

"Now your turn," Maddie said.

"My turn?"

"You must have some questions about my profile."

"Just one," Phinn said.

"Well, that's no fun." She took a sip of wine. "Go on, you may commence with the interrogation."

"You mentioned that you're a dog lover, but recently..." He stopped when he saw her face change. "I'm sorry."

"No, that's fine. It's a fair question. I included it in my profile, so..." She took another sip of wine. "My dog, Raymond, passed away earlier this year."

"I'm so sorry."

She nodded. "We were together for fourteen years. I couldn't have asked for a better boyfriend."

He smiled compassionately. "I bet."

"And speaking of boyfriends, I have one final question."

"Okay."

"Why aren't you with someone, Phinn Reed?" she asked.

Phinn could feel some of the air leave his lungs. He'd never met anyone as transparent as Maddie. "I was," he said, "for a few years. But she wasn't the right one for me. I guess you can say I was broken for a while, but…"

"And now?" she asked.

"Fully whole."

"Good to hear," she said.

"And you?" he asked. "Are you wounded?"

"Not me," she said, shaking her head. "I've had two serious boyfriends, one in high school and the other in college—which means two breakups with lots of tears that I can barely remember." She smiled. "Timing is everything, isn't it?"

"It sure is," he agreed.

Jonah stopped by the table. "Still haven't cracked open those menus, have you?"

Phinn began shaking his head when Maddie flipped hers open. "We'll be ready to order in three minutes," she promised.

Jonah smiled. "I'll be back in two." He hurried away to tend to another table more interested in eating.

"I like this menu," Phinn commented.

Maddie nodded in agreement. "There are so many choices to pick from," she said.

As promised, Jonah quickly returned. "So what are you folks thinking?" he asked, his order book in hand.

Maddie peered over her menu at Phinn. "What do you think about sharing a caprese salad to start?"

Phinn nodded and then looked up toward Jonah. "And let's get another carafe of the chianti. It's delicious."

Maddie's eyes went wide. "Another carafe? I guess we'll be staying here for a while then."

"That's the plan," Phinn muttered.

Jonah smiled. "And for your main course?"

"I'm going to have the veal parmesan," Maddie said before snapping her menu shut and handing it back.

"I'll try the Bolognese," Phinn said.

"With ziti or fettucini?"

"Fettucini."

Jonah nodded, reaching for Phinn's menu.

"Do you mind if we hold on to one of them?" Phinn asked.

Nodding, Jonah scampered away.

Although she never questioned it, Maddie's eyebrow danced.

"In case we want to try something else," Phinn explained with a half shrug.

Maddie grinned.

"Ever since I can remember, I've always held on to the menu," he said, completing his shrug. "I'm not sure why."

She chuckled at his quirkiness.

When the dishes arrived to the table, Maddie's plate looked like it could easily feed a family of five. Phinn laughed.

"What on earth am I supposed to do with this?" she asked.

"You need to finish it," he teased. "I'll be very upset if you don't."

"Then get comfortable because we're going to be here for a week."

"That works for me," he said without smiling.

Grinning, she blushed just a little.

My God, she's beautiful, he thought, feeling high on more than just the wine.

As they ate, Maddie said, "I really don't get it."

"Get what?" he asked.

"How on earth are you still single?"

Phinn laughed. "You know, I've been wondering the same thing about you."

She studied his face for a while. "Be honest with me, Phinn. Are you done with the ex? No emotional ties?" Before he could answer, she said, "Because I don't have the time or interest to travel down some dead-end street."

"I'm an open highway," he said, smiling, "honest."

She returned the smile, clearly believing him. "Then that's all I need to know. You can keep the details to yourself."

Phinn laughed before taking another sip of wine. "It's funny," he said, "but I've never used an online dating service before." For whatever reason, he felt embarrassed about it. And then it struck him. *Maddie did the same.* "Not that there's anything wrong with it," he added, trying to yank his foot out of his mouth.

"That's right," she said, grinning, "you met me, didn't you?"

Instinctively, he reached across the table and grabbed her hand. Feeling awkward over the impulsive move, he began to pull away when she grabbed it and held on.

"Relax," she said, "you're doing fine."

Phinn laughed again; this time, it was an awkward laugh that made his face burn red.

Maddie graciously ignored it, refocusing on her meal. Although she was barely putting a dent into the massive platter in front of her, she was clearly enjoying the dish, releasing moans that could have mimicked a more intimate experience.

"You really like Italian food, huh?" he said.

She nodded. "I'm obviously not finicky."

He ignored the self-deprecating comment. "Just so you know," he said, "I make a mean lasagna." He grinned. "I'm just sayin'."

"I look forward to it." She smiled. "That was an offer, right?"

He nodded. "An offer that stands any time," he said, hoping that she couldn't hear his heart trying to kick itself out of his chest.

After sharing a decadent chocolate dessert and nursing two cappuccinos, Phinn snatched the check as soon as Jonah delivered it.

"We can split it," Maddie suggested.

Phinn shook his head. "Not on a first date," he said. "My mother raised me better than that."

"Yeah, she did," Maddie agreed, "smart woman."

Phinn grinned. "She sure was."

"Your mom's passed?" Maddie asked, treading lightly.

He nodded. "I was in college. It was so devastating that it nearly broke me."

"I'm…I'm sorry."

He shook his head, surprised that he felt comfortable enough to share something so personal—so soon. "My mom always taught me that life is temporary," he added, almost involuntarily, "but that the afterlife, or heaven, is eternal." He nodded. "Those exact words are what sustained me."

Maddie never flinched. "Very smart lady," she repeated.

Phinn nodded again. "And more kind than smart."

"Even better." After a moment, she smiled. "Thank you for dinner, Phinn. It was amazing."

"The food or the company?" he teased.

"The food was okay, I guess." She grinned.

As they stepped out into the rain, Phinn noticed a homeless man—with a leathery face and dark eyes—taking shelter under the restaurant's forest green awning.

"Hey buddy," the man called out, "you gonna eat those leftovers?"

Without giving it any thought, Phinn marched straight to him and handed over his doggie bag. Not a second later, he felt something brush against his shoulder. He looked up to see Maddie standing beside him, handing the man her bigger bag.

"Here you go, sir," she said, "this should hold you over for a while."

"God bless you both," the homeless man said, already digging into the larger bag.

Phinn and Maddie stepped down the sidewalk a few feet.

"Let me walk you to your car," he suggested.

"I appreciate it," she said, "but it's raining and…"

"I don't melt," he said, gesturing for her to lead on. "Come on, I insist."

When they reached Maddie's car, she jumped in to escape the pounding rain. She quickly rolled down her window.

Phinn squatted until he was eye level with her. "I had an amazing time tonight," he confessed.

"Me too," she said, "but you're going to get soaked."

"It's fine. I don't mind," he said, leaning into the window to kiss her on the cheek. "Can I see you again?"

She nodded. "You're making me lasagna, right?"

He instinctively went in to kiss her cheek again. This time, she moved her face just enough so that the kiss landed on her lips. It was sweet and gentle, nothing passionate.

"I certainly am," Phinn said, winking at her.

"Let me see your phone," she said.

"Ummm okay, but if this is about that witness protection thing…" he joked, handing it over.

Laughing, Maddie punched her number into his phone. "This is me," she said, handing it back. "Goodnight, handsome."

He couldn't believe it. After only a few hours, Maddie Renaud's voice had already become his new favorite sound. "Goodnight, beautiful," he said before floating away in the rain, never feeling more whole or alive in his entire life. *Thank you, Mason Sterne!*

• • •

On her ride home, Maddie realized, *I've been kissed before, but this was different.* As she smiled, she felt enough warmth in her chest to defog the windshield. *This was my real first kiss.*

• • •

When Phinn arrived home, there was an email waiting for him. *Hi Phinn, Thanks again for a great night. I hope you've dried off. Kidding aside, I'm so happy I joined the dating site. And I'm glad you did too. Looking forward to seeing you soon. I'll bring the wine and garlic bread. Maddie xo*

Phinn read the email a half dozen times before leaving it in his inbox, knowing he'd be reading it a dozen more.

CHAPTER 6

Maddie finished up the day's last assignment at her new job, Ally Rose Photography. As she stepped into the parking lot, she spotted Phinn leaning on her car and holding a covered dish, a clear plastic bowl filled with colorful salad and a bottle of wine. Her skin tingled at the sight of him.

"Can Maddie come out and play tonight?" he called out, smiling.

Oh, absolutely, she thought, picking up her pace. She grabbed the warm dish from him. "Ahhh, Phinn's famous lasagna?" she purred, inhaling deeply to take in the aroma. She then looked at the plastic bowl. "And a salad to go with it?"

He nodded. "You gotta take the bad with the good, right?"

She chuckled.

Phinn shrugged. "It seemed a bit forward of me to ask you back to my place for dinner on our second date, so I decided to bring it to you."

"So we're on our second date right now?"

"We are," he said.

"Good," she said, "so where are we going to eat it?"

"I know the perfect place," Phinn said, walking around the car and opening the passenger door for her. "Can I take you there?"

Smiling, Maddie started for the open door. *A gentleman, indeed,* she thought, feeling all warm and fuzzy inside.

It was nearly sunset when they pulled into Brayton Point Park. "That's unusual," Phinn commented.

"What's unusual?" Maddie asked.

"My friend, Mr. Tetreault, is normally here at the park walking at this time of day," he explained, "but he's nowhere in sight."

"Maybe it's a little too nippy for him," she suggested.

"Nah, not Mr. Tetreault. He's a hearty soul."

"Well, at least we don't have to share our lasagna," Maddie teased, still surprised at how comfortable she felt in his company.

"Oh, that's right!" Phinn blurted, "I forgot."

"Forgot what?"

"Did you hear about that massive fire out in the Berkshires?"

"Yeah."

"Well, he sent me a text that he was headed out there to help," Phinn explained.

Help? she wondered, but let it go with a nod.

Phinn jumped out of the car and ran around to the passenger side to open her door. As he did, Maddie spotted two silhouettes walking toward them—one tall and the other short.

"Hi Phinn," the smaller shadow called out.

"Oh, hey Mason," Phinn replied.

As they met in the grass, formal introductions were made. "This is my dad, Bobbie," the small boy said. "Dad, this is Phinn."

Phinn shook the man's hand. "Nice to meet you." He looked down at Mason. "You have quite a boy here, Bobbie."

The man laughed. "Oh, you don't know the half of it, Phinn. My wife, Amy, and I are always joking that Mason's looking after us." He ruffled the kid's walnut-colored hair. "He's something, all right."

Chuckling, Phinn introduced Maddie.

Mason grabbed her hand and gave it a shake. "Nice to meet you,

Maddie," he said, grinning. He then looked back at Phinn. "So did you find it?" he asked, his penetrating gaze locked on.

Phinn smiled wide enough to bust his cheeks wide open. "I did," he said.

While shivers cascaded down Maddie's spine, she watched as Mason's smile mirrored Phinn's. "Good," the little man said, before he and his father stepped off into the shadows.

"What was that all about?" Maddie asked, taken aback by the odd exchange.

Phinn shrugged once before continuing their stroll. "I met Mason at this park not too long ago. I think he's an old man stuck in a little kid's body—and I'm not even kidding." He paused to glance over at the two fading silhouettes. "He actually helped me find something."

Maddie's brow creased. "And what's that?"

Phinn stopped to kiss her. "My way," he whispered, offering no further explanation.

Your way? she repeated, deciding to let it go for the time being. "Well, he's a handsome old man, that's for sure," she commented.

"That, he is," Phinn agreed, squeezing her hand.

It was only a few hundred yards to the riverbank. While Maddie held the lasagna and salad, Phinn spread out a blanket on the ground and lit a candle.

"Wow," she said, impressed. *Is this the real Phinn,* she wondered, *or is he just auditioning for the role of boyfriend?*

"It's important to set the right mood," he joked.

Comfortable in their thick sweatshirts, they settled in and began to eat. "This is absolutely delicious," Maddie said sincerely. "You can really cook."

"Thanks, but that's only true for one or two dishes."

She laughed. "What about entertainment?" she asked. "Will you be providing entertainment tonight, as well?"

"Just name it," he said, smiling. "Song? Dance? Some really bad juggling?"

"Tell me a story," she said, teasing him, "I love stories."

"Fair enough." He nodded. "Do you prefer romance? Fantasy? Comedy? Horror?"

"Horror," she blurted, amused.

"Fact or fiction?" he asked.

She was intrigued. "Hmmm, how can I not go with fact for the first round?" she joked.

"First round," he repeated, chuckling, before his eyes drifted off in thought. "A few years back, to pay for my college tuition—along with every other bill attached to adulthood—I took employment at a woodworking shop that produces giant spools for wire companies. On my third day, I was sanding a massive reel on a belt sander, when I heard a grown man release a blood-curdling scream, 'Mommy!' the guy yelled out. Wiping the sawdust from my goggles, I turned to see the table saw operator, Ricky Smeaton, holding his hand. I took one step closer before I saw it. Poor Ricky had run his hand into the saw, splitting his middle finger right down the middle...like someone slicing a banana in half."

"Really," Maddie asked. "this is the story you picked to tell during a lasagna dinner?"

He chuckled. "There was blood everywhere," he quickly added, "making me want to vomit."

"Oh...okay," she said, pushing her plate away.

Laughing, he continued, "Men rushed over and, while my stomach churned, the shop's foreman called for an ambulance. After offering Ricky's fingertip to the paramedic, the older man told everyone get back to work."

"Ugh…" Maddie moaned.

"I returned to the belt sander, when the shop's foreman patted me on the shoulder. 'Get on the table saw, Reed,' he told me. 'We have a big order to get out.'"

"You're kidding me," Maddie said, taking a sip of wine.

"Nope, I'm not. That beady-eyed donkey told me to either get on the table saw or go home."

"So you went home, right?"

Phinn shook his head. "Not quite. I cleaned off the blood and fired up the saw—as slowly as possible. All the while, I was hoping that OSHA would show up and shut the sweatshop down." He looked at her and shrugged. "With every board I cut, I kept reminding myself that I needed to finish my degree and get out of there as soon as possible." He stopped.

"That's right…an optimist," she commented.

He laughed. "Horrific enough for you?"

"More than enough," she said, looking at her half-eaten lasagna. "As soon as I picked the category, something told me that I should have gone with comedy."

He cleared his throat. "Oh, I have plenty of those too."

"Here we go," Maddie said, laughing.

"My first roommate's name was Matt Woodcock. He was a drummer in some up-and-coming garage band. Fortunately, we got along well, which was a good thing because the apartment's one-bedroom barely fit Matt's massive drum set alongside a set of second-hand bunk beds."

Laughing, Maddie reached for her unfinished lasagna.

"At six hundred dollars a month," he continued, "we paid much more in rent than we should have. The only benefit was that heat was included, so…" He smiled. "…we exercised our sense of fairness and used this benefit any chance we could. In fact, when the rest of the world was frozen under a sheet of ice, we were prancing around in our boxer briefs with the apartment's front door flung wide open."

"Boxer briefs," she muttered under her breath, smirking.

"And being as poor as we were, the only decent thing in the apartment was the new stereo system." He stopped to laugh. "I remember telling Matt, 'You can probably build your credit if you rent a stereo and make the payments each month.' And the idiot agreed."

Maddie stopped chewing to laugh.

Phinn nodded. "Within two months, Matt was twenty pounds lighter and completely broke. And I knew it was the end of the line when a pair of big dudes arrived at our front door—dressed in long coats—to repossess the stereo."

"Oh no," Maddie said.

He half shrugged. "After months of Matt's parents begging him to come home, he finally agreed—without any further argument. The only thing left to do was for him to make good on the five hundred bucks he owed me for outstanding bills." He finished the shrug. "So I told him to sell me everything, and he did." Phinn laughed. "His ceramic cobra cost me twenty dollars; the DVD player—which could only play the disc stuck inside it—was a steal at forty bucks."

Maddie laughed.

"I also scored a strobe light, some pots and pans, and various other odds and ends that Matt had begged, borrowed, and stolen." He shrugged again. "The only thing left to do was find a new roommate."

Sighing heavily, he shook his head. "His name was Barry Amaral, and we don't have nearly enough time to get into him tonight."

"You are too funny," Maddie said.

Under a cornflower blue sky, they settled in on the bank of the river, watching as the giant sun deflated in the pink and coral horizon, ushering in the quiet of night. Just as the final sliver of sun went down over the sparkling river, Phinn swallowed his last bite of cheesy pasta and looked at her. "Good show?"

"I can't imagine a better one," she replied.

"Me either."

"I love sunsets," she said, "but sunrises always feel a little more hopeful to me."

"I like that," he whispered, "I'll have to remember it."

I hope you do, she thought. "You didn't eat any of the salad," she noted.

Phinn smiled. "I've always liked the idea of salad, but…" He stood and extended his hand.

She grabbed it. Hand-in-hand, they started a leisurely stroll along the river's edge.

"So how was your day?" she asked, as if they'd just started a new date.

"Well, it got a lot better when you agreed to have dinner with me," he said, playing along.

She smiled.

"Which is more than I can say about last night."

"What happened last night?"

"I had to attend an awful dinner with a bunch of pompous asses." He gave her hand a squeeze.

"Tell me about it," she said, excited to hear the story.

Phinn shook his head. "I was seated at a table with some incredibly pretentious snobs," he began, "people who couldn't stop rambling on about their success and wealth. At one point, one of them finally asked me, 'So what is it that you do for a living?' And I couldn't resist." He started laughing.

"What?" she said, completely hooked.

"Well, while everyone looked down their noses at me, waiting for an answer, I finished chewing. Slowly, I looked up from my plate. 'I work in a button factory,' I told them, keeping a straight face. 'I make buttons.'"

Picturing the scene, Maddie began laughing.

"If you could have seen the judgment in their faces," Phinn said between laughs, "it was priceless." He shrugged. "I told them, 'Everyone needs buttons, right?' Then I looked across the table at one of the women and told her, 'Those are some really nice buttons you're wearing.'"

"You didn't," Maddie said, snorting.

"I did," Phinn said, "I swear it." As the laughter subsided, he shook his head. "I considered telling them the truth, but decided not to."

"Why not?"

"I figured these folks are a lot happier looking down on others."

"You're too funny," Maddie repeated, impressed with his sense of humor.

"So I never said another word," Phinn added, "and went back to my plate, trying not to laugh at all the discreet glances being exchanged around the table." He shrugged. "When I think back on it now, I'm pretty sure I did them a favor."

"How do you mean?" she asked.

"I made them feel good about themselves," he said, grinning, "more superior, you know?"

"Wow, you're tough," she said. "I like it."

Phinn lifted her hand to give it a kiss. "Only with people who deserve it," he said.

"Okay," Maddie said, "you obviously have a great sense of humor and can make someone sick while eating lasagna, but how are you with serious?"

"Try me," Phinn said, grinning.

"Ummmm, okay, tell me something about yourself that won't make me laugh…or want to throw up."

Although he laughed, he was somewhat reluctant. "I love writing poetry," he finally admitted.

Really? she thought, instinctively moving closer to him. "Wait a minute—you hate rap music, but you love writing poetry?"

His grin and a subtle shrug arrived at the same exact time.

"Poetry, huh?"

"Yup, but no one's ever read it," he added, "and I'd really prefer it stayed that way."

"So you wouldn't even share it with me," she teased, "even though I wrote that I love reading poetry in my dating profile?"

"It's not that good."

She smiled. "And you're not a good liar."

He laughed. "We'll see," he whispered. "And now you, tell me something about you." He shrugged, playfully. "Maybe a dream you've had for as long as you can remember."

"Now that's random," she said.

He laughed. "I like random."

"Me too." She looked into his eyes and smiled. "Are you sure you want to hear about the sappy dreams of a little girl?"

He nodded. "I'm sure."

Maddie usually kept her dreams locked within, where she could visit them any time of the day. *But it's different being with Phinn*, she thought, feeling both safe and free with him. "Since I can remember, the only thing I've ever wanted in life is to have a family."

He flinched slightly, clearly taken aback by her sincerity.

"A husband and children," she added, realizing at that moment that she was emotionally incontinent around him, incapable of holding anything back.

But he never flinched again, and his eyes never left hers.

"Now how crazy is that to hear on a second date?" she asked, hoping for a kind response.

"Not crazy at all," he said, pulling away from her to peer into her eyes. "What makes you think little boys don't have the same dreams?"

She could feel the unbelievable chemistry between them, a connection unlike anything she'd ever experienced. *This guy's too good to be true.*

They made their way back to the blanket just as pinpoints of white light appeared up and down the river, cast from the windows of the houses that bordered the waterway. This was followed by swaths of shimmering light—reverse shadows—that danced on the dark, rippling water. It was quiet but hardly silent. The water gurgled. The wind whispered. And even when a stiff chill crept into the air, it was too perfect to leave in search of warmth.

This is heaven, Maddie thought, paralyzed from contentment.

As if reading her mind, Phinn shuffled closer to her. Wrapping his arm around her shoulder, he looked back toward the sky. "I think

God's done a wonderful job," he innocently commented.

She looked at him. "Do you go to church?" she asked.

"I used to." As if stalling for time, he looked around. "I love the message. It's the messenger that I have a problem with."

She kept her eyes locked on his, but said nothing.

"Let me ask you something," he said. "Do you believe that God is unconditional love?"

"Absolutely."

"Me, too," he said, "so why does the church teach us to fear unconditional love?"

Although her lips parted to reply, she had no idea what to say.

"To control the masses through fear," he quickly added. "If we're taught that God loves us completely, unconditionally," he explained, "then how can we possibly face an eternity of torment if we break certain rules or wander off the right path?" He shook his head. "I've never been able to reconcile it." He paused for a moment in thought. "I just don't think the church can have it both ways."

She nodded in complete agreement.

"And I also can't imagine that today's church is what God intended," Phinn said, grinning. "Not that I can talk for Him."

Maddie returned the grin. "You mean Her, right?"

He laughed.

"Actually, I don't think God's either," she said. "I believe that wherever there's love, that's God."

"I guess I'm not the only poet, huh?" He looked back at the stars. "It's funny. I think these stars are the very reason I became an architect. I love the perfection in their design, the raw beauty."

"Phinn, the architect and the poet. Now how do you suppose that happened?"

"It's a mystery to me, for sure," he said, shrugging. "For some strange reason, I've always been drawn to the creative process."

"Promise that you'll show your poems to me," she said, leaning in to him.

"Why don't I just show you the one I'll write for you?"

"It's a good start," she said, nuzzling her head into his shoulder.

It was late when they returned to her car, the parking lot completely empty except for her vehicle.

"Thank you for such an incredible night," she told him. "It was the best restaurant I've ever been to."

"You're welcome," he said before slowly leaning in toward her mouth.

She couldn't help herself; she grabbed his face in both hands and kissed him hard on the lips.

When they came up for air, he was smiling from ear to ear. "I think I'm going to cancel my online dating service subscription," he whispered.

You'd better, she thought, but said, "I was just thinking the same thing."

"And the next time we go out…"

"And when is that?" she asked.

"I've been invited to a Halloween party and was hoping you'd join me," he said.

"A Halloween party?"

"Yeah," he said, nodding, "I hate them."

She laughed. "In that case, it's a date."

They kissed again.

• • •

On the ride home, Phinn's mind reeled. For the first time in his life, he actually felt scared to be with a woman. *What if Maddie realizes she's too good for me? And then she doesn't want to see me anymore?* he thought. *What then? Now that I know how great life can be, I could never go back to one without her.* He realized it was very early to feel as strongly as he did. *I mean, we just met,* he told himself. But it didn't matter. He was at Maddie Renaud's mercy now, the beat of his heart controlled by her very hand. He considered texting her right then and there, but decided, *I should wait until I get home.*

CHAPTER 7

Phinn bellied up to the bar alongside some guy dressed as a suave devil, his smirk adding nicely to the role. *I hate Halloween parties*, Phinn thought, as he ordered a vodka and soda. Turning toward one of the massive windows, he could almost feel the darkness that loomed over the creepy night. Taking a sip of his cocktail, he thought, *I can't wait for Maddie to get here.*

Twenty minutes passed before Maddie arrived, dressed as a voluptuous witch.

"There's my angel," Phinn joked, grabbing her hand. "You look as beautiful as ever tonight."

"Well, thank you. I'm sorry I'm late, but…"

"Forget it," he said, dragging her toward the dance floor. "I need to dance with you right now."

She started to giggle.

When they reached the center of the floor, he turned and pulled her in close. For the next few minutes—an eternity—they swayed back and forth, while the faces in the room disappeared, one after the other.

As the last few notes rang out, Maddie leaned into his ear. "Let's go outside," she whispered, "where we can be alone."

Grabbing her hand again, he made a beeline for the door.

In the abandoned park across the street, they took a seat on a green wooden bench. The autumn night was thick with energy. A crescent moon, a strand of light, dangled in the black sky, revealing mere shadows. While an eerie wind rustled through the oaks, Maddie said, "I really love this time of year." She rested her head on Phinn's shoulder to gaze up at the stars. After a few minutes of uninterrupted silence, she revealed her thoughts. "My Nana used to say that we're like particles of dust, blowing around aimlessly and bumping into each other, trying to discover where we fit into the grand scheme of life."

"Wow, that's deep," Phinn said.

She pulled her head away. "Don't tell me you're afraid of going to the deep end of the pool, Mr. Reed?"

"No, not at all," Phinn said, shaking his head. "I'm very comfortable on the deep side." He shrugged. "It's just that I'm used to swimming there alone."

"Well, that's no fun," she said, returning to her muscular pillow.

He laughed. "Your Nana sounds like a wise woman."

"She was."

Another moment of silence hung between them.

"So what do you think," he finally asked. "about why we're here?"

"I think it's all planned out long before we get here." She looked up at him. "We just need to find our purpose."

"I like that," Phinn said.

She returned her head to his shoulder. "It's hard to find passion in life when you don't know your purpose."

He cleared his throat. "I'm pretty sure I could find some passion right beside me."

Giggling, she met him face-to-face. "So tell me about Phinneas Reed," she said, kissing him, "where you came from...who you are." She nodded. "It's time to peel back the onion, so to speak."

He laughed. "I think I'll take a rain check, thanks."

"Sorry, no rain checks."

"Well, it wasn't easy growing up," he told her. "Sometimes, I'm surprised I even made it—with the braces, orthopedic shoes, glasses with the corrective tape in the corners."

"Poor guy."

"And I had to wear all three when I was in elementary school," he joked.

She laughed. "That's nothing. A few years ago, I saw an old schoolmate I haven't seen in years. 'Wow,' she said, 'you've really put on some weight, huh?'"

Phinn's entire body tensed.

"So I told her, 'No, I actually just lost forty pounds.' 'Then you look great!' the wench said." Maddie started laughing.

Phinn leaned in closer to her. "I think you look perfect," he said, his words brightening her eyes and lifting her shoulders.

She kissed him. "As long as I look perfect to you."

"You do," he said, "and I'd rather learn about you...about where Madelyn Renaud comes from?"

Maddie took a deep breath. "Well, let's see, my mother's a saint, and my brother, Jake, is the best man I've ever known." She smiled. "You're going to love them both."

"I am?" Phinn asked, thrilled at the prediction.

"You are," she said, "that is, if you ever decide to pick me up at my house like a real gentleman would."

He started laughing. "Next date, I promise." He smiled. "Then maybe I can stop feeling like a stalker."

She laughed. "But my father," she said, her face turning serious, "he was a different story." Her eyes drifted off.

"Was?" Phinn asked softly.

She nodded again. "He passed away nine years ago."

"I'm so sorry," he said.

"Oh, don't be," she said, almost too quickly. "I suffered my father's verbal abuse as payment for three meals a day and a hot shower," she explained. "He died when I was eighteen, getting ready to graduate from high school. I felt guilty about his death, because although I loved him, I couldn't cry when I found out he'd passed." As if on cue, her eyes filled. "I know this sounds horrible, Phinn, but a big part of me wasn't all that sorry when he was no longer around to belittle me." She looked away. "He could be really cruel, you know."

"That doesn't sound horrible at all," Phinn said, "I get it." He wrapped his arm around her shoulder. "Tell me about him."

"Well, he wasn't around much, but when he was you never knew what to expect. He was mentally disturbed, I think." She took a deep breath. "People either loved him or hated him—and most people didn't love him. There was no middle ground when it came to my dad. He was a nut in every sense of the word, and the stories that prove it are endless."

"Really?" Phinn said, prodding her to get it all out.

"It's been told that at an early age, his game of choice was playing undertaker for the neighborhood animals. Whether or not he intentionally killed any of his clients was always a bit hazy, but once their hearts no longer pumped blood, he gave them a proper burial in the small graveyard he'd founded." She locked eyes with Phinn again. "For anyone with an understanding of the human psyche, this is obviously not a normal start at life."

Phinn nodded, remaining silent.

"He was the type of man to engage in a conversation with Russian or Chinese people who didn't understand the English language,"

Maddie continued, "most never realizing that they were serving as the butt of his sick sense of humor. They also said he was a true prankster, even though most of his unsuspecting victims didn't appreciate it." She raised an eyebrow. "I'm no psychologist, but it seems pretty clear that my dad wasn't so much funny as he was mean." She shrugged. "Sometimes I think his need to constantly strike out came from his frustrated perspective on life and all of the disadvantages he'd fostered within himself. In either case, he was really tough on me." She paused to collect herself. "Not to mention, he was the worst thing that ever happened to my mom." She shook her head. "Oh, my poor mother, enduring each day in a mutually miserable marriage, unwilling to make a move—until there was nothing but kids who stayed in their bedrooms, avoiding parents who argued all the time." She shrugged. "Fighting apathy can be exhausting, I guess."

"I don't ever want to find out," Phinn muttered.

"And do you want to know the craziest thing about being that monster's daughter?" she asked, clear about the deep disdain she felt for him.

"I do," he said.

Her eyes glistened with old tears. "I actually loved him," she said, shrugging. "But I loved him for reasons I don't think I'll ever understand."

Phinn hugged her.

Some time passed before Maddie cleared her throat. "In the end," she said, "the cigarettes he smoked for all those years proved even meaner than he was."

Phinn squeezed her tighter. *And I thought my father was a loser,* he thought. Although he felt sorry for Maddie's suffering, he was grateful that she'd opened up to him. *I feel so close to her right now,* he realized, the idea that she'd shared something so intimate not lost on him.

• • •

Phinn finally found the time to meet Micah at the local YMCA.

"Thanks for coming down to shoot hoops, Phinn," the kid said, swishing another shot.

"I've been looking forward to it," Phinn said, fetching the ball. "I was hoping to get down here sooner, but…" He stopped, tossing the ball back to the smirking boy.

"But?" Micah asked, hitting another shot.

Phinn smiled. "I recently met a girl," he said, electing to be honest.

The kid's eyes lit up. "Good for you, player! Have you guys already…"

"Be respectful," Phinn warned. "I really like this girl, and I don't want to hear anything stupid from you."

"I wasn't going to say anything stupid." He skipped the ball to Phinn, who took an outside shot and missed badly.

"Sure you weren't," Phinn said, hustling for the rebound.

"Is she hot?" Micah asked, clearly unable to help himself.

"And there it is," Phinn said, laughing. He held onto the ball for a moment. "Micah, there's never been a more beautiful creature made by the hand of God." His eyes glassed over, as he stared off into the distance. "I'm already done for."

"What does that mean," the boy asked, "you're already *done for?*"

"It means that this woman could either break my spirit with a single look or heal my soul with those same eyes." He nodded. "It means I'm all in."

"Wow," the kid said.

"Yeah," Phinn agreed, "wow." He took another shot and finally made it. "Now it's up to me not to screw it up."

"And how would you do that?"

"By failing to treat her like she's the only woman on the entire planet."

Micah shook his head. "I think I'd rather stick with a variety."

"But that's only because you haven't lived long enough to know the difference," Phinn said.

Smirking, Micah took a three-point shot and missed.

• • •

After fixing his shirt, Phinn rang the doorbell and waited with flowers in hand like some nervous schoolboy.

The door opened, revealing a middle-aged brunette with short-cropped hair and Maddie's amazing smile. She extended her hand. "You must be Phinn," she said.

He shook her hand. "It's nice to meet you, Mrs. Renaud," he said, his anxiety peaked.

"Call me Julia, please," she said. "I'm too young for anything else."

"Okay, Julia," he said, feeling weird about it.

Julia escorted him to the couch. They were just about to discuss the weather, when a couple entered the living room, both of them smiling. "Hi, I'm Jacob, Maddie's favorite brother," the man said, extending his hand for a shake, "and this is my wife, Sarah."

Phinn stood and shook their hands. "Nice to meet you both. I'm Phinn."

"And Jake's Maddie's only brother," Julia clarified.

Everyone laughed.

The four started in on some small talk before Jacob said, "I know I probably shouldn't be telling you this, Phinn, but it's been a really long time since I've seen my sister so happy."

Sarah slapped her husband's arm. "No, you shouldn't be telling him that."

"Maddie would have your neck," Julia quickly added.

Jacob laughed. "But it's true," he said, rubbing his arm. "Whatever you're doing, Phinn, keep doing it." His face suddenly changed. "But if you hurt her, then you'll have to deal with me. Got it?"

Phinn was taken aback. "Ummmm…."

Sarah slapped Jacob again. "Stop it, you big goof."

Jacob started to laugh. "I'm just playing with you, man."

Although Phinn chuckled, his heart continued to race.

"Don't pay any attention to him, Phinn," Julia said, "he thinks he's funny, though we all know better."

They all laughed.

"I wasn't joking about Maddie being so happy though," Jacob added.

Offering a subtle shrug, Phinn smiled. "I haven't done anything," he said, "and I probably shouldn't tell you this, but the feelings are mutual. I know it's been a relatively short time, but I can't remember ever feeling this happy."

"I'll be sure to let her know," Julia teased.

"Me too," Sarah said.

Jacob chuckled again. "Oh, I see, so it's okay if you two…"

As Maddie walked downstairs, Phinn took one look at her and was removed from Jacob in mid-sentence. Phinn and Maddie stared into each other's smiles until Phinn remembered the lilacs. He handed them to her. "These are for you, beautiful."

"Thank you," she said, blushing.

Not thirty seconds down the road, Maddie turned to Phinn. "I'm sorry about the welcoming party back there. It's just that…"

"Please, don't even worry about it. Your family seems very nice. And your brother Jacob is something else."

"Yeah, Jake's an incredible person. Unfortunately, he's had his fair share of sorrow." She caught herself and stopped.

"Sorrow?' Phinn repeated.

"I'm sorry," she said, "I shouldn't be burdening you."

Picking up on the depth, Phinn placed his hand on hers. "Don't apologize. I'm interested. Go ahead, finish."

She looked deeply into his eyes. "A few months ago, we all moved here because of Jake and Sarah. Their daughter—my niece, Miranda—died from SIDS a year ago."

"Oh, I'm so sorry."

She nodded her appreciation. "Jake and Sarah took off for a while to heal. They came back to Connecticut and ended up talking me and Mom into moving to Massachusetts." She shrugged. "So here we are."

"With Jake's attitude, I would have never guessed," Phinn said.

"He is amazing. But if you asked him, he'd just tell you that it's his faith."

"Faith," Phinn whispered. "Good for him."

Maddie interlaced their fingers.

Crushed white sea shells crunched under the car's tires. Situated on the front end of a 29-acre farm in Westport's historic central village, Bittersweet Farm was a big barn with an antique buckboard covered in seasonal potted plants sitting out front.

Phinn parked, jumped out of the car, and ran around to the passenger side to open Maddie's door. Stepping out, she extended her hand. He gladly took it.

Hand in hand, they moved past the massive colonial-framed windows at the back of the restaurant, revealing the patrons dining in soft candlelight—generated by hurricane lamps—at linen-covered tables. Most couples leaned in to each other, betraying the quietness of the large room. As Phinn and Maddie made their way to the front of the rustic oasis, clever landscaping of ornamental grasses—capable of surviving the sweltering heat and frigid winters of New England's extreme seasons—bordered a winding walkway all the way to the front door.

Throwing open the heavy door, Phinn took note of the large room, its rough-hewn barn beams supporting a loft where more small tables were located. Tiny white lights illuminated a menagerie of glass and wood. *Great spot*, he thought, silently patting himself on the back for picking such a romantic location.

As they approached the hostess station, a young family was making their way out of the restaurant. "Come on, Lola," the man called out, extending his hand toward a small porcelain doll that lagged behind him.

The woman—Lola's mom—scooped up the little girl and met her husband in the foyer.

"She's so cute," Maddie told the woman, "and I really love the name Lola."

"Do you want her?" the man joked.

"I do," Maddie said, her face serious.

Well, okay then, Phinn thought, immediately understanding Maddie's thoughts on children.

"Sorry," the smiling woman said, kissing the little girl's cheek, "but you'll have to get your own."

Maddie looked at Phinn.

He swallowed hard.

"I love that name, Lola," Maddie repeated, waving at the little girl as she and her family left.

"I guess you do," Phinn said, noticing that the atmosphere on the main floor was quaint and rustic, while live acoustic music could be heard playing in the tavern below. He looked at Maddie. "Do you want to stay up here or…"

"I have a fireside table downstairs," the hostess interrupted, "if you guys are interested."

Maddie quickly nodded.

"That would be great," Phinn told the girl. "We appreciate it."

As they descended the stairs, the room was significantly darker, the ceilings lacking the height of upstairs. *This is even better*, he thought. The tavern was cozy, but when adding the fireside table—*Man, did we score,* he thought.

The hostess handed them two burgundy menus—a pigment similar to Cabernet wine—with gold embossed letters. "Ellie will be your server tonight, and she'll be right with you."

Phinn nodded, the menu feeling good in his hand.

"How was your visit with Micah?" Maddie asked, as they took their seats.

"Good," Phinn said, "the kid's either going to run the world or become a professional finger painter." He shrugged playfully. "I honestly don't see any middle ground for him."

"You're terrible," Maddie said, laughing.

Phinn nodded. "I think I'm exactly what that boy needs."

"He's not the only one," she muttered from behind her menu.

"What was that?" he asked.

"I wish I could order one of everything," she said, changing the subject.

"Go ahead," Phinn said, "taste it all."

She laughed. "Imagine?"

"I really like an a la carte menu," Phinn said, as he read. "It's a little more pricey but at least I'm not going to be served something I won't like."

"I don't know," Maddie said, shrugging. "Some of my favorite foods started off as things I thought I'd never like."

"Do you think you'll ever agree with me on anything?" he asked.

She grabbed his hand. "What fun would that be?" She deepened her voice. "Sorry, honey, but Mama didn't raise no bobblehead."

He stared at her. "I think I need to have a talk with your Mama."

"Good luck with that."

Laughing, they both dove back into their menus. While they browsed an incredible selection of appetizers and entrees, an acoustic soloist with a gifted voice performed the James Taylor classic, *Carolina In My Mind*.

"What do you think about sharing the stuffed mushroom caps?" she asked.

He shrugged. "I've never had them."

She raised an eyebrow. "Well, we're just going to have to take care of that today, aren't we?" She looked back at her menu. "The surf and turf looks good," she said. "Imagine if I order the last steak they have?"

"Then I'd have to fight you for it."

She grinned. "Oh really? How hard would you fight?"

He looked up from his menu. "Like I was the third monkey on the ramp of Noah's Ark."

She laughed. "Wow, that's all in."

"For steak, you'd better believe it."

While they laughed, Maddie ordered the mushroom caps, as well as the surf and turf. Phinn chose the filet mignon wrapped in bacon. Both cuts of meat were in supply. "And I'll take a side salad, as well," he said.

"Why?" Maddie asked with the waitress listening in. "We both know you're not even going to touch it."

Phinn shrugged. "You gotta take the bad with the good, right?" He looked up at Ellie. "I'll take the salad," he confirmed, "and if it's okay, I'd like to hold on to the menu."

Offering an apathetic shrug, the waitress stepped away.

"Have you ever actually ordered something different after you've gotten your meal?" Maddie asked.

Phinn shook his head. "Not once." He shrugged like a little boy. "I don't know why, but I like holding onto it. Always have."

"And what's with—*you gotta take the bad with the good?*" she asked.

"You got me, beautiful," he said. "I've been saying it since I can remember." He shrugged. "I'm not sure where that came from either."

"Whatever makes you happy, weirdo," she teased, raising her glass of Westport Rivers pinot noir. In turn, Phinn hoisted his sweating glass of Buzzard's Bay pale ale. They toasted. "To us," Maddie said before he could get a word out.

Those two simple words lit a flame in his heart. *Us*, he thought, loving the sound of it. "To us," he repeated, touching her glass hard enough to make it sing.

While Billy Joel's *She's Always a Woman* played in the background, Phinn watched Maddie take the first bite of the seafood-stuffed mushroom caps—like she was a canary heading into a coal mine. She moaned once, signaling that it was safe for him to jump in. Within minutes, they were wrestling in the shared plate for the last one.

"I can see that you're not a very good sharer," he teased.

"That's because you don't know me well enough yet," she replied.

I can't wait, he thought, happy to continue the playful banter.

Don McLean's *American Pie* was just coming to an end, when a monstrous slice of toll house cookie pie landed on the table. Both Phinn and Maddie looked up.

Ellie laughed. "Yeah, and good luck with that," she joked.

"If we finish it, do we get our photo on some wall of shame?" Phinn asked.

"Nope," Ellie said, lowering her tone, "but you'll have a pretty decent shot at diabetes."

Phinn laughed hard. "I like her," he told Maddie, as Ellie stepped away. "It's rare to find a waitress with such a good sense of humor."

Although Maddie nodded in agreement, she was already moaning over the sweet, gooey dish.

Phinn marveled at his dinner date, thinking, *Could this woman be any more perfect for me?*

Maddie moaned again.

When he offered to pay the bill, she teased, "Mr. Big Bucks."

He laughed. "Hardly," he said, "and if you're looking for a guy with money, then…"

She grabbed his arm. "But I'm not looking for a guy," she whispered. "Not anymore."

Phinn nearly lay his upper body on the table so he could kiss her.

On the ride home, Phinn pulled into Brayton Point Park. "I was hoping we could walk off some of that dessert," he said, realizing it was too late to run into Mr. Tetreault or his little buddy, Mason.

"We'd better march until morning then," Maddie said.

He laughed.

As they headed toward the river, she asked, "So when are you going to let me read your poetry? I've been waiting too long already, and for the record, I'm not a very patient person."

"You don't say," he teased, leading her to a grassy knoll where they took a seat.

She giggled. "I'm serious. I really need to…"

Placing his index finger to her lips, Phinn reached into the back pocket of his pants and retrieved a square of paper. Carefully unfolding it, he read, "A Poor Man." He looked up and smiled. "For Maddie," he added.

A subtle squeal of joy escaped her throat.

He began, "A poor man I've been called by most,
with gains enough to live.
But wealth, my love, is like a ghost,
from me, there's more to give.

"The moon and stars that paint the night,
a bubble bath with wine.
Dinner served by candlelight,
the promise of my time.

"Fresh-cut flowers from the wild,
the freedom to be you.
A constant mirror for your smile,
the giggles when you're blue.

"Dancing to the tap of rain,
each sunset, sharing tears.
A faithful heart that beats your name,
strong hugs to soothe your fears.

"An ear to catch your silent screams;
long kisses, soft and sweet.
Songs that bring peace to your dreams,
massages for your feet.

"Though the list goes on, I do confess,
as a poor man, I shall live.
Yet without man's gold, I have been blessed,
for the world is mine to give."

Maddie pulled him to her, where passionate kisses were exchanged until everything but the rhythm of the lapping river melted away.

Phinn placed his hand on her upper thigh, giving it a squeeze that left little doubt about his desires.

Maddie covered his hand with hers, squeezing it back.

Breaking off the kiss, he looked at her. "I'm sorry, Maddie," he said, "I didn't mean to…"

"Please don't apologize," she said, clasping both of his hands in hers. "It's fine." She grinned. "I hate to break it to you, but I'm not a virgin."

"I…I never thought…"

"Nor am I a prude," she added, interrupting him again, "but at this point in my life, I want to do it the right way. I need to do it the right way." She paused, remaining in his gaze. "I'm older now, a little wiser, and I know exactly what didn't work in the past." She kissed him gently on the lips. "You and I feel like a fresh start, Phinn, and I really want this to work." She locked eyes again. "I need this to work."

"Me too," he whispered, kissing her again.

CHAPTER 8

On their last official date, Maddie and Phinn ended up at their favorite spot, sitting on the river bank. As they sat together, huddled against the cold, Maddie studied his profile. *I thought I'd fallen in love before,* she thought, *but this is different. This is my first real love. Everything feels like the first time with Phinn—fresh and exciting.* Suddenly, there was no one before him. *And there certainly won't be anyone after him,* she decided. *He's it. He's my one and only.* She placed her head on his shoulder. *My love.* The dating phase was over; they were now an item.

At the absence of Maddie's relentless prodding, Phinn finally relented and shared his collection of poems with her. "These aren't to be seen by anyone else," he said, handing over a worn notebook. "They're my deepest thoughts, and I'd never share them with anyone but you. They're way too personal." He searched her eyes. "You promise?"

She snatched the book out of his grasp. "It's our little secret," she vowed, adding a wink.

She read through the table of contents. "The Past, Ice Cream Cone, Fields of Granite, A Poor Man." She looked up and kissed him before returning to the list of poems. "In The End," she read, her forehead wrinkling from curiosity. "What's that one about?"

As she scanned the curled pages for the poem, he answered, "My thoughts about death or the impossibility of it."

She read the poem to herself, her eyes filling with tears. "It's beautiful," she whispered, kissing him again. "*You're* beautiful."

He blushed.

"So you don't fear death?" she asked.

"I wish that were true," he admitted. "I had a terrible dream once, warning me that I'm going to pay dearly for all of my mistakes here on earth."

"Oh, I'm sure you'll be fine," she said, smiling, "I mean, what's the worst you could answer for?"

He hesitated, his face flushing.

Oh no, she thought. "Please don't tell me..."

"My ex-girlfriend had an abortion," he blurted, "and I feel like it's something that needs to be answered for."

An abortion, Maddie repeated in her head, taken aback. "Did you ask her to?" she inquired, without judgment.

"No," Phinn said. "The truth is, I didn't even find out about it until she'd already gone through with it."

Maddie slowly closed the collection of poems.

"I want to be an open book with you, Maddie," he said. "No secrets."

"Good," she said, "I want the same thing."

"Maybe I should have told you sooner, but..."

She shook her head, halting him. "You told me, Phinn," she whispered, her eyes swelling with tears as she felt the weight of the moment, "and that's all that matters."

He nodded. "Thank you," he said, giving her a grateful hug. "You're so perfect," he told her. "I bet you've never done anything wrong in your life."

Wow, now there's some naïve thinking, Maddie thought. "And I wish that were true," she said before taking off her coat and rolling up her sleeve to reveal a tattoo of a faded bloody rose. "I'm scarred, too," she whispered, "in more ways than one."

He never cringed. Instead, he gently touched the old ink. "I like it," he said.

"I'm glad," she said, putting her coat back on, "because it's part of the package." As she prepared to share the details, she immediately flashed back to her sordid youth.

• • •

Maddie—the lost teenager—answered the kitchen telephone. "Hello?"

"Oh, hi Maddie," Aunt Phoebe said, sounding surprised. "I was expecting your mom to answer."

Maddie cringed. The old woman's voice had the same effect as listening to a cat trying to climb a chalkboard. "She's at work, Aunt Phoebe," Maddie said. "Do you want me to give her a message?"

There was a pause. "Actually, I was calling her about *you*, dear."

"About *me*?" Maddie confirmed, swallowing hard.

"Yes," the old maid managed before clearing her throat. "But now…now that I have you on the phone, maybe…I should give you a chance," she stammered, "to tell me the truth."

Maddie remained silent, listening to the poor woman's heavy breathing.

"When you showed up at my house for a visit last week, I…I have to admit I was very surprised but I was also so happy, I can't tell you." She swallowed hard enough to be heard over the phone. "Sometimes being old can be lonely," she added, her voice cracking.

Maddie could feel the start of tears.

"Are you still there, dear?"

"Yes," Maddie squeaked. "I'm here."

"But then I noticed a few days later that some of my pills were missing. Not just some pills but a full bottle. I've searched and searched and still can't find them." She paused for a long while. "The only thing that's come to mind is that…"

"…is that I took them?" Maddie finished, defensively.

Aunt Phoebe gasped. "Well, it does seem peculiar that…that the pills were there before you visited, and when you left…"

"I didn't take them, Aunt Phoebe!" Maddie barked. "And I'm hurt that you'd even…"

"I'm sorry, dear," she said, upset. "It's just that…I need those pills for my nerves."

"I'm sorry your pills are missing, Aunt Phoebe, but you need to look somewhere else."

"I…I will, Maddie. I'll do that." There was a pause. "I'm so sorry I thought…"

"It's fine, Aunt Phoebe," Maddie said, tears streaming down her cheeks.

"I didn't mean to hurt you," the old lady said, her heavy breathing now laden with guilt.

"It's fine," Maddie repeated. *You can't hurt me any more than I've hurt myself*, she thought, hanging up the phone before her aunt could hear her sobs.

• • •

Maddie returned to the present. "When I was a teenager," she confessed to Phinn, "I went through a pretty rough patch. I started popping pills—any pills I could find. I even stole them from my elderly aunt once." She began to cry.

Phinn wrapped his arm around her. "Whoa, whoa, I didn't mean to get you upset."

She shook her head.

"That was a long time ago," he reminded her.

"I was fortunate enough to get off that bad path," she explained, "but I knew a few kids that never did." She took a few deep breaths, calming herself.

Phinn hugged her tight.

"But without my struggles," she added, "I would have never known my own strength."

"I'm sorry you had to go through that," he said, "but if it helped make you who you are today, I'm also grateful for it."

She kissed him. "How did I ever get this lucky to find a man as wonderful as you?"

He returned her kiss. "I hate to break it to you, babe, but I'm the lucky one in this deal."

They sat for a while in silence. "So what's the worst thing you ever did as a kid?" Maddie asked.

"What is this, confession time?"

She nodded. "Yup, it's good for the soul."

Phinn's eyes grew distant before he visibly cringed. "When I was a kid, I betrayed my best friend, Joshua."

"How?" she asked.

Phinn's mind warped back to that fateful day.

• • •

At thirteen years old, Phinn and his best friend, Joshua, strolled Westport Fair's bustling midway.

"I have a cotton candy allergy," Joshua said, grinning. "If I eat too much of it, my face gets swollen."

"You mean fat?" Phinn said.

Joshua nodded. "Zactly," he joked.

They both laughed.

Amidst the flashing lights, hectic sounds, and wide array of smells, a vendor—an older man, wearing rags for clothes, hawked, "Candy apples, get your candy apples here!"

Phinn grabbed Josh's shoulder to conspire a plan; peeking over at the vendor, he told his best friend, "Just because we don't have any money doesn't mean we can't enjoy a couple of candy apples, right?"

Joshua shook his head. "Are you crazy, dude? I'm not stealing anything!"

"You're such a chicken. Fine. I'll do it."

"Candy apples," the man yelled out to the thick crowd. "Get your candy apples here!"

"Your mother would kill you, if you get caught," Joshua pled.

Phinn smiled. "Then I'd better not get caught, right?" He slithered toward the vendor, with his reluctant friend in tow.

"Candy apples, get your candy apples here!"

While the man was distracted, trying to solicit customers, Phinn moved in. He was just about to grab two apples on a stick, when the vendor spotted both boys near his wares and grabbed them by the arms. "Trying to steal from me, are you?" he roared.

Phinn froze. "Na...no," he stammered, "we...we weren't trying to steal anything from you."

"You're a liar," the man screamed, looking around. "You know what, why don't we just go see what the cops think?"

Panic flooded Phinn's mind. "Cops? There...there's no need to call the cops."

"Sir, it wasn't him," Joshua blurted. "It was me."

The vendor looked at Joshua. "You?" he asked, skeptically.

"I'm the one who tried to take your candy apples," Joshua confirmed before gesturing toward Phinn. "My friend had no idea."

The man glared at Phinn. "Is that true?"

For a moment suspended in time, Phinn looked at his best friend—and then chose fear over honor. "Yeah...yeah, that's right. I didn't know he was trying to steal."

The scowling vendor immediately let go of Phinn's arm—who quickly ran away—before dragging Joshua off to talk to the police.

• • •

Phinn moped back into the present, shaking his sorrowful head. Though it clearly wasn't easy to share, he explained, "We were together at a town fair, and I had the bright idea of stealing a few candy apples."

She grinned. "That's kid stuff. Lots of..."

"But we got caught," Phinn interrupted her, "and even though he had nothing to do with it, Joshua knew I was going to be in deep trouble with my mother, so he took the blame."

"Oh," Maddie said.

"And I let him," Phinn said, his voice thick with torment.

She grabbed for his hand.

His eyes swelled with old, painful tears. "And do you want to know what the worst part of that betrayal of my best friend was?"

"I do," she said, clutching his hand.

"That my guilt and shame wouldn't allow me to remain friends with him." He shook his head, his throat choked off with emotion. "So I abandoned him, as well."

"Did you ever apologize to Joshua and make it right?"

He shook his head.

"Then you should."

"That was so long ago, Maddie. I'm not sure…"

"It's never too late to make things right, Phinn," she whispered, "and I'm guessing it'll be good for the both of you."

Phinn thought about it. "He lives just outside of town now, with his family. I'll go see him this week," he said, nodding.

"Good," she said, "and then you'll finally be able to let it go."

• • •

It was Friday afternoon. Maddie was on her phone, texting plans with Phinn. *I can meet you after the wake tonight.*

Wake? he texted back.

Yeah, one of the women I work with, her niece just passed away.

Oh, I'm sorry.

Me too. She was just a few years younger than us.

Oh man, what did she die from?

A drug overdose, Maddie wrote, sadly.

A few moments passed. *Do you want me to go with you?* he replied.

Not unless you enjoy wakes? she teased.

I don't.

Then I'll meet you afterward.

Okay, he quickly replied, and she could feel the relief in his text. *I'm going to go look in on my young friend, Micah.*

You're such a good guy, spending time with that kid.

Not really. I have a friend, Katie, who's so good that some of it rubbed off on me.

I look forward to meeting her, Maddie wrote.

And I look forward to seeing you later.

Me too.

• • •

Taking a few deep breaths to steady herself, Maddie stepped into the funeral home. From the moment she signed the guest book, she could feel the sorrow that blanketed the carnation-scented room. Slowly, she marched to the casket, took a knee, and offered two prayers: one for the deceased and the other for the suffering family. After conveying her condolences to each person in the receiving line, she found an empty seat in the second row.

Looking to her right, Maddie spotted the deceased girl's grandmother sitting beside her. Surprisingly, the elderly woman was smiling, peace illuminating her ancient eyes.

"I'm so sorry for your loss," Maddie whispered, offering her heartfelt sympathies.

The woman nodded her appreciation. "This world can be a cruel test for us all," she said before looking toward the casket, "and even more so for some. My granddaughter's gone home to her Father."

Pondering this, Maddie scanned the receiving line to see the deceased's dad swaying slightly, an unrelenting grief betrayed in his catatonic face.

"And I expect I'll be following soon," the old lady added, reclaiming Maddie's attention.

Wow, Maddie thought, taken aback by the woman's strong resolve. *Death is clearly not high on her list of fears.* Oddly, the woman's angelic smile eased some of Maddie's own fears about death.

As if reading her mind, the old woman patted her knee. "There's nothing to fret about, dear," she said. "Fear is for the faithless."

"I'll have to remember that," Maddie muttered.

"Be sure you do," the wrinkled sage concluded. "It's the path to peace."

• • •

Although Phinn valued his time with Micah, he couldn't wait to see Maddie. *I hope she's not too bummed out because of the wake*, he thought and turned to find her standing in his living room doorway, staring at him. A grin worked its way into the corners of her beautiful mouth. *There's my girl*, he thought. "How was the wake?" he asked, knowing it was a ridiculous question just as soon as he'd asked it.

"As terrible as any other wake," she said, joining him on the couch.

"I know," he said, "stupid question. Sorry." After kissing her, he thought about it. "Besides losing my mom, I've been pretty fortunate." Pretending it was a block of wood, he knocked on the side of his head. "I haven't lost anyone else who's close to me."

"I wish I could say the same," Maddie admitted, "though some were worse than others."

"How do you mean?"

She shook her head. "When I was young, I had a good friend who took her own life."

"Oh no…"

"Her name was Gail and she had a glass eye," Maddie explained. "And although kids can be unkind, they were no more cruel to Gail than she was to herself."

Phinn nodded that he understood.

"So one day, I guess Gail decided that she'd finally taken enough," Maddie said. "She was walking on the sidewalk of a busy street when, without warning, she stepped out into traffic—right in front of a speeding pickup truck." Maddie paused a brief moment; it was long enough for Phinn to grab for her hand. "They said she died instantly."

"Ugh," Phinn muttered.

"Gail committed suicide and even at my young age, the grief was consuming," Maddie said. "There was so much guilt and regret—everything that keeps you up at night. We'd been so close. I mean, our backyards bordered one another. We'd played together. We even shared our first kisses, with two neighborhood boys down near the railroad tracks. I always thought that awkward experience was going to bond us together for life. But after Gail took her life, even the funny memories we'd shared were a terrible source of pain."

Phinn let go of her hand to wrap his arm around her.

"A few weeks later, I was riding my bike home. It was late, getting dark, and I remember I was praying for Gail, when I started to pass an empty cornfield. Suddenly, I felt a presence, a familiar presence. I searched the field for shadows, but there was no one there. And that's when I heard a cowbell. I started pedaling faster, squinting to search the field as I passed. Still, there was nothing there." She sighed heavily. "I prayed harder than ever that night."

"Oh, wow," Phinn said, momentarily unable to access his vocabulary.

"That was such an awful year," Maddie said.

Phinn hugged her.

"A month later, my Uncle Victor passed away."

Phinn remained silent, awaiting more details.

"He was gay and had been infected by his new partner," she explained, shaking her head.

"Well, that sucks," Phinn blurted, immediately wishing he'd either chosen better words or bitten his tongue.

Maddie nodded. "I've been praying for the both of them—Gail and Victor—every night since they passed."

He hugged her tighter. "I'm sorry," he whispered, kissing her cheek.

She nodded her gratitude. "So how was your visit with Micah?" she asked, clearly wanting to change the subject.

"Good," Phinn said, shrugging. "He's a great kid, but he's definitely a one-man reality show."

She chuckled.

"Micah's the product of an entitled generation and the easy life that technology's provided."

"So he wouldn't get off his phone, huh?"

"Exactly," Phinn said, smiling. "But I see a lot of my younger, foolish self in him, so I'm hoping I can eventually steer him in the right direction."

"I think we forge our own way," Maddie said, with a half shrug, "for the most part, anyway." She thought about it and nodded. "The best we can do for others is to make sure they know they're not alone and that we're right there beside them, offering our love and support."

"Whoa," Phinn said, "that's heavy."

"The rest is on them," she finished, playfully slapping his arm.

"I think someone's going to make a great mom," he told her.

She peered into his eyes. "And I know someone else who's going to make an amazing father."

Phinn swallowed hard. *God, I hope so*, he thought. *I'd give anything for a second chance.*

They lounged on Phinn's couch, both content to be in each other's quiet company. After a while, Maddie grabbed Phinn's poetry book off of the coffee table and flipped to a random page. "A Walk in the Clouds," she said, and began to recite the piece.

"I walked amongst the clouds today
and then I took a seat
to try to understand the world
that spun beneath my feet.

"It was the grandest picture
my eyes had ever seen.
I couldn't make out colors,
except for blue and green.

"And yet, I could see people;
a whole race on the run.
To tell the truth, from where I sat
they clearly moved as one.

"With fear, they searched for answers
they thought were on the ground
and though they spoke in different tongues
they made the sweetest sound.

"They had the wrong perspective
with no way they could know:
There are no individuals,
but just parts of a whole.

"And so I made a wish for them
that someday they would see:
Only when they really love
is when they're really free.

"I'll dance amongst the stars tonight,
while others search in vain.
For just above their point of view
there's no such thing as pain."

She looked up at him, her right eyebrow standing tall. "Whoa,"
she said.

He offered a subtle shrug. "When I write, it's important that I
consider perspective," he explained, "and I figured that the farther
we get away from everything around us, the easier it must be to see
the truth."

She nodded. "Beautiful and wise," she said, impressed. "I'm not
sure which one looks better on you."

He laughed.

She thought about it. "I like both," she said, returning to Phinn's
tattered notebook.

• • •

The following morning, Maddie found an envelope tucked under her windshield wiper. She removed the lined paper from the envelope, unfolded it, and read, "One Favor—for Maddie." Her eyes were already misting over.

You've lived within my sweetest dreams,
your voice, your smell, your stare.
And on the night an angel spoke,
I found you standing there.

Kindness, truth, a hint of love
betrayed within a glance.
As if I was still dreaming,
I prayed for just one chance.

For all the struggles I endured;
the wrongs I tried to right.
I always knew I'd walk through hell
to find you on that night.

And there you were—just smiling,
aglow with peace and love;
the answer to my every wish
I'd sent to God above.

I dare not ask for one more thing
from God—He's done His part.

She smiled and finished,
From you, I beg one favor,
please take care of my heart.

Wiping her face, Maddie collapsed against the car's fender. "Thank you, Phinn," she said, holding the poem against her heaving chest. She then looked skyward. "Thank you, God."

• • •

Phinn peeked his head into Steve Nichols' office. "Do you have a minute, boss?" he asked, his tone all business.

"Of course," Steve said. "Come in; take a seat."

Phinn did as instructed.

"So we finally got you down to forty hours a week, huh?" Steve teased.

Phinn smiled. "Yeah, it's been great," he said, trying to maintain a serious demeanor. "Actually, my hours are the reason I wanted to talk to you."

"You want less?" Steve asked, looking concerned.

"No," Phinn said, hurriedly, "I was hoping to take on more again."

"Really? Money problems?"

Phinn grinned. "No, future plans."

Steve leaned back in his high-back leather chair and smiled. "Phinn, this business wouldn't be where it is today if it wasn't for your hard work. Take whatever hours you can handle."

Wearing an enormous smile, Phinn stood. "Thanks, boss."

"Maybe it'll even inspire Karl into giving me forty good hours?"

Phinn shook his head. "Getting Karl to accomplish anything is like trying to take a sip of water from a fire house," Phinn joked. "It's just painful."

While Steve smiled at the analogy, Phinn returned to his desk to work harder than he'd ever worked before.

• • •

That night, Phinn and Maddie talked for nearly two hours on the phone. "Steve's asked me to take on more hours at the office," he fibbed.

"Really?" she said, sounding disappointed. "Why?"

"I guess business has picked up and he needs to get the work out." He smiled.

"I hope not too many more hours," she commented.

"Whenever I'm not there, I'm all yours."

"Yeah, you are," she whispered.

As they prepared to hang up, Phinn told her, "Meet me in my dreams tonight, babe. I'll be waiting for you."

"I'll be there," she promised.

CHAPTER 9

Nearly a year and a half had passed since Phinn and Maddie's first date. It seemed like a lifetime ago; all of the loneliness and insecurity vanished in fifteen magical months of laughter and an ever-growing love.

Phinn found it more and more difficult to find the time for Micah, but he also felt compelled to keep his commitment. *No matter how busy I am,* he thought.

It was late afternoon when he pulled into the basketball court's parking lot. Micah was nowhere in sight. *Late, as usual,* he told himself, turning on the radio and leaning back in the driver's seat. Four full songs later, Phinn looked up to scan the court. *Still not here.* Aggravated, he picked up his phone and dialed Micah. It rang four times before the teenager answered.

"Hello?"

"Hey Micah, it's Phinn. Where are you?"

"I'm at my boy Gavin's house, why?"

"Gavin? Isn't he the kid you were telling me about? The bully?" Phinn asked. But before Micah could answer, he added, "We become the company we keep, right Micah? How many times have I told you that?"

"But Gavin's not the bully," Micah said. "That's Garrett and I'd never chill with that jackass."

"Okay, good," Phinn said, taken aback. "Weren't we supposed to meet at the courts today?" he asked, adjusting his line of questioning.

There was a pause. "Oh…right, I'm sorry."

"Sorry?" Phinn said, perturbed. "You can't be that sorry, right?" he said, "I mean, you've blown me off three times in the last couple of months."

"Yeah, I know. My bad. It's just that…"

"I'd rather you steal money from me than my time, Micah," Phinn snapped, cutting him off.

There was silence on the other end of the line; Micah was obviously surprised to find himself on the business end of Phinn's tirade.

"Listen, if you don't want to hang out anymore, that's cool. Just let me…"

"That's not it at all," Micah interrupted. "It won't happen again, I promise."

Phinn took a deep breath. "Then I'll see you back here next week, same time?"

"I'll definitely be there," Micah swore.

"Good," Phinn said, "I'm looking forward to it."

"I'm sorry, Phinn," the teenager repeated, his tone sincere.

"Forget it," Phinn said, "I'll whoop your butt at some hoops next week."

"Yeah, I don't see that happening, but…"

Phinn laughed. "Be good, kid. Talk next week." He hung up.

• • •

Julia, Maddie's mom, answered the phone. She listened for a few minutes before bubbling over with joy. "I understand, sweetheart. Mum's the word," she said. "But what a beautiful idea." She pulled the phone from her ear. "Maddie," she yelled up the stairs, "it's Phinn!"

The sound of quick footsteps danced across the ceiling above her. She placed the phone back to her ear. "She's on her way, Phinn."

"Thanks, Julia," he said on the other end of the line.

"Why is he calling the house phone," Maddie asked, as she descended the last few stairs, "and not my cell?"

"Because he wanted to speak with me," Julia said, seriously. *And that's the truth.*

"You need to get your own boyfriend, Ma," Maddie teased, "and while you're at it, you might want to trade in this old landline for a cell phone."

Julia made a funny face at her.

Smiling, Maddie grabbed the receiver from her mother. "Hi boyfriend," she said, wrinkling her nose at her mom.

Julia stepped off into the corner, trying to appear invisible as she listened to her daughter's one-word answers.

• • •

"Sorry to tell you this, babe," Phinn began, "but I need to work late again."

"Again?"

"Yes, and if I could get out of it, I would."

"Uh, huh."

Phinn felt awful; the entire conversation was clearly making Maddie frustrated and angry. *But she'll find out soon enough why I've been working so hard,* he thought. "At least we have the trip to the Berkshires to look forward to," he reminded her.

She remained silent.

"But I need to go for now," he said.

"Fine."

"I'm sorry, babe. I'll make it up to you. I promise."

"Sure."

"Bye, babe," he said, rolling his eyes—happy she wasn't there to catch it.

"Bye," Maddie said, hanging up the phone.

It's a good thing this charade's coming to an end, he thought, *because I don't think I can keep it up much longer.*

• • •

Julia emerged from the shadows.

Maddie looked up at her mother. "He's working late again," she said, her jaw muscles nearly clenched closed.

No kidding, Julia thought, trying not to smile. "Phinn's a hard worker," she said. "You're fortunate. It's much better than the alternative."

"Is it?" Maddie asked before storming out of the room.

Julia wiped her hands on her apron. "It sure is," she said under her breath. "Just you wait and see."

• • •

Phinn ended the call and re-read the Berkshire Whitewater brochure:

Thanks to scheduled water releases on the Deerfield River, we are able to enjoy whitewater rafting in Western Massachusetts from April through October. The Deerfield River runs through the foothills of the Berkshire Mountains along the historic Mohawk Trail. Known for its excellent trout fishing, the Deerfield has become an outstanding venue for whitewater rafting. The scenery is breathtaking and the river is clean and clear. From first-time families to whitewater enthusiasts, the Deerfield River offers an exciting whitewater rafting experience for everyone.

The Fife Brook section of the Deerfield River is the most popular rafting trip in Massachusetts. With several Class 1 & 2 rapids, this section of river is the ideal introduction to whitewater rafting for families.

To learn the basics of paddling, we start with a brief warmup. We then get right into action at Hurricane Hole, a great introduction to the rapids of the Deerfield River. We continue our trip by floating, relaxing, swimming, and soaking up the beautiful New England scenery. This theme of shooting fun rapids, refining our paddling skills, and keeping a keen eye for wildlife follows for about six miles until we approach the Class 3 Zoar Gap rapids—the only thing that stands between us and a riverside picnic.

After lunch, we're back in the rafts, on our way to the take-out through some more rapids.

"This will be perfect," Phinn said aloud, excited that he was finally able to execute his long-laid plans.

• • •

Maddie stormed back into the room. "God, I can't believe Phinn," she said, still frazzled.

Her mom emerged from the corner of the room. "What is it?" she asked, continuing to fight off a smile.

Maddie shook her head. "I've hardly seen him in weeks, and it really doesn't seem to bother him. We've even started arguing, which we've never done. He says he's just been busy at work and can't break away, but I think it's more than that. He's been distant. I...I don't know how much longer I can..."

Smiling slightly, Julia patted her frustrated daughter's shoulder. "Don't be so impatient," she interrupted. "The best things in life are worth waiting for, sweetheart, trust me."

"I don't know, Ma. Maybe Phinn's the one who should be doing the waiting," she said, storming out of the room again.

Julia's smile widened.

• • •

Phinn and Maddie checked in to the Warfield Inn at Berkshire East. Built in 1915, it was a comfortably-furnished bungalow located just a couple of hundred yards from the main house. *And we have it all to ourselves*, Phinn thought.

"I love it," Maddie said, kissing him. "Thank you for taking me here."

He laughed. "But you don't even know what we're doing here."

"It doesn't matter," she said, kissing him again. "I'm here with you, and we're finally going to spend some time together."

After unpacking the coolers and loading the fridge, Phinn suggested that they take a tour of the grounds. Maddie grabbed his hand.

From the top step of the front porch, they paused to take in the breathtaking view. Green rolling hills, peppered with pines, oaks, and white-trunked birch trees, were protected by a range of mountains that loomed over them. Even from this distance, it was clear that thick swaths had been carved into the mountainside to create ski runs.

Inhaling deeply, they began their stroll. The landscaping was pristine, with beds of wild flowers and acres of deep green pastures for the livestock to graze. Up the hill and past a small frog pond, they approached the first of several red barns—with two llamas waiting to greet them. Maddie hurried toward the fence.

"Be careful," Phinn warned. "I'm pretty sure they spit."

"That's okay," she said, "so do I."

He was still laughing when he noticed a dozen Adirondack chairs circling a stocked fire pit. *Definitely something to revisit later*, he thought.

As they headed toward the back houses and out buildings, they passed a stack of shrink-wrapped hay that looked like giant marshmallows. "Maybe we'll make some s'mores later," he suggested.

Maddie nodded. "We'd better find some massive graham crackers," she joked, never missing a beat.

As they happened by the second barn, they watched as a new calf was being bottle-fed by a man in high rubber boots and a worn John Deere hat. Pleasantries were exchanged before the farmer pointed to a dilapidated barn across for them. "That used to be an old lumber mill, but I'd steer clear of it if I were you," he warned. "One stiff breeze and she might come right down on top of ya."

"Thanks," Phinn said, "we'll stay away."

"There are some horses in the upper field," he said. "If you folks are lucky, you might get a glimpse of the new foal."

They walked for a while until they spotted the horses concealed within the tree line.

"They look like mares," Maddie said.

Phinn squinted to get a better look. "Well, not all of them," he said, laughing.

Maddie looked again. "Yeah," she said, "one of them is definitely a boy."

"Yup," Phinn confirmed, still laughing.

Back on the front porch, the happy couple shared dinner—pasta with chicken and spinach in a light vodka sauce—and a bottle of good red wine. Maddie also spooned out some salad for Phinn. "You gotta take the bad with the good, babe," she teased, with a wink.

He laughed, having no intentions of taking one bite of it.

As the sun played hide-and-seek with the mountains, a row of coach lights softly illuminated the winding pathway through the property. The thing that stood out most, though, was the quiet. With the exception of a few active crickets and some peepers, a peaceful stillness blanketed the vast farm.

"Do you want to sit by the fire pit?" he asked.

She stood and reached for his hand. "Lead the way, babe."

She's calling me babe again, he thought, smiling to himself.

Before they even reached the spot, Phinn spotted the glow. *I hope nobody's beat us to it*, he thought, feeling selfish. He breathed a sigh of relief when they got within sight and saw nothing but empty chairs. *Good*, he thought, *I don't have to share Maddie.*

Beneath a sky full of stars, they'd just settled into their chairs—Maddie's head buried into his shoulder—when four shadows slowly approached, two large and two small.

"May we share the warmth of your fire?" the woman asked, as though they were living at the turn of the century.

"Of course," Phinn said, disappointed with the intrusion.

"I'm Heather," the woman announced, "and this is my husband, Frank. These are our girls, Carly and Nora."

"Nice to meet you folks," Maddie said, "I'm Maddie and this is Phinn."

"Honeymooners?" the woman asked.

Phinn cringed.

"No," Maddie said, "just two people who love to sit by a quiet fire."

Phinn nearly laughed out loud.

"We're from the North Shore," Heather said, oblivious to Maddie's less than subtle message.

Frank, her husband, stared at the dancing flames. Phinn wondered whether the zombie was considering jumping in.

"Where did you two meet?" Heather asked, preferring to engage in mindless banter than to contemplate the shimmering Milky Way above.

"It's a funny story," Phinn said, sliding to the edge of his seat. He looked at Maddie. "Do you mind if I share it, dear?"

"No," she said, smirking, "by all means."

Phinn smiled. "Maddie served a few years at the women's penitentiary up in Framingham," he began.

Even in the dim light, the color in Heather's face changed. And for the first time since they'd crashed the party, Frank looked up from his coma, clearly amused by where this might go.

Maddie shrugged. "We all make mistakes," she said, looking Heather right in her judgmental eyes.

"Anyway, when she finally got paroled," Phinn said, "she was assigned to my case load. At first, it seemed inappropriate to become romantically involved, but my supervisor was kind enough to transfer her to another parole officer." He smiled. "We've been an item ever since." He grabbed her hand.

Maddie nodded, her face as serious as death. "Sometimes I think going to prison is the best thing that's ever happened to me." She looked at Phinn googly-eyed. "I would have never found my soul mate."

"Wow," Heather managed, "that's quite a story." There was a moment of silence before Heather slapped Frank's leg. "We should probably get the kids off to bed," she said.

"Already?" Carly complained.

"Yeah," Nora whined, "it's not even our bedtime."

"It's getting late," Heather said and stood, signaling the rest of the North Shore clan to do the same. "Nice to meet you two," she said. "Have a good night."

"You too," Phinn and Maddie said in unison, both struggling not to break out in laughter.

After the four shadows disappeared over the hill and out of earshot, Phinn raised his fist into the air. "Nice work, convict," he said, still staring into the fire.

Maddie bumped her fist on his. "You, too, boss man."

They both laughed.

As silence reclaimed the farm, Phinn and Maddie began kissing passionately.

When Maddie came up for air, she whispered, "I realize that this night has been a fairy tale, but I was hoping we could wait just a little while longer to seal the deal."

He pushed back to look her in the eyes.

"Everything's been so perfect with you," Maddie explained, "with us." She shook her head. "I know it may sound crazy, but I don't..."

Grinning, he kissed her again—ending her ramble.

"Believe me," Maddie added between kisses, "I want to be intimate with you more than anything in the..."

He kissed her again. "I know," he whispered. "I understand."

"You do?" she said, surprised.

"I do." He smiled wider. "But I do have one question."

"Sure, anything."

"Can we still sleep together?"

She kissed him again. "Of course," she said, "that couch didn't look too comfortable." She grinned. "And besides, I don't see anything wrong with a little heavy petting."

• • •

An hour after the sun arose, they sat on the porch in their pajamas, sipping coffee and eating Maddie's French toast. "It was my Nana's recipe," she said. "I've been trying to get it right for years, but I still haven't been able to pull it off."

Phinn took a bite and quickly looked up at her. "If your grandmother made better French toast than this, then she must have been a saint."

"I always thought so," Maddie said. "She left me her recipe."

Phinn took another bite. "She left you a fortune," he said.

Maddie smiled. "…along with a true feeling of being grounded." Her eyes drifted off. "Nana was my constant reminder that I could never be a nobody because I came from a long line of somebodies."

Phinn swallowed another bite. "I like that," he said.

"She spent years sharing our family's history with me. When I was young, I never realized how priceless that was." She nodded. "But I do now."

"Good," he said, "you should."

The morning air was still and crisp, a nice change from the oppressive humidity they'd endured all summer.

"It felt wonderful to be in your arms last night," Maddie said. "It felt right."

"It did," he agreed.

"Thank you for being patient with me."

"Please don't thank me," he said, "I loved last night too."

She kissed him.

"Are you ready?" he asked her.

"Ready for what?"

"To do some whitewater rafting?"

"You're not serious?"

He nodded. "I am. I hope that's okay?"

She nodded. "I've been wanting to try it my whole life but never got the chance."

"Well, today's your chance, pretty lady."

Given the conditions—and the fact that the dam was scheduled to be released up river within the hour—Phinn and Maddie checked in to Berkshire Rafting Center at ten o'clock sharp. After signing waivers, they opted out of the wetsuit rental and took a seat on one of the long benches to await the pre-trip orientation.

Once all of the rafters had arrived, everyone was equipped with vests—also referred to as PFDs, or personal flotation devices—a helmet and paddle. With everyone properly outfitted, the safety briefing commenced.

A thickly bearded, barrel-chested man, wearing a green biker's bandana, entered the large room. "The name's J.D.," he said in a commanding voice, "but everyone calls me Bison." He smiled.

Phinn looked at Maddie. "I guess we know who's in charge," he whispered.

"I know I wouldn't argue with him," she said under her breath.

After explaining what each piece of equipment would be used for, Bison covered proper paddling techniques. "So what happens if you fall out?" he asked, scanning his wide-eyed audience. "And some of you will fall out."

A middle-aged clown in the back of the room raised his hand. Bison pointed to him. "Then we'll go for a swim," the guy joked.

A few people started to laugh before noticing that Bison's face remained stoic. "What you *will do* is flip onto your back, keep your legs up and float," he said, using maximum volume. "Otherwise, you'll smash them on the rocks beneath you."

The room went silent.

"I will then throw you a rope. You will grab onto said rope and hold on while I pull you back onto the raft." He scanned the room again through squinted eyes. "Any questions?"

Everyone remained silent, and although the safety briefing was frightening enough to walk away, each person stayed.

"Good," Bison said, his smile returning. "We depart for the river in two minutes. Spend the time emptying your bladders and then get on the bus. It's a scenic ride to where we put in." He stretched out his back, resembling a grizzly bear emerging from hibernation. "We're going to have a great day out on the river," he said. "I just got that feeling."

Phinn looked at Maddie. "I hope Bison's in our raft."

As fate would have it, Phinn and Maddie drew the long straw and ended up in Bison's raft. Once they put into the river, they took their seats on the edge of the raft, wedging their feet into the bottom of the rubber boat. Seated across from each other, they exchanged smiles; it was a combination of the excitement of embarking on an adventure together, as well as the fact that Maddie's helmet kept sliding just below her sight line.

"To get us started," Bison yelled out, "we're going to take a picture, which means you need to paddle as hard as you can when I tell you to. We're going to turn the nose of the boat into Hurricane Hole." Sitting up high at the back of the raft, he smiled. "If we get it right, it'll be a great shot."

Both Phinn and Maddie braced their legs and drove their paddles into the water, paddling hard and fast while following every barked instruction from their giant guide.

Phinn was just starting to get beyond his fears to enjoy the challenge when the raft bounced off of a rock, throwing Maddie straight up into the air. One second, she was in the boat and the next, she was gone—under the water. *Oh, no!* Phinn thought, lunging across the raft to grab her. But she was nowhere in sight. His blood turned to ice water. *Please God*, he thought, his throat closing off in fear. He looked back toward Bison just in time to see the big bear fishing Maddie out of the churning whitewater like he was snatching up a flopping salmon. With one hand on her life vest, Bison yanked her into the boat and tossed her toward the front. "Keep paddling," he yelled to the rest of the rowers.

Maddie scrambled to retake her position and began paddling.

Phinn did the same. *What was I thinking?* he wondered, his body still rocked from the fear. *This is supposed to be fun?*

A moment later, they received a thumbs-up from the cameraman on the bank.

This had better be a really good picture, Phinn thought.

"They got the shot," Bison screamed out, quickly turning the boat down river with his paddle. "Now let's go have some fun."

Fun? Phinn repeated in his head, his heart still pounding out of his vest. He looked across to Maddie and shook his head.

"How long was I under?" she asked over the roar of the water.

"Long enough to scare the life out of me," he yelled back to her. She lifted the helmet off her eyes and smiled.

He shook his head, still trying to take in the air he'd lost. *I knew I loved Maddie and that I'd be lost without her,* he thought, *but I never realized just how much until now.*

"Relax, babe," she yelled back at him, "I'm fine."

He nodded. "I will," he told her, "as long as you stay in the boat for the rest of the trip."

She lifted her helmet again. "I'll try my best."

They were a half mile past the trauma when they hit a rapid called Amtrak.

"Everyone paddle," Bison screamed from his back perch.

Everyone did just that, working together to keep their raft upright.

"Good job, everyone," Bison yelled, as they exited the thrill ride. "You can rest for now."

Phinn looked at Maddie. She was smiling from ear to ear. *Relax,* he told himself, *she's fine.* He realized that he wasn't worried about himself falling in; he was worried about her. *But she's loving it,* he told himself.

As the river continued to howl, they rode the "bubble," speeding into one stretch of whitecaps after the next. Ranked from Class 1 through Class 3 rapids, Bison warned, "It's the rocks that you don't see that'll bounce you into the drink," he said, grinning at Maddie. "Am I right?"

"You're right," she yelled back.

"Now paddle," he screamed, as the small crew tackled a rapid named the Mine Field.

"Keep an eye out for hidden rocks," Bison called out.

Phinn leaned in and paddled hard, bracing himself against some unseen rock. They made it through without anyone taking a swim.

Other rapids included Miami Beach and The Gap. As each one was conquered, a sense of pride and camaraderie was left in their frothy wake.

Along the way, they bumped into their share of concealed rocks, several of the crew being catapulted out; each time, it was as if they'd been plucked out of the boat by some invisible force. Somehow, Phinn and Maddie managed to stay in the raft.

As Bison began pointing out a few of the rocks in the river—by name—he spotted some of the wildlife moving along the river bank. Placing two fingers in front of his mouth, he began screaming, "Beaver...beaver...beaver!"

Phinn laughed. *This guy's nuts*, he thought, *but he did scoop Maddie out of the water like he was saving a child, so the madman's all right in my book.*

The crew celebrated their success with a riverside picnic: turkey wraps and iced tea, finished off with some homemade cookie-brownies.

"I wonder if Bison baked the brownies?" Phinn whispered to Maddie.

She chuckled. "If he did, then you know he put something special in them and we probably won't remember the rest of the trip."

They both laughed.

Although they tackled a few more rapids, Phinn got the sense that they'd survived the worst of it. During the second half of the trip, they spent time drifting down the river—Tom Sawyer-style—until Bison showed off his skills by popping wheelies with the raft. At one point, Phinn and Maddie were laying back, looking straight up into the blue sky.

Other games included ramming rocks, which was not Phinn's favorite, and spinning through the rapids—with one side of the boat paddling forward and the other side paddling backwards. Just before the take-out, a water fight broke out between all of the rafts, five-gallon buckets being supplied for such a purpose. Phinn watched as Maddie laughed so hard she began to cry. He couldn't take his eyes off of her. *She's soaked from head to toe*, he thought, *and she's more beautiful than ever.*

Back at the Rafting Center at Berkshire East, the happy couple held each other close as they watched a slide show presentation of their rafting journey. Once Maddie bought some pictures, they were on their way back to the inn.

"Thank you for today," she told Phinn on the ride. "I can't remember the last time I had so much fun."

"That's great," he said, "but unfortunately, it didn't start that way."

"I was fine, babe," she said, shaking her head. "Besides, I needed a bath."

• • •

"Can you wait on the front porch for a minute?" Phinn asked Maddie when they got back to the bungalow.

With a creased brow, she nodded. *What's this about now?* she wondered.

Disappearing into the house, he was back within seconds, looking nervous.

"What is it, Phinn?" she asked, feeling some of his anxiety.

He took a step closer to her. "I was going to wait until tomorrow and do it up on the mountain, but I can't wait another minute." He took a knee.

Oh, my God! Her hand immediately went to her mouth. "Oh Phinn," she squeaked, her eyes misting over. *Is this really happening?*

He removed a piece of paper from his pocket, unfolded it and read, "A Lifetime Proposal for Maddie."

"Take my hand and walk with me,
it's just a simple choice.
Close your eyes and you will see
the future in my voice.

"To count your breaths while you have slept,
I've memorized your face.
In hopeless love, I've even wept,
yet known no better place.

"In crowded rooms, I've held your hand,
but felt we were alone.
If only you could understand,
where you are, I am home.

"I've seen my children in your eyes,
your smile; my twilight years.
Together, there can be no lies,
united, no more fears.

"Take my hand and be my wife,
my soul's eternal mate.
What I offer is my life,
the rest we'll leave to fate."

By now, Maddie was down on her knees with him.

Phinn extended the ring box and opened it. "Marry me, Maddie...please," he said, his words dripping with emotion. "I swear I'll love you for the rest of my life."

She began to cry. "Yes," she managed, "yes!" She kissed him. "And I promise to love you for the rest of mine."

He slid the ring onto her finger. It was a perfect fit.

Hysterical, she kissed him in between the laughter and sobs.

"Should we go tell Heather and Frank?" Phinn teased.

"No," she said, "I want you all to myself." She looked at him, feeling overwhelmed with all the love she felt for him, as well as the sudden realization that she was going to spend the rest of her life with him.

"I'm sorry I've been working so many hours, babe," he told her, "but I knew we'd need the money for the wedding."

She nodded, her mind too overloaded to properly process the information.

"I don't want your family worrying about having to pay for any of it."

"Thank you," she said, feeling bad about her recent frustrations with him.

He shook his head. "And we can wait to be intimate until we're married," he said.

"Really?" She offered a mischievous smile. "Because I was thinking…"

"I know what it means to you, Maddie." He nodded a few times, as if steeling his resolve. "As long as it doesn't take too long to plan our wedding."

She laughed through the sniffles. *Not a chance*, she thought.

"Because I need you badly," he said, kissing her again. "I am a man, you know."

"I know," she purred, "you're my man." *And always will be.*

CHAPTER 10

Maddie had taken multiple photos from the bungalow's front porch and then pieced them together to create a panoramic view of the exact location where Phinn had asked her to be his wife.

Jacob looked at the massive picture before slapping his future brother-in-law on the back. "You hopeless romantic," he said, "it didn't take you long to pop the question, did it?"

Phinn shrugged. "When you know, you know," he said, winking at Maddie.

"I do know," she whispered.

Phinn turned back to Jacob. "I know Maddie wants you to give her away, Jake, but I was wondering if you wouldn't mind staying up there with us as my best man?"

"I'd be honored," Jacob said, taken aback, "but I thought you'd be asking your friend Karl to be your best man?"

"Karl and I have been friends for years. He'll understand." Phinn smiled. "You're family."

"Family," Jacob repeated in a whisper, "I like the sound of that." They shook hands.

Maddie turned to Sarah. "And since you're the sister I never had…"

"Yes," Sarah screamed, "of course I'll be your maid of honor!"

• • •

The night before the wedding, Phinn called Maddie's phone.

"Are you nervous?" he asked her.

"No. I'm excited."

"Meet me in my dreams tonight," he whispered. "I'll be waiting."

"I'll be there," she promised, "but we both need to go to sleep first."

"Goodnight, beautiful," he told her.

"Goodnight, babe."

• • •

Even for August, it was really hot, the type of heat you could feel yourself walk through. As Phinn paced back and forth in his tailored suit, Jacob approached him, grinning. "You guys couldn't wait until the fall, huh?"

"Nope," Phinn replied, "couldn't wait another day."

"Fantastic," Jacob said, patting Phinn's back, "that's exactly what I wanted to hear."

"I love her, Jake," Phinn vowed. "I really do. And I'm going to take good care of her."

"I know that, Phinn. And I also know my sister. She absolutely adores you, man." Jacob nodded. "You guys have found a rare love in each other. I couldn't be happier for the both of you."

"And I couldn't be more grateful." They hugged.

"Listen, I need to go collect the bride." Jacob winked. "I'll see you out there on the field."

Phinn tried to chuckle off some of his nerves. "Wow, you make it sound like we're going into battle."

Jacob shook his head. "For some families, I'm sure that's true. But not ours."

"Thanks, brother," Phinn said, trying to keep his emotions at bay. "You got it, brother," Jacob replied, his eyes misting over.

Sakonnet Vineyard, New England's oldest winery, rested on 150 plush acres of land, a portion of which produced some remarkable award-winning wines. Their grapes were grown locally, picked by hand, and barrel-aged in oak. Nestled between two waterways, Sakonnet's cool air combined with a humid subtropical climate, rarely found in northern America. These conditions fostered a longer ripening season and a later-than-average harvest. While slight winds blew in from the water, Phinn looked out onto the sprawling grounds. Tucked into the heart of the vineyard, their wedding ceremony and reception were surrounded by rows upon rows of grapevines on all sides. *Maddie picked the ideal place for us to tie the knot,* he realized.

Rows of chairs—bride's side and groom's side—were divided by the center aisle. As the music started, Phinn and the minister stood together at the flower-covered gazebo, awaiting the rest of the party. Phinn scanned the crowd to see Julia smiling at him. He returned the smile. Young Mason Sterne and his parents were seated beside Mr. Tetreault, who was sitting in front of Katie and Micah. The teenager was looking at Phinn and smiling from ear to ear. He winked at his young friend. *The only one missing is Mom*, he thought, immediately looking skyward. *But I know you're with me today, Ma,* he told her in his mind. *I can feel you here.*

In the distance, several groomsmen and bridesmaids were making their way across the lawn, followed by an overzealous flower girl and a ring bearer who'd recently learned how to walk. As the hushed laughter of the guests subsided, Jacob and Maddie appeared. *Oh, my God,* Phinn thought, momentarily losing his breath, *she's so*

beautiful and…and she's walking toward me…to…to become my wife.
He struggled to take in oxygen. *Whatever you do*, he told himself,
don't pass out.

As the smiling siblings stopped before him, Jacob kissed Maddie's cheek before whispering something into her ear.

She nodded. "I will," she mouthed, smiling.

Jacob then took three steps forward and turned, taking his place
beside Phinn.

Maddie grabbed Phinn's hand. "Hi, handsome," she whispered.

"Hi, beautiful."

"I hope you didn't wait too long?"

"I would've waited forever for you."

The minister cleared his throat. "Welcome family and friends, as
we celebrate the blessed matrimony of Phinneas and Madelyn." He
gestured toward the vineyard with his sweeping hand. "Surrounded
by the Lord's chosen drink, I'm predicting a joyous night for us all."

Everyone laughed, most being polite.

"Phinneas and Madelyn have…"

Maddie coughed loudly.

The man smiled. "Phinn and Maddie have elected to write their
own vows," he said, looking out into the small audience for effect,
"which makes my job a lot easier."

There was less laughter.

"Phinn, if you would," the minister said.

The groom squared his body to be able to look directly at his
bride. "Maddie, you are the one, my one, and I knew it from the very
moment I laid eyes on you." He blinked away the tears that began to
form. "I've been waiting for you my entire life, never realizing how
much I missed you until the night we met."

The crowd cooed.

"You have my heart, now and always, and I promise to be the best man I can be for you, for us, from this day until my last." He squeezed her hand. "I love you with everything inside of me, Maddie, and it's my honor to become your husband."

"Wonderful," the minister said, turning toward the bride. "Maddie, you're up."

Everyone laughed.

Maddie took a deep breath to compose herself. "Phinn, you are my dream come true, the dream I've had since I was a little girl. From the moment I looked into your eyes, I saw that one piece of me that had always been missing. And this may sound crazy, but I believe I've known you for much longer than I have."

Another wave of coos traveled through the crowd.

"From this day on," she continued, "there is no more me without you." She returned the squeeze. "Becoming your wife means everything to me, and I will always be your lover, your confidant—your best friend. Thank you for loving me and for letting me share all the love I have inside of me." Overwhelmed with emotion, she stopped.

"Beautiful," the minister finally said, unsure whether she'd finished. "The rings, please."

The tuxedoed ring bearer shook his head. There was a pause, followed by a brief struggle and another wave of laughter.

After wrestling the jewelry from the little boy, the minister turned to the smiling groom. "Phinn," he said, "do you take Maddie to be your lawful wife, promising to respect and love her all the days of your life?"

"I do," Phinn answered, loud and clear.

The minister turned to face the bride. "Maddie, do you take

Phinn to be your lawful husband, promising to respect and love him all the days of your life?"

"I do," Maddie said, just as robustly.

"Phinn," the minister said, smiling, "you may kiss your bride."

With tearful eyes, Phinn and Maddie met halfway, pulling each other close and sealing their future with a kiss.

Applause echoed through the field.

Phinn leaned in and kissed his wife again. "I love you, Mrs. Reed," he whispered, realizing, *I finally have a family again.*

"You'd better, Mr. Reed," she whispered back, "'cause you're stuck with me forever now."

As they walked up the center aisle, across a plush green lawn that rolled and dipped, Phinn felt like his feet weren't even touching the ground.

Maddie's boss, Ally Rose, snapped off one photo after the next, while music—*Summer Wind* by Frank Sinatra—seeped out of an alabaster white tent. *How appropriate,* Phinn thought. Hand in hand, he and his wife made their way toward an informal receiving line to greet their smiling guests.

While Maddie and Katie talked for a few minutes, meeting for the first time, Phinn spent the time with Micah. "Thanks for coming," he told the dapper-looking teen. "It means a lot to me."

"I wouldn't have missed it," Micah said, smiling. "It's not every day I can go on a date with a teacher."

"Don't you dare…"

"I'm kidding, Phinn. I'm kidding." He started laughing.

Phinn smiled. "Make sure you thank Ms. Fleet for bringing you."

"I already have."

"Good man."

Micah nodded. "Congratulations, Phinn. I'm happy for you."

"Thanks Micah," he said, giving the kid a hug.

Within the reception tent, long linen-covered tables with padded folding chairs were lit by flickering hurricane lamps—a special place setting dedicated to Phinn's mother. He smiled at the sight of it. *Thanks for sharing this day with us, Ma.*

The D.J. waved from the portable dance floor located beside an open bar that was stocked with all the beer and wine their guests could consume. *I'm sure someone will be carrying Karl home tonight,* Phinn thought. Beyond the clean portable bathrooms, the bake master and his young apprentices were working away on the far end of the field.

Several servers carrying trays of champagne cocktails, as well as the clambake's signature cocktail—a "Dark 'n Stormy," Goslings Black Seal Rum, and ginger beer, served over ice in a mason jar—scurried about. Other smiling servers, a mix of young men and women, carried silver trays of hors d'oeuvres, snaking their way through the crowd and pausing at each person they passed. These bite-sized delights included cocktail-sized stuffed quahogs, risotto croquettes with fontina cheese, scallops wrapped in bacon, and peppercorn-crusted tenderloin on sliced baguettes with horseradish cream sauce.

A loud bell suddenly rang out in the corner of the field, signifying that guests were invited to view the opening of the clambake.

Families dressed in suits and light summer dresses—led by a swarm of rambunctious kids—hurried across the field to where the bake master stood, leaning on his long rake. Phinn and Maddie followed the stampeding hoard.

The bake master, a large man in denim overalls, wiped his forehead with a red handkerchief from his back pocket. As he worked his steel rake, he said, "You good folks are about to enjoy a traditional old-fashioned clambake." Explaining the tradition as well as the process in his thick New England accent, he gave everyone the feeling that they'd just traveled back in time. "The entire menu is cooked over hot rocks, covered with seaweed." He wiped his brow again. "We started early this morning by digging a hole and starting a fire that turned those rocks cherry red. After that, we covered the rocks in fresh kelp, or seaweed, before wooden crates were stacked on top, each one filled with a different food like clams, mussels, and potatoes. The whole thing was then covered in the heavy tarps you see covering this pile." He wiped his forehead once more.

Phinn looked at Maddie, who was beaming with joy. Although the molehill emitted some very strong smells, she predicted, "This is going to be delicious."

"It had better be for what we paid," Phinn whispered.

She slapped his arm.

Playing to their enthusiastic crowd, the bake master and his staff transferred the steaming food into the steel baskets for serving.

"What did Jacob whisper to you before we got hitched?" Phinn asked his new bride.

"He told me to take good care of his brother."

Phinn's eyes filled. "I still don't know what I did to be so blessed." He grabbed her hand. "Finding you was a miracle, but when you throw in your family…"

"They love you, too, babe," she said, grabbing his hand and following the bake master and his sweaty assistants back to the tent.

At each table setting, a wedding favor awaited—corks holding place cards intended to be used as picture holders later on. There were also two different wines available on each table. For a white, Phinn and Maddie had selected the 2014 Expedite Happiness, containing surges of green apple, grapefruit, and a touch of honeysuckle; it was a light-bodied Chardonnay with a clean taste—perfect with seafood. For the red, they went with the NV Blessed Blend, a mix of Cabernet Franc, Lemberger, Merlot, and Cabernet Sauvignon; this medium-bodied blend exhibited notes of black cherry, dark chocolate, and oak.

In preparation for the toasts, Blanc de Blancs was being poured out—a dry and crisp white bubbly, glinting with citrus and apple combined with notes of almond for a balanced flavor.

Sarah grabbed the microphone. "Maddie, thank you for letting each one of us share in your dream today," she said in a shaky, high-pitched voice. "You've been my sister from the moment we met, and I'm so happy that you've finally found the love you deserve." She looked toward the groom. "Welcome to our family, Phinn," she said, "your family." She lifted her trembling champagne glass and took a sip.

Everyone followed suit before applauding.

Phinn nodded his gratitude.

Keeping his glass raised, Jacob grabbed the microphone from his wife. "To Madelyn and Phinneas," he said, winking at his sister in jest. "I have never met two people better suited to spend the rest of their lives together. I could not be any more thrilled that you found each other and are beginning your lives anew." He winked at Maddie again.

This time, she smiled.

"Remain best friends, always," Jacob added before focusing on

Phinn, "and when she gives you a hard time, I'm always here to listen, brother."

Everyone laughed.

Jacob hoisted his glass a bit higher. "To Maddie and Phinn," he concluded.

Everyone drank, applauding again.

With their glasses still raised, Maddie looked at her grinning husband. "To us," she whispered.

"To us," Phinn repeated.

Once the applause subsided and the bride and groom kissed, the D.J. resumed the ballads at a lower volume. Phinn and Maddie remained seated to be served, while their happy guests headed for the buffet line.

It started with a chowder station offering Rhode Island-style clear broth quahog chowder. From that point forward, a culinary paradise could be found: steaming trays of Maine soft-shelled steamed clams, Prince Edward Island mussels, and a mountain of perfectly steamed pound-and-a-half lobsters. These were followed by a supporting cast of sweet corn on the cob, red bliss potatoes, a spicy Portuguese sausage known as chourico, onions, and finally, filets of steamed cod. Plates of mixed green salads and hot brown bread and butter were waiting back at each table.

"Who's Barry Amaral?" Maddie asked, looking over at the smiling man. "You've never introduced me to him."

"Barry isn't a bad guy. He's just not a good friend," Phinn said, thinking, *Though I probably would've ended up in prison if I kept hanging out with him.* "I guess it's not so much a friendship that we share now," he added, shrugging. "It's more like just memories."

"And Karl?" she asked.

"Karl's different," Phinn said. "He's the type of guy to wear a shark fin hat in a public swimming pool."

She laughed.

"How can you not be friends with a knucklehead like that?" he said.

"What's he like at work?" Maddie asked.

Phinn glanced over at Karl to see him goofing around with the guests at his table. "Let's just say that most children grow out of the days of innocence and their childlike sense of wonder, but Karl's eyes have remained blind to adulthood."

She laughed, drawing everyone's attention. Several spoons struck wine glasses, requesting that the young couple kiss.

"I'm so happy that your friend, Joshua, accepted our invitation," Maddie said after their orchestrated smooch.

"Me, too," Phinn agreed. "If it wasn't for you, I'd still be lugging that burden around with me."

She kissed his cheek. "Consider it part of your wedding gift."

"There's more?" he asked, joking.

"Oh yeah," she said, seriously, "much more."

"I'm hoping Joshua and I can resurrect our friendship and pick up where we left off," Phinn said, looking over at his childhood friend and the man's wife, Sylvie.

"You will," Maddie said.

For dessert, platters of fresh watermelon and assorted mini-pastries were served, along with fresh brewed coffee and tea. While women fanned themselves and nibbled on sweets, men found their comfort at the bar, sampling the generous beer selection.

"Can I buy the happy couple a drink?" Karl asked Phinn, as he passed by the head table.

"Thanks, buddy," Phinn said, "but it's open bar."

"Oh, I know," Karl said, smiling, "so it looks like you're the one who's buying then."

Maddie laughed, finding the comment much funnier than her husband did.

"Please don't encourage him, babe," Phinn said, trying not to smile.

After the delicious dinner, everyone—from grandparents to the stumbling ring bearer—headed for the dance floor. And through the hot and muggy night, the music blared. Light blue shirts quickly became dark blue shirts, while a camaraderie was cultivated between families, two clans fusing into one. There was an occasional breeze off the river, which should have broken through the stagnant air and offered some relief, but the dancing mob preferred to sweat it out.

"I love you so much," Phinn told his wife, as they danced.

"How much?" she asked, grinning.

"More than I have words for," he admitted.

"Then show me without words," she said, hurrying out of the tent.

Phinn took chase, gladly following his playful partner to discover paradise among the grapes. Giggling, they ran through the rows of vines until the music and their howling guests were nothing more than a distant echo. "We're finally alone," Maddie said, stopping at a grassy path between the high rows.

The night was serene, a million stars twinkling above. Feeling buzzed on a strong mix of alcohol and love, Phinn studied his beautiful wife's face and smiled. *I don't just love this woman*, he thought, *I adore her*.

Returning his smile, she began to remove her wedding dress. Phinn quickly stripped off his suit. Naked for the first time, they embraced, kissing passionately beneath the waning summer moon. The kissing quickly turned to heavy petting until they were making love among the vines, the music still pulsating in the distance.

Phinn was as nervous as a virgin, and in many ways, he was. He'd never experienced such an unconditional display of love. As physical as it was—their two bodies intertwined, rocking as one—it was also a spiritual experience, his mind completely free of anything and anyone other than Maddie. He was completely with her in the moment. Everything else in the world just faded away. There was only Maddie and his intense desire to prove his love for her with every move he made.

Once they finished, both breathing heavily and grinning, they lay on the grass and looked up at the open sky.

"Hopefully, no one will notice that we've been gone," Maddie said, panting for air.

"I couldn't care less," Phinn said, rolling over to kiss her sweaty neck, "I just want to get home and make love to my wife again."

Satiated and disheveled, they returned to their guests. As they slithered their way through the crowd and back onto the dance floor, Sarah approached Maddie. "Nice night for a walk, huh?"

Red-faced, Maddie nodded. "The best."

Sarah looked at Jacob and then at Phinn.

"The best," Phinn confirmed.

They all laughed.

Guests were starting to bid their farewells when Phinn watched Mr. Tetreault approach, smiling.

"Tonight was a magical night," Mr. Telreault said. "Thank you for letting me share it with you."

"Of course," Phinn said, as Mr. Tetreault hugged Maddie, "it wouldn't have been the same without you."

"And your brother was right, you know," the man said, looking into Maddie's eyes. "The most important thing is that you two remain best friends."

"We will," Maddie said, wrapping her arm around Phinn's waist. Phinn did the same.

"Good," Mr. Tetreault said, before hugging each of them and stepping off into the dark night.

Arms locked around each other's waists, Phinn turned to his wife. "He's right."

"About staying friends?" she asked.

"Yes," Phinn said, nodding, "and that this was a magical night." From the romantic location and delectable food to the boundless love that filled the humid tent, he couldn't imagine a more enchanted evening.

Maddie nodded in agreement. "I hope all our guests had a great time," she said.

"It's a night they'll never forget," Phinn said. "I know I won't."

• • •

Back at their apartment, both the grass-stained wedding dress and wrinkled suit never made it past the living room.

This time, the foreplay was extended, with Phinn kissing every inch of his wife's quivering skin. He inhaled her scent, locking it into his brain for all time. And unlike his past, he was much more interested in satisfying his partner than himself. It was a mix of tenderness and passion, like a pendulum that brought them into perfect synch—exchanging hot breaths and sweat and involuntary moans.

After making love again, they showered together, Maddie giggling while Phinn lathered up every inch of her squirming body. As the warm water rinsed her clean, Phinn kissed her rose tattoo. "There is nothing about you, Mrs. Reed, that I don't love."

"Ditto," she whispered between kisses.

Wedding night sex is hardly sex, he thought, *at least not how I've ever known sex to be.* It didn't feel ordinary or meaningless. *It was anything but meaningless,* he thought. *It was amazing.* As Maddie gave herself completely to him, he'd done the same. *I've never experienced anything like it,* he realized, *not even close.*

CHAPTER 11

Maddie had decided that they'd honeymoon in St. Lucia, the world's leading destination for newly married couples. The enchanted honeymoon package included a bottle of champagne and two commemorative glasses, a tropical fruit plate and a flower arrangement upon arrival, a 50-minute couples massage, celebration dinner for two, and a room upgrade to a king-sized bed that featured a third floor ocean view from a private balcony.

Phinn had been hoping for flip flop weather: but from the moment they stepped off the plane, he was concerned that his melting sandals might actually fuse with the steaming asphalt. *It's hotter than hell*, he thought, *or at least on par*.

After a seven-hour flight, Phinn and Maddie hobbled on sleeping legs through the tiny airport, which definitely had a third world feel about it. Two customs officials, slow enough to avoid any chance of heart disease, processed their paperwork.

The taxi ride to the resort—in an older model Mercedes that reeked of incense—sped through the hilly jungle terrain. While Maddie snapped off one photo after the next, the grinning driver maneuvered through switchback after switchback, all the way up the narrow mountain road. Speeding past plush countryside, the green blur was broken up by the occasional banana farm. A few times, Phinn thought he might actually lose his continental breakfast. To distract from the onset of car sickness, he began a relentless line of questioning about the island. Thankfully, the driver was happy to answer each one, as he raced into 180-degree turns at 45-degree angles.

"What's the one thing we should absolutely do while we're here?" Phinn asked.

"Besides make a baby?" the man said, smiling.

"Yeah, besides that," Phinn said, while Maddie continued to take pictures as though she hadn't caught the comment.

"Make sure you visit Soufriere, our old capital, and the Pitons."

"Thanks," Phinn said, deciding to cease the interview.

The car wound through several traditional Caribbean fishing villages, tropical rainforests, and banana plantations. The scenery was stunning. As they passed one shanty town after the next—consisting of cinder block shacks, barefooted children running about, and the occasional roadside stop with signage of cold beer and bottled water—Phinn worried that he might puke up his guts at any moment.

Maddie looked at him. "Are you okay?"

He nodded. "I'll be fine."

She winked. "You gotta take the bad with the good, right?"

The St. James's Club at Morgan Bay was a vibrant, all-inclusive resort, promising relaxation, romance, and adventure.

Phinn and Maddie met their bags at the room. After tipping the bell hop, they shut the door behind them. Phinn hurried to the balcony to check out the view. Beyond the white sugar beach, peppered with vacationers enjoying different water sports, the aqua blue and teal Caribbean Sea met a sky of baby blue. There was a warm breeze, making the palm trees sway to the rhythm of the island's calypso music. To the left, a giant thatched hut—one of the resort's many restaurants—was perched on the end of a long dock. To the right, there were several pools, with people swimming up to the bars to order their colorful cocktails. Phinn felt Maddie's arms wrap around him from behind.

"It's paradise," she whispered, tickling the hairs on the back of his neck. "I'm going to take a shower, Mr. Reed," she said. "Do you care to join me?"

Phinn slammed the glass slider shut, nearly catching his fingers.

• • •

Feeling liberated in their new bathing suits, they toured the resort, with its many poolside bars and beautiful restaurants. After grabbing two frozen strawberry banana daiquiris from the Tiki Bar, they headed for the beach. The place was packed with couples and families; by their accents, many of them were Europeans on holiday. It didn't matter. For all intents and purposes, Maddie and Phinn existed all alone in the world. Draping their towels over two blue lounge chairs, they finished their drinks before running for the surf. *Paradise,* Maddie repeated in her head.

Holding each other in the warm bath water, they swayed to the ebb and flow. "I wondered if I'd ever make it here," Maddie said.

"St. Lucia?" Phinn asked.

She shook her head. "No," she whispered, hugging him tighter, "in the arms of the man of my dreams, looking forward to sharing the rest of my life with him."

"Well, I'm here," he said, kissing her lips, "and I still can't believe I get to spend the rest of my life with you."

Yeah, you do, she thought, returning his salty kiss. As they stood waist-deep like two wrinkled raisins, Maddie whispered, "I just had the best idea."

"What is it?"

"How 'bout we head back to the room and make love before dinner?"

Phinn sprinted out of the shallows like he'd just spotted a shark. Laughing, Maddie followed his lead.

• • •

Located directly over the lagoon, Morgan's Pier Restaurant was an open kitchen that put together a seafood platter that could have fed five. Although there was an amazing view of the Caribbean Sea right before him, Phinn preferred watching the flickering candlelight dance across his wife's angelic face. *This must be what heaven looks like*, he thought.

When the waiter reached for the menus, Maddie handed hers over but said, "Can he please keep his menu?"

The man's sun-kissed face contorted in confusion.

She shrugged. "I find it a little strange myself, but it's a thing for him."

As the waiter hurried off, Maddie smiled.

"A *thing*?" Phinn asked.

She nodded. "A strange thing," she reminded him, reaching for his hand. "Fortunately for you, I love strange things."

Phinn laughed.

As they drank frozen blended drinks, Maddie said, "I don't think we're supposed to have these with dinner."

Phinn laughed. "Why," he said, "it's not like there are any adults here to stop us."

"That's true."

After a moonlit walk down the beach, occasionally stopping to make out like two middle school kids, they were lured toward the Sunset Bar & Lounge, an open-air pavilion that served as the resort's main bar. As a local band played Caribbean music, Phinn and Maddie found a poolside table where they enjoyed a candlelit nightcap.

"So what do you think of married life so far?" he asked.

Keeping a straight face, she shrugged. "It's okay, I guess."

"What?"

She started to laugh.

"Keep it up," he said, "and I'll put you over my knee and give you a good spanking."

"Promises, promises," she whispered.

They quickly finished their drinks and raced back to the room.

• • •

After enjoying the breakfast buffet at the Palms Restaurant, Maddie and Phinn met the smiling concierge at the front desk.

"We'd like to book a day trip to the volcano and mud baths for tomorrow," Maddie said, considering that the term *mud baths* might be a contradiction.

The concierge smiled wider. "Great choice," he said, "great choice." He opened the brochure and then began to explain the details of the trip, as he'd undoubtedly done a thousand times before. "You'll enjoy a leisurely stroll through the town of Soufriere," he said. "Once there, you'll visit our twin Pitons, the Diamond Botanical Gardens, and the Sulphur Springs. At the volcano, you'll see the bubbly waters from a viewing platform. After that, you'll visit the Diamond Falls Botanical Gardens, whose centerpiece is the beautiful Diamond Waterfall. This 56-foot waterfall is one of St Lucia's most treasured natural wonders," he added with a proud nod.

Maddie returned the nod, impressed.

"And when you stroll through the lush tropical gardens," the man continued, "keep an eye out for native birds that live in the mahogany and red cedar forest."

"Sold," Phinn said, grinning, "we'll take two tickets."

"Two tickets, it is," the concierge said, extending his hand to accept the credit card.

Wrapping up a full day of drinking and eating and drinking some more—alternating their time between the pools and the beach—Phinn and Maddie arrived for their reservation at The Bambou, an al fresco beachfront restaurant with modern Caribbean décor located just steps away from the lapping shore. Their eclectic offerings included Asian fusion and contemporary Caribbean cuisine for the evening fare. "The concierge said we were lucky to get this reservation tonight," Phinn said, perusing the oversized menu.

Maddie grabbed his hand and stared into his eyes. "It feels like everything I do with you is lucky."

"Me too," he whispered, kissing her hand.

In the restaurant's soft light, they enjoyed a quiet dinner at a leisurely pace.

"Another great meal," he told Maddie, as the waitress cleared their dinner plates.

"It sure was," she said, radiating. "Are you sure you want the sorbet for dessert?"

He shrugged, picking up the single menu he'd kept at the table. "I don't know," he said. "What else were you thinking?"

"Me," she whispered.

"Check, please," Phinn called out in jest. Removing the napkin from his lap, he threw it onto the table and stood. "Let's go," he said, grabbing her hand. "I don't know what just came over me, but all of a sudden I have a wicked sweet tooth."

"Good," she said, giggling all the way back to their room. *Let's go burn off some of these calories.*

• • •

In the morning, the yawning newlyweds waited on the deserted beach with a couple dozen strangers for the Calypso Cat, a 42-foot power catamaran, with a sound system that could have rivaled a concert stadium.

"You look tired," Maddie teased.

"Tired, but happy," Phinn said, feeling more content than he'd ever felt.

"If I'm too much for you," she said, "just let me know."

"Never!" He shook his head. "I'd die first."

She laughed.

A half hour down the island's coast— just beyond the picturesque harbor of Marigot Bay—the party boat passed a sheltered fishing village. Flanked by tall cliffs that overlooked a charming hillside village, they stopped in its cove to do some snorkeling.

After donning masks and fins, they stepped off the boat and plunged into the warm water. They weren't twenty feet from the boat, when several canoes and kayaks approached, native vendors peddling their wares. "Looks like we found the Walmart of the seas," Phinn joked, before he and Maddie swam up to the hawkers to do some browsing. There was an array of cheap bracelets and coconuts. Phinn chose a bracelet for Maddie. "But you'll have to wait to get paid until I'm done snorkeling," he told the salesman.

"Of course, man," the paddling vendor said, "I'm not going anywhere."

With the mighty Pitons looming overhead, they finally reached Soufriere.

"This is going to be awesome," Phinn said, excitedly.

Maddie giggled. "It already is."

From the boat dock in Soufriere Town, the beautiful former French Capital of St. Lucia, they immediately boarded a bus to visit the gorgeous Botanical Gardens and Diamond Waterfall. After a brisk walk through the rainforest, they finally reached the breathtaking waterfall. Along with forty other honeymooning couples, they waited in line to take a picture.

"Is it me," Maddie commented, "or does this entire experience seem a little too rushed?"

"It's a tourist trap, for sure," Phinn said, handing the bus driver his cell phone to capture a few well posed shots.

Back on the bus, they quickly arrived at the mineral baths. "These baths were once commissioned by Louis XIV," the tour guide announced, "and we still believe they have therapeutic powers."

Phinn and Maddie stripped to their bathing suits before carefully navigating the slippery rocks. Once into the mucky stream, they took handfuls of mud and lathered each other up. *This could be really erotic*, Phinn thought, *if it wasn't for the fifty strangers standing around us.* Stinking of sulphur, their entire bodies were covered—faces included. "This is so crazy," Maddie said, giggling like a little girl. Phinn pulled her close, kissing her hard—as though no one was watching.

After rinsing off, they were back on the bus to be transported into the heart of Soufriere, where the day trip continued on foot.

The town had a cool island feel about it—like a huge street party—with the pounding beat of reggae helping to create the laid-back vibe. Right away, Phinn could see that Soufriere was a busy hive of activity with the local fishermen taking to the sea in their colorful boats or *pirogues* and returning with the day's catch—snapper, tuna, dorado, barracuda, Spanish mackerel, lobster, and crabs. The plethora of sea dwellers quickly made their way to the villagers' coal pots and grills, which lined the beachfront.

"Finally," Phinn said, excitedly, "we're going to rub elbows with the locals and experience some of their culture."

Maddie stopped in her tracks and turned to face him. "That's exactly what you wrote in your dating profile," she said.

"Really?"

"Really."

He smiled. "Are you sure about that, babe?"

"Absolutely," she said, nodding, "I memorized it."

Salivating, they followed their noses toward an unforgettable lunch.

After washing down a few final bites, the couple wandered the streets, finding that the crowd was a nice blend of locals and visitors. Behind brightly covered tables, friendly artisans and artists—happy to trade their handmade goods for American dollars—were set up among rum shops, bars, and impromptu cafes. With music playing in the background, Phinn and Maddie browsed—and bought—while sampling some of the locally made rum and traditional cassava bread.

On the boat ride back to the resort, Phinn sat with his back against the rail. Sitting between his legs, Maddie leaned against his chest. "What was your favorite thing we did today," he asked his wife, "the mud baths, the shopping, the..."

"Right now," she said, interrupting. "this is my favorite."

He kissed the top of her head. "Good answer."

"What about you?" she asked.

"I'll let you know in an hour when we're back in our room."

Giggling, she leaned back harder into his chest. "*Great* answer," she said.

The following day was spent on the beach, laying beneath the shade of three palm trees, a Caribbean breeze blowing straight at them. Although the Tiki Bar was only a stone's throw from their blue lounge chairs, they opted to use the beach service by raising a red flag, rallying a platoon of white-pants waiters to deliver their cold libations—one after the next.

"I could really get used to this," Maddie slurred, sipping on a fresh rum punch.

"Me too," Phinn said, "but unless we hit the lottery, you might want to enjoy it while it lasts."

After a full day of drinking dark rum beneath the sun, both Phinn and Maddie were completely intoxicated.

"You're tho drunk," she told him, giggling.

"I'm *tho* drunk?" he repeated, laughing.

"Sop it," she said, careful to pronounce the *s*.

"You *sop* it," he said.

She slapped his arm, her giggles turning to snorts.

"The beach party's tonight," Phinn said, "but I doubt we'll make it."

"Oh, we're bein' there," she said, getting up from the chair and stumbling her first few steps.

He laughed. "Oh, we're *bein' there*, all right."

From a row of Tiki torches that lined the dark beach, flames danced to the rhythm of the lapping surf. Phinn and his staggering bride perused the bountiful buffet-style dinner, with Maddie taking photos of everything her eyes met. While a steel drum band set the mood, actors dressed in native costumes—fire jugglers, a grim reaper, and three skeletons walking around on stilts—worked the crowd, providing the entertainment. But thanks to a full day of drinking, everything was a blur. Phinn looked at his wife and chuckled. *It's a good thing she's taking pictures*, he thought, *or we'd never remember any of this.*

They approached a man using a machete to open coconuts, throwing a straw into each one. Maddie accepted one and took a sip, her face contorting at the unfamiliar taste. Phinn laughed again.

"Ooh, a limbo contest," Maddie said, walking sideways like a sand crab in that general direction.

Phinn grabbed her arm and spun her into him. "We should probably take a rain check on that, babe," he said, hugging her.

She looked confused.

"In our condition, that's just an invitation to a bad head injury," he explained.

She shrugged.

They returned to the buffet where Phinn took out his phone and snapped a picture of the roasted pig on a spit, his bleeding-heart wife frowning beside it.

"One more drink?" Maddie suggested.

"What can it hurt," he said, "it's not like either of us has to drive."

While the crowd thickened and music filled the warm air, Phinn felt like he was in the middle of some surreal dream. *At least we'll sleep good tonight,* he thought, looking to his right to find Maddie on one knee, taking more photos. He laughed again. *I hope she gets at least a few good shots.*

She looked back at him and grinned, her eyes fogged over.

But I doubt it, he thought. "What are you going to do with all of these pictures you're taking?" he asked, teasing her.

"I'm going to say *you're welcome* years from now when you're thanking me for taking them."

Wow, he thought, smirking, *I guess someone's not as drunk as I thought.*

On the last full day of their honeymoon, they tried to get in everything they could, while Maddie continued to capture each moment with her overworked camera. At her prodding, they finally visited the Choc Bay Café, which served specialty teas, local coffees, and sweet homemade pastries. Although they passed on the full afternoon tea with finger sandwiches and fresh fruits, Phinn was able to feed his actual sweet tooth with some gooey chocolate concoction.

Saving the best for last, the newlyweds made a dinner reservation at Le Jardin Restaurant, a quaint bistro that promised romantic, upscale dining in air-conditioned comfort. From French Creole cuisine to savory steaks and seafood, Phinn and Maddie looked forward to an intimate evening filled with fine wine, decadent desserts, and first-class service.

At precisely eight o'clock, they were seated beside the pianist. "You look beautiful tonight, Mrs. Reed," Phinn told her, opening his menu.

"Well, thank you, Mr. Reed," she said, radiating true contentment. "I hope this place is worth the thirty-five-dollar surcharge."

"There's a price to pay for everything, babe," Phinn said before looking around, "and we're not here to save money, that's for sure."

She laughed.

"Although we definitely need to buckle down when we get back, if we're going to build our own home."

"Our own home?" she repeated, excitedly.

He nodded, taking a break from the thought for Maddie to order her dinner.

"A glass of Riesling," she said, scanning the menu one last time, "and I'll have the lobster." She surrendered her menu.

With a nod, the woman looked toward Phinn.

"I'll have a glass of the cabernet, and I'd like the best steak you have, cooked medium." He thought for a moment. "And throw in a side salad."

Maddie snickered.

Nodding again, the smiling server waited for his menu for a few moments before walking away without it.

While the piano player tickled the ivories, Phinn reached across the table and grabbed Maddie's hand. "So tell me about your dream house," he said, excited to resume their talk of the future.

"My dream house?"

"Yeah, when you picture the house of your dreams, what does it look like?"

Although it was subtle, a squeal escaped Maddie's lungs. "That's easy," she said, "I've been imagining it for years now."

He grinned, waiting.

"I picture a full-dormered Cape…"

"A Cape?" he repeated.

"Of course," she said, nodding. "We live in New England, right?" He laughed.

"With three bedrooms and two full baths," she added, "decorated in rustic design, but with all the modern amenities." Her eyes widened. "And there's a wraparound porch in the front." She nodded. "Definitely a big, wraparound porch."

"I like it," he said, smiling, "and what can you see from that big, wraparound porch?"

"I see a small residential neighborhood where the land rolls and the emerald-green lawns are perfectly manicured." Her eyes were distant now. "I see mulched, kidney-shaped flowerbeds sprouting wildflowers of honeysuckle and lilac, black-eyed Susans and tiger lilies sharing space with columbine, clover, and Oriental poppy. There are a couple of small Japanese cedars shading hydrangeas, pansies, and impatiens, with green and red ornamental grasses mixing nicely with silver mound, Russian sage, and juniper." She looked at Phinn. "Colors that'll steal your breath away, you know?"

"I do," he said, nodding. "So what do you think about working toward making that dream come true when we get home?"

"Are you serious?" she asked, even more excited.

"I am," he said. "It'll take some sacrifice and a lot of hard work but…"

"I love the idea, babe, but I don't want to trade in our time together for a house."

"I get it." He nodded again. "We'll definitely have to find a balance."

"You promise?" she asked. "I'd love for us to build our own home, but not at the price of..."

"I promise," he interrupted.

She kissed his hand. "My family has always rented," she said. "We never owned a home, so this really would be a dream come true for me."

"Then let's make it happen together," he said, thinking, *I still don't know everything about Maddie, not even close.* He smiled. *And I hope that never changes.*

After savoring a remarkable meal, they finished the night—as well as their unforgettable honeymoon—singing Billy Joel's *Piano Man* with the rest of the restaurant's happy-go-lucky patrons.

• • •

As the plane lifted into the air, banked left, and headed for home, Phinn looked out the small window to memorize the turquoise waters that surrounded Saint Lucia.

"It was the trip of a lifetime," Maddie said, patting his knee.

"It was awesome," he said, nodding, "but we have a lot more trips ahead of us." He then watched as they flew over the mountains and a terrain ranging from sandy beaches to lush rainforests.

"The trip of a lifetime," she repeated.

He came out of the window and rested his eyes on her. "Whatever you say, dear," he teased.

She smiled. "Now you're starting to get it," she said, patting his knee once more.

CHAPTER 12

The first snow of the season blanketed the world. In their cozy corner of that dream-like reality, Phinn was kissing Maddie when she grabbed his face in both hands. "Hon," she said, softly, "what do you think about having a baby?"

"Of course I want to have kids."

"I mean, now."

"Already?" he asked. "Are you serious?"

As if she'd just come up with the brilliant idea, she nodded. "I've never been more serious about anything in my life."

"But we never talked about having a child now. I thought we were going to build a house first and get a little more settled financially." He placed his hands on hers. "You never mentioned this before, babe. What's going on?"

"I don't know," she whispered, grinning, "but something's changed. I have this strong sense that my life will never be complete without having your baby."

"I'd love nothing more than to be a dad," he said, a bolt of excitement ripping through him. "You know that." He kissed her again, this time more passionately. It was their first step in the baby-making process.

• • •

Although life had become insanely busy, Phinn continued to visit with Micah. He wasn't spending as much time as he would have liked with the teenager, but he felt it important to stay in Micah's life.

"So what's going on with your math grade?" Phinn asked.

"What do you mean?"

"I mean, you have a C average right now. Is that good enough for you—a C?"

"How do you know?" Micah asked.

"Katie, I mean, Ms. Fleet..."

"Is a snitch," Micah interrupted, preparing the video game console for battle.

"No," Phinn said," she's actually a great teacher who cares about your future." He nodded. "I wish I'd had one of those when I was your age."

Micah said nothing; he just handed Phinn his video controller.

"Do you need a tutor?" Phinn asked. "Or I can help you..."

"Math's different now, harder. It's not like the olden days when you did it."

Phinn chuckled.. "Fair enough. We'll get you a tutor then."

"How's married life?" Micah asked, his eyes locked on the television screen.

"Don't change the subject."

"Not that great, huh?"

"I love it," Phinn said, working the video game controller, "I couldn't be happier."

"Really?" the teen asked, clearly skeptical.

"Really," Phinn said, chuckling.

"She must be special," Micah said, easily slaying Phinn on screen.

"She is," Phinn said, "though she basically has the same needs as any other female."

Micah smirked. "And what are those?"

Phinn grinned. "It's the simple things that make them smile," he said, fighting to stay alive on screen. "The trick is to be thoughtful and put them first." He thought for a moment. "I'll never forget my mother's advice about the opposite sex. It seemed so ridiculous at the time, but when I think back now…" Phinn's mind instantly rewound to his adolescent years.

• • •

Frustrated and confused about the third girl he'd liked in six months, Phinn sat beside his mother at the kitchen table.

"Why the long face?" she asked, offering her complete attention.

"I don't think I'll ever figure girls out." He sighed heavily.

His mom grinned. "That's probably true," she whispered.

He looked at her, taken aback by the comment.

"Your opposite sex," his mother said, clearly trying to wipe the grin from her face, "is mysterious by nature." She nodded. "We only reveal what we wish, leaving the rest to those who have the courage to explore us further."

I wish my dad was still around for these talks, Phinn thought. "Why can't it just be easy?" he asked. "Straightforward?"

His mom chuckled. "Because women live by their feelings, Phinn, and rely on their instincts. Some even wonder why their needs aren't understood without ever explaining them." She offered a subtle shrug. "Women will test your heart and constantly check its depth," she said. "Without even being in your presence, we can sniff out wandering eyes or anything less than the truth."

I'm already sorry I asked, Phinn thought, putting on the same face he wore when pretending to pay attention in class.

"We only want to be placed first," his mom continued, "though we'll never request it. We want solid communication, but will rarely say it. And we want someone who'll understand us completely, though we'll never, ever show our entire hand." She chuckled at her own words.

This isn't helping, Mom, Phinn thought, his head abuzz.

"All women are maternal and protective, almost territorial, when it comes to those they love," she added. "The truth is found more in what we don't say than in what we'll have you hear. And it's the little things like flowers and poetry that mean more to us than anything." She smiled.

"Ummm...okay," Phinn muttered, hoping to put an end to the painful lesson.

The smiling woman looked into Phinn's eyes, preparing to drive her next point home.

Phinn slid to the edge of his seat, ready to stand and make his escape.

"Most women like to feel the safety a man can provide," his mom continued, "though we'll fight to hold onto our independence. We're compassionate and sensitive, and though we desire the same from a mate, we're also attracted to raw masculinity."

Oh, dear God, Phinn thought, *please make it stop.*

Shrugging, his mom chuckled again. "I suppose the word *mysterious* doesn't begin to explain who we are."

Phinn couldn't take any more. He finally stood. "Yeah, thanks mom," he said, leaving even more confused than when they began the awkward heart-to-heart chat.

• • •

Phinn returned to the present to find a comical expression on Micah's face. "It may seem odd to you," Phinn said, chuckling, "but you had to know my mom. She was both mother and father to me." He nodded. "She was everything."

"I can relate," Micah muttered, nodding, "but if your mother was right, then understanding girls seems like way too much work to me." He worked his controller like it was an appendage he'd been born with.

"Oh, but the incredible joys you can reap in return," Phinn said before catching himself.

Micah paused the game, his face lighting up. "Oh yeah, like what?"

Phinn grinned, saying nothing.

"Tell me," the kid said.

Phinn shook his head.

"That's not fair," Micah said, reluctantly resuming the game.

"Life's not fair, my friend," Phinn said just before watching his final life on screen terminated by the smirking teen. "And you'll be working with a math tutor this week. I'll arrange it, okay?"

"Okay," Micah said.

"You're welcome," Phinn added.

"I appreciate it," Micah said, maintaining his smirk.

• • •

It was eternal dawn. Two silhouettes stood in the soft light of a cloud. Through the veil of fog, the shorter shadow held a thin burgundy-colored book the approximate size of a menu. Phinneas Jr.

was having a conversation with God before being sent into the world. The silhouettes remained faceless. There was a faint sound of birds chirping and a whistling wind. "So you're sure you're ready, P.J.?" God teased in mid-conversation.

"Oh, I've been ready!"

"As I've explained, there's a perfect plan for all people," God said, still grinning.

"But I'll still have to learn everything I already know?" P.J. asked, dumbfounded.

"Trust that everything you'll ever need for the journey, you already have inside of you. The catch is, you can't remember it, or the experience would be compromised. There would be no reason to create what you already know will be, right?"

Although he was still confused, P.J. nodded. "But if I can't remember, how will I know the path I'm supposed to follow?"

"The heart knows...the soul knows," God said.

P.J. was at a loss.

"Intuition, faith, unmistakable signs," God embellished. "I'll also send angels to guide you."

"How much time will I have?"

God shook His majestic head. "Although the measurement of time is required on earth to create the illusion of order and control," He gently explained, "time is non-existent to me. Here..." He swept His hand across the shimmering firmament. "...there is no past or future; everything is happening *now*." He shrugged. "Unfortunately, by default, time brings forth fear." He shook His head again. "As soon as the clock starts ticking, everyone begs for more without ever knowing the truth." He smiled. "Contrary to popular belief, you are all spirits having human experiences, and not the other way around."

"So you're not going to tell me how long I have then, huh?" P.J. prodded.

God laughed. "You'll be on that plane of existence for as long as you need to be, my boy. But you belong home."

P.J. surrendered with a nod.

"P.J.," God said, "some people live an entire lifetime in one single moment. It's what you make it."

"And you'll be with me, right?"

"You have my word."

"But don't you have to be with others, as well?" P.J. asked.

"Each and every one," God said, grinning again.

"Then how can you be everywhere at once?"

"Can love be everywhere at once?" God asked. "And what does *once* mean?"

"At the same time," P.J. fired back.

"Here we go again with time." God draped His warm arm around P.J.'s shoulder. "Trust me, it's not easy to wrap your head around it." He smiled. "It's more a matter of faith."

"Faith," P.J. repeated.

"That's right," God said, "knowing something to be true without having to experience it through sight or any of the other senses I'll give you."

"If I need to talk to you, how…"

"In prayer," God answered, "I'm always listening."

"Do you ever answer?" P.J. asked.

"Sure I do, though not always with words." God peered into P.J.'s eyes. "It's impossible to hear anything, to hear me, until you learn to be still. You must learn to be aware of your surroundings without being *of* them, if that makes sense."

"But how…"

"By allowing your thoughts to come and go without paying any real attention. Permit them to just flow through you, with you as an observer who makes no judgment—or feels nothing for them." He nodded. "This is what I mean by being still. And only when you're still will you be able to hear me."

Although P.J. sensed that the message was invaluable, he struggled to internalize it.

"You'll never find me in the chaos, P.J.," God added, "and the more you succumb to temptations or sin within the chaos, the more you'll feel separated from me—until there's such a great distance that you feel alone."

"Alone?" P.J. repeated, feeling anxious.

"Which couldn't be any further from the truth," God promised. "We can never be separated. We are one, just as you are connected to all other human souls."

P.J. nodded in relief. "Is that the worse I can expect to encounter…in the unknown?" he asked.

God nodded. "That's right. The truth is, you're all parts of a whole, and I am able to experience all I created through each of you. You are never alone—not ever. Nothing could be more impossible."

"Then why would I ever feel alone?"

"If you believe strongly enough that something is real, then it's real. It becomes part of your reality." He shook His head. "One of the greatest challenges you'll need to overcome on earth is to ignore the many lies you'll tell yourself."

That one was far beyond P.J.'s intellectual reach. "And when I mess up, which we both know I will," he inquired further, "will I be…"

God laughed hard, halting P.J.

"Will I be punished for my mistakes?" he finished.

"I don't punish," God said. "That was never the design. With free will, the punishment is already built in through consequences." He shook His head. "None of my children can escape their own words and deeds."

"And there's no good without the bad, huh?" P.J. said, still trying to make sense of it all.

"That's right," God said.

P.J. handed the menu back. "I'll take it all then."

God chuckled. "You remind me so much of your father."

"My father? I thought you were my father."

God pointed down from the cloud and showed P.J. his mortal father. Phinn was happily going about his business. "Your earthly father," God explained. "He also had many questions. And he asked for many of the same things."

P.J. looked down at Phinn and smiled.

"He'll teach you all you'll need," God whispered, "and remind you of who you are."

P.J. felt relieved but continued to stare. "What's his name," he asked, "…my earthly father?"

"Phinn."

"I like that," he said, continuing to stare. "What did you tell him before he was sent into the world?"

"I told him to take an active role in his own life—to participate." God nodded. "And I'll tell you the same thing: Drive hard, my son. Don't accept the passenger seat. You're not meant to be a spectator. There's no greater waste. Your true destiny is to experience all that's been given you, so give it all you have and don't leave any of it to chance. Live intentionally. Love. Laugh. Cry. Sweat. Bleed. Even when things get dark, be fearless and have the courage to live with reckless abandon, squeezing out every drop you can." He nodded. "And do your very best to leave the world a better place than how you found it."

"How can I do that?" P.J. asked.

"It's simple," He said. "Just be kind."

"Okay. I will."

"P.J., in all creation for all eternity, there is only one you—*one*. There's no other like you. There never will be. So please do your best not to be something or someone different from that." He nodded. "You cheat humanity when you do."

"I'll do my best."

"I know you will," God said, pulling him close. "Do you still want the same purpose for your life?"

P.J. nodded. "Yes, I'd like to find my soul mate." He looked at God and shrugged. "I honestly can't think of a better reason to live."

"Me either," God said, hugging him tight.

As though he'd been waiting in line, P.J. took a step forward before turning back. "I feel like I'm leaving my best friend," he told God.

The Divine smiled. "I'll be with you every step of the way, my boy." He winked. "Although your life will only last a moment within this realm, it will have an eternal impact on every single soul you touch—so be sure to make it a great one, okay?"

P.J. nodded. One deep breath later, he was travelling along a river of light.

• • •

Phinn returned home from work to find Maddie standing in their doorway, waiting for him—and smiling.

"What's going on?" he asked, her goofy grin rubbing off on him.

"I have something for you," she said.

"Oh yeah?" He quickly moved in for a kiss.

As they broke apart, she lifted a pair of pale green booties until the tiny socks were at eye level. "Congratulations, Daddy," she whispered.

"Wha...what?" he stammered. His hair stood on end, while the skin on his forearms turned to sandpaper. Instantly, his mind flashed back to the promise he'd made to God at Brayton Point Park. *If you ever allow me to have a child in this lifetime, I swear I'll be the best dad I can be. You have my word. Whatever that child is destined to experience, joy or pain, I'll be right there by his or her side.*

"Are you happy?" she asked, diving back into his arms.

His eyes filled with tears. "No, Maddie," he whispered, "I'm beyond happy." He hugged her—carefully. "I'm complete."

Within a few short weeks, Maddie was kneeling on cold bathroom tiles, retching into the toilet. "Oh, God," she said, wiping her mouth. "I never knew I could feel this sick," she gasped, happy to share the joys of her debilitating morning sickness with her husband.

"I'm sorry," Phinn said, sitting on the edge of the bathtub, holding her hair back.

Maddie heaved again; this time, nothing came out. Her stomach was finally empty. "If it's a girl, we need to name her Lola," she announced between the dry heaving.

"Why do you love the name Lola so much?" Phinn asked, rubbing her back.

"I don't know," she said, wiping her mouth on a hand towel. "Ever since I can remember, I've loved that name." She began to shrug when she dry heaved again. "I don't know why," she managed.

"And if it's a boy?" he asked, grinning.

"Then you can have a say," she teased, finishing the latest retch session.

"Deal," Phinn said, clearly in no position to say otherwise.

• • •

Weeks later, as they lay side-by-side in bed, Maddie asked, "What's worrying you?"

"It's nothing," Phinn said.

She put her worn copy of *What To Expect When You're Expecting* down and grabbed his hand. "Tell me," she said. "No secrets, remember?"

He nodded. "I guess I'm just worried about being a good dad."

Maddie was taken aback. "Oh my God, Phinn, you're going to be the best dad ever!"

He inhaled deeply. "I can't imagine wanting to be anything more than that in this world," he said. "I just wish I'd had a better example to follow." Suddenly, he drifted off to the time he'd confronted his father over their parents' unexpected separation.

• • •

"But you guys haven't even been fighting," eleven-year old Phinn told his father, confused by the whole nightmare.

"And that's the point, son," his dad explained. "Your mother and

I haven't really fought in years." He shrugged. "I suppose it's been that long since either of us has cared enough to fight."

"But how can you guys break up? After all these years and everything you've been through, how…"

"It was going to happen anyway, Phinn," his old man confessed. "It's been a loveless marriage for as long as I can remember. And we've been waiting a long time to put an end to it. If it wasn't for you…" He stopped.

This unexpected claim took a moment to sink in. When it did, Phinn's heart overflowed with hurt and anger. "Don't you dare put that on me," he hissed, "…you and Mom staying together for my sake."

"I didn't mean it that way," his father said.

Twenty minutes later, the man emerged from his bedroom, carrying the last of his boxes and loaded them into his truck.

Phinn couldn't imagine what was in those boxes. He remembered looking at his dad and not knowing what else to say or feel. He knew this breakup wouldn't change their family history or all they'd been through together. *And it can't change one single memory*, he thought. But he also knew that, *Going forward, the world will never be the same again*. Life, as he'd always known it, was going to be very different. *Good in some ways, bad in others*. Part of him was resentful that his parents didn't fight to save their marriage, their love. But he also felt relieved that the painful charade had finally come to an end. It wasn't easy reconciling it all, seeing his mom and dad as people and not just parents, the roles they'd always played so well for him. *But they're just people*, he realized.

"I'll see you this weekend," his dad said, spreading his arms for a hug.

"But I have a baseball tournament this weekend, remember?" Phinn told him after the long embrace.

"Next weekend then?"

"Sure, Dad, next weekend."

• • •

Phinn emerged from the daydream and sat in silence for a while, contemplating how his life had changed from that moment on; how the natural drift that came with growing up had been significantly sped up. "But that next weekend never came, and my dad basically disappeared from my life," he told Maddie, shaking his head. "If I'm being honest, my dad is more dead to me than my mother—and he's still alive."

"I'm sorry," Maddie said. "When you didn't invite him to our wedding, I knew it had to be really bad between you. I just didn't know how it all happened."

"Relationships end," he said. "I understood that even when I was a kid. But that shouldn't apply to parents and their children, right?"

Maddie rubbed his arm. "There'll be no relationship-ending under this roof, babe, I can promise you that," she said. "And you're going to be the greatest dad, Phinn." She grinned. "You don't think I would have let you get me pregnant if I didn't know that, right?"

Phinn smiled. "So you control it all, huh?"

"You silly, silly boy," she teased, "are you just starting to realize that now?"

• • •

After being lulled to sleep by his neighbor's sweet voice, P.J. floated freely in his warm pool of serenity. Suddenly, there was a loud pop, startling him from his slumber. *What was that?* he was wondering, when his safe haven was immediately transformed into a combat zone. While the syrupy pool emptied from beneath him, the walls that had always provided a sense of security now served as a torture chamber; they closed in on him for a few horrible moments before easing up, and then squeezing him harder each time. *This cannot be happening*, he thought, terrified by the chaos that enveloped him.

As the walls pressed in on his skull, he felt nauseous, his head throbbing with a sensation he'd never known existed—pain. *Please God*, he thought, closing his eyes, *spare me from whatever this is.*

Strangely, there was no fight or flight decision to be made. Instead, he was paralyzed with fear, his limp body surrendering to the crushing walls that were now closing in on him, faster and stronger. His heart thumped hard, laboring to push blood out to his rubbery limbs. *Please*, he thought, his dizzy mind already beginning to forget who he was talking to.

The walls crashed in on him again. *This must be it,* P.J. thought. *This has to be the end for me.*

• • •

"Put these on," the maternity ward nurse said, handing Phinn a set of blue scrubs. "Your wife will be having the baby right in this room."

Phinn quickly donned the baggy costume, spending a few extended moments at the hand sanitizer station, rubbing his hands together as though he were preparing for surgery.

Maddie moaned from the increasing convulsions. "This kid's really making me pay," she gasped.

Phinn hurried to her side, and while she endured the pain—nearly crushing his hand to offset it—he offered a silent prayer for his young family. *Please Lord, protect my wife and shroud her in your angels. And bless our child with a safe journey.*

While his wife huffed and puffed, he recalled those who'd asked, *How can you bring a child into a world that's so messed up?* He had to smile, remembering his reply. *Because it's the only world I know and we need more good people than bad to fill it.*

Still awaiting the doctor, the nurse took a seat between Maddie's spread legs and reached in with her gloved hand. "You're ten centimeters, Mrs. Reed," she announced. "It's time to start pushing."

"What about the doctor?" Phinn asked. "Shouldn't we wait for the doctor?"

Another nurse entered the room. "Your child could be attending first grade by the time the doctor shows up," she said, snickering.

That's not very comforting, Phinn thought.

The first nurse leaned in, making solid eye contact with Maddie. "You already have everyone you need in this room," she said, confidently, "so start pushing."

After a deep breath, Maddie bore down and pushed.

"Good," the nurse said, "and again."

Maddie pushed harder with each contraction, groaning in pain.

"You're doing great, babe," Phinn told her, feeling more useless with each word he muttered.

Maddie clamped down on his hand, nearly fusing all of his fingers into one.

"The baby has had a bowel movement and will be covered in meconium," the nurse warned Maddie and Phinn, "so please don't be alarmed when you see it." She smiled. "Your baby will be covered in green muck."

"Okay," Phinn said, never feeling more out of control—or more trusting of others—in his life.

Maddie sipped in air, hyperventilating through each contraction and subsequent push.

"You're so amazing," Phinn told her, feeling overwhelmed with emotion.

Maddie bore down again and grunted.

"Wonderful," the nurse announced, excitedly. "The head is starting to crown."

Phinn glanced between his wife's trembling legs to see a patch of wet matted hair. His heart began to race. *Our baby's almost here*, he thought, no longer able to hold back the tears.

Maddie pushed once more, when the baby's head popped out, its eyes closed and green face scrunched.

Oh God, Phinn thought, losing his breath and feeling his knees buckle. *Be strong, man,* he yelled in his head, righting himself.

"Just a few more pushes," the nurse announced.

Maddie gritted her teeth and pushed so hard that Phinn could see a map of red capillaries bursting just beneath her puffy cheeks.

"You're almost there, babe," Phinn said, his words garbled from emotion.

At that moment, the doctor arrived and elbowed the veteran nurse out of the way.

"One more push," he said, the nurse's compassion missing in his voice.

Now, babe, Phinn told Maddie in his head. *Now!*

As if reading his thoughts, Maddie released a war cry, pushing their child completely out and into the world.

For a second, Phinn held his breath, while the doctor held the flaccid newborn in his arms for a cursory inspection. "It's a boy," he announced without emotion. Flicking the bottom of the baby's foot, the boy let out a whimper.

Phinn began to sob.

"Cut the cord," the doctor told him, "so we can clean out your son's lungs. He's ingested a lot of fluid."

Phinn made his work quick. The baby was then rushed to the corner of the room, where a pediatrician—a different doctor—snaked a long tube down his throat and began to extract brown fluid with a massive syringe.

Holding Maddie's hand, Phinn held his breath again. *Please God,* he prayed, *let our son be...* His body shuddered. *...let him be okay.*

The newborn wailed, this time his voice loud and unobstructed.

Thank you, Father, Phinn thought.

Smiling, the pediatrician carried the naked boy directly to his mother, placing him belly down on Maddie's heaving chest. "Congratulations," he said, "you have a healthy baby boy."

"Yes," Phinn blurted; the word sounded like a squeal. He quickly inspected the tiny package. *Ten fingers, ten toes, my light hair, and his mother's dark eyes. He's perfect!* Through blurred vision, he kissed the boy's pink cheek before looking to his wife, the cornerstone of their family. "I'm so proud of you," he whimpered.

They sat quietly for a while. "Well," Maddie said through her sniffles, "what name should we give your son?"

"Son," Phinn repeated, his chest swelling with pride. "What do you think about Jacob…Jacob Phinneas Reed?"

She shook her head. "You know I love the name, Jacob, but this little guy looks more like a Phinn to me."

Phinn began to cry. "Phinn Jr.," he managed.

"P.J.," Maddie whispered.

Phinn placed his face inches from the baby's. "It doesn't matter what you do in this world, P.J., or who you try to become," he whispered to his boy. "From this moment on, you'll always be the only person you can be—my son. And regardless of the roads you travel, I'll be proud." He kissed the newborn. "And I'll always be with you," he vowed. "You have my word."

As the new family bonded, Phinn pondered the miraculous experience. Medical staff aside, he'd felt like he and his wife weren't the only ones present in the delivery room. "You're going to think I'm crazy," he told Maddie, feeling the need to share it with her, "but I felt like there were other people in the room with us—like my mom, people who love us and came to help P.J.'s spirit pass over." His eyes filled. "Like they helped our boy find his way to us, you know?"

Maddie nodded, the color beginning to return to her drained face. "That's not so crazy, babe," she said. "If you want to know the truth, I felt like P.J. just passed through me as though…" She thought about it. "…as though I was some kind of portal delivering his spirit into the world." The sacred experience had clearly humbled her. "Deep in my heart, I know I wasn't alone during this miracle. And for the rest of my life, every time I pray, I'll be giving thanks to the good Lord for allowing me to deliver our boy into this world."

Phinn nodded, and as he lay beside the two people he loved most in the entire universe, he realized, *I've discovered heaven.*

• • •

Humbled by the miraculous gift, Phinn understood that he'd been given a second chance at fatherhood. Beyond grateful, he also felt inspired to capture the moment on paper for his baby boy. He wrote, *Daddy's Boy.*

With wide eyes focused on the birth of his child,
two feet were planted firmly for the new arrival of hope.
Every freed inch of the baby's head
made his heart beat faster.
Then, as the newborn completed his journey home,
Daddy held a breath, while the boy took his first.
Through misty eyes, he instantly recognized the face.
It was Phinn Jr., his best friend,
raging out at the cold air, loud sounds and bright lights.
In turn, a silent vow was taken:
As partners, they would tackle the cruel world together.
With the love and time of a gentle teacher,
P.J. would grow.
It was all they would ever need.
A new beginning for them both, they would each learn...
P.J.—the simple, yet invaluable lessons of childhood.
Daddy—a second chance to discover the world through
the eyes of innocence, goodness and love.

CHAPTER 13

It was nearly dawn, and as the first rays of morning light began to penetrate the house, Phinn paused at the window. *This gives me an idea*, he thought before quietly sliding back into bed.

Maddie sat up, her wide eyes signaling that she was in full maternal mode. "The baby?" she asked.

"He's fine," Phinn said, yawning. "I just changed his diaper and laid him back down. He went back to sleep."

Her head collapsed back into the pillow.

"I think our days of power sleeping are long gone, babe," Phinn said.

Through squinted eyes, Maddie looked at him. "Quit your squawking," she teased. "We'll get plenty of sleep when we're dead."

He started to laugh before nodding off from sheer exhaustion.

• • •

Phinn heard the heart monitor flatlining. Confused, he mumbled, "Where…where am I?"

Death popped up out of nowhere and stood before Phinn, startling him.

"Can I help you?" Phinn asked, taken aback.

Death snickered. "At this point, you can't even help yourself." He thought about it and laughed. "That's actually pretty funny. I'll have to use that one again."

"Who the hell are you?" Phinn asked.

"Who the hell am I?" Death repeated, shrugging. "Heaven, hell—it makes no difference to me, pal. I'm only the delivery boy."

"The what?"

"I'm your chauffer," Death interrupted.

"Chauffer? I never called for a car service."

"No, you didn't," Death agreed, "but God did." He checked his watch. "So let's get going. I have an unusually heavy workload tonight." He nodded. "There are a few countries at war, you know."

"Listen," Phinn said, nervously, "I don't know if this is some twisted joke, but I'm not going anywhere with you."

"Oh, but you are, my simple-minded friend. When death comes calling, even kings must abide."

"Death?" Phinn repeated, skeptically. "Where's your sickle? The hooded cloak?"

"Hooded cloak?" He sighed heavily. "Times change, man. Fashions change. I don't see you wearing a Pilgrim's hat and buckle shoes."

Phinn was in shock. "This...this can't be happening," he mumbled to himself. "There's no way this dude's the Grim Reaper."

Death cleared his throat loudly, reminding Phinn that he was still standing there. "Ummmm....hello, I'm right here." He waved at Phinn. "Grim Reaper, the Angel of Death—call me whatever you want, but the bottom line is this: The boss wants to see you, and He ain't too happy. Now let's get a move on."

"So you've come here to punish me?" Phinn asked.

"No, not at all!" Death barked back, clearly frustrated. "Here we go again with the punishment thing." He took a deep, calming breath. "Listen, death isn't a punishment, knucklehead. Everybody has to die, right?"

"Sure, but..."

"And for the record," Death interrupted, "you determine your own punishment by the life you've lived." He fixed his hair. "I'm just the handsome chauffer who transports you to that judgment."

"I...I thought I had more time," Phinn stammered. "I thought I could make up for..." He shrugged. "...you know."

"Yeah, believe it or not, I've heard this same spiel a few times before."

"But I'm not ready," Phinn said, "I...I need more time."

"Ahhh, time," Death said, "the one thing promised to no one." He shook his head impatiently. "Listen, we really need to get going. Oh yeah, and here's your life's ledger," he said, handing Phinn a book. "If you ask me, it feels just a wee bit light."

Phinn felt insulted. "Light? I've spent years building a career that..."

"And every second of it was wasted time, knucklehead," Death interrupted. "God couldn't care less about your career success." He placed his hand beside his mouth and lowered his voice to a whisper. "If you ask me, He's a little more partial toward the poor." Death shrugged. "No matter, the boss has called for a reckoning and He doesn't like to wait, so let's roll."

Phinn felt panicked. "If...if I go now, I'll suffer for all eternity. I know I will."

Death chuckled. "Well, at least you're not as stupid as you look." He nodded. "That's something, anyway."

Phinn became more panicked. "I...I need more time," he began to negotiate. "I can make this right. I know I can. But I need more time."

"Not happening," Death said. "Your hourglass is empty."

"Please, there must be something I can give you to buy more time?"

"Are you actually trying to bribe me?" Death asked, snickering. "Do you have any idea how long I've been at this gig? How many people I've watched beg and grovel at my feet, pleading for a couple more hours...a few measly minutes? It's not gonna happen, baby brain. I only have one job to do..." He smiled. "...and you know what? I'm pretty damn good at it."

Phinn placed his hand on Death's cold arm. "What...what if... what if I bring someone with me...someone who can testify on my behalf?" he asked in desperation.

Amused, Death placed his bony finger on his chin, considering the idea. "Even if I agreed, it wouldn't make a difference. Since the beginning of time, I've never met anyone willing to leave this earth for someone like you." He shook his head.

"But what if I can find someone," Phinn desperately negotiated. "Would you let them come along to put in a good word for me?"

Death checked his watch.

"Well?" Phinn pled.

"I'm still listening, aren't I?"

"Okay then," Phinn said, feeling relieved, "would this person have to be alive?"

Death grinned. "No one is beyond my reach."

• • •

Panting like an overweight dog, Phinn awoke and sat up straight in bed.

"What is it?" Maddie asked, reaching for him.

"I just had another dream that I died and death came to get me."

She struggled to keep her eyes open. "It was only a dream, babe," she yawned. "Go back to sleep before the baby gets up again and you won't be able to."

Phinn nodded. "I will," he said, knowing full well that it was wishful thinking. *No matter how much I've tried,* he thought, *I still can't shake my fear of being punished.*

• • •

At P.J.'s baptism, Jacob and Sarah were honored as godparents. As the water ran down the coffee-eyed infant's forehead, his healthy wails echoed off the church's cold stone walls. Standing with his young family at the altar, Phinn was absolutely consumed by a divine sense of contentment and gratitude.

The family was leaving the church, when Jacob grabbed Phinn to share a moment alone. "Thanks for asking Sarah and me to stand up for P.J., brother," he said. "It means the world to us."

Phinn patted his back. "Of course, Jake. Honestly, I don't know a better man than you."

"I appreciate that," Jacob said, "but I have to thank my daughter for that."

Phinn's right eyebrow rose to attention.

"Since the moment we lost her," his brother-in-law explained, "I've spent every day trying to be the best man I can be."

"Miranda would be very proud of you, Jake," Phinn said, unsure whether he'd chosen the right words.

Jacob's eyes immediately glossed over from emotion. Although he cleared his throat, he never uttered a response. Finally, he nodded his gratitude.

Phinn matched the nod. "As far as being P.J.'s godparents, it's actually nice to know that if anything were to ever happen to me and Maddie…"

"Well, that's not going to happen," Jacob interrupted. "Sarah and I are just grateful to play such an important role in another child's life." He peered into Phinn's eyes. "I want you to know that we'll always be there for your son."

Phinn patted his brother-in-law's back. "I know, Jake," he said. "It's why you were chosen."

After the baptism party, Phinn headed off to the park for a quick power walk, happy to discover that Mr. Tetreault was finishing up his own daily stroll.

"Haven't seen you around here lately," the good man acknowledged.

"That's because you're always off somewhere, saving the world," Phinn teased.

Mr. Tetreault chuckled. "How's the baby?"

"Couldn't be better," Phinn announced, beaming. "I think he might weigh ten pounds already."

"Wow, big boy! And Mom's also doing good, I hope?"

Phinn half shrugged. "Maddie's been in a bit of a funk since P.J. was born."

"A funk?"

"She's constantly tired. I keep telling her to go get checked, but she says she's just run down from the baby."

Mr. Tetreault nodded. "A new baby will do that." He smiled. "Welcome to fatherhood."

"I didn't know you have children?"

Mr. Tetreault offered a wink. "Children are amazing. It doesn't matter how many you have; each one shows you the world through a different set of eyes."

"I can imagine. Sometimes, late at night, I just sit and stare at P.J.," Phinn said, incapable of wiping the grin from his face. "And he usually smiles back at me, a big smile like he wants to tell me a secret but doesn't have the words."

"Then he probably does." Mr. Tetreault said, looking skyward. "Some people believe that we're closest to God at the beginning and end of our lives."

Phinn nodded. "I can believe that."

After shaking hands, Phinn started down the bluestone path.

"Any resemblance to his father?" Mr. Tetreault called out.

"Spitting image," Phinn yelled back, his words overflowing with pride.

Mr. Tetreault laughed aloud. "Wonderful!"

• • •

The months ticking away P.J.'s growth were even more magical than Phinn and Maddie could have imagined. It seemed like one minute they were taking the baby into their bed to bond with him, and the next, they were at the local mall, handing the boy over to Santa Claus for a Christmas photo.

Three winks later—or several months—they were at Grandma's house for their weekly visit, when P.J. decided to speak his first word.

"Dada," the boy mumbled.

"Yes!" Phinn said, already celebrating. "He said Dada!"

"Very good, P.J.," Maddie said, ignoring her gloating husband. "Now say Mama. Ma…ma."

P.J. smiled. "Da….da…da…da," he rambled on.

The entire family laughed, everyone applauding.

"Mama," Maddie repeated, "Ma…ma…ma…ma."

"Dada," the baby replied.

Beaming with joy, Phinn turned to Maddie. "Always remember that he said *Dada* first," he teased.

She punched his arm. "Oh, I'm sure you'll be right there to remind me if I ever forget."

"It won't be an easy job," he joked, "but someone has to do it." He looked over at P.J. "Right, buddy? Tell Mama."

"Dada," the boy said.

"That's right," Phinn added, laughing hard, "you got it, kid."

After lunch, Maddie approached Phinn, wearing her mischievous smile; it was a look he hadn't seen since the little man had come into their lives. "My mom's suggested that we let P.J. stay the night with her," she told him.

"The whole night?" Phinn said, surprised.

She nodded. "We could go rent a room for a quick getaway."

"I don't know, babe. We're saving for a house," he said. "I'm not sure we should be spending money on…"

"So spending time with your wife isn't worth the investment?" Maddie interrupted, the glorious mischief in her eyes gone.

Phinn quickly shook his head. "Of course I want to be with you." He thought about it and grinned. "And I didn't say we couldn't go to a hotel and hang out, but there's no reason we can't dance the night away in our own bed and sleep at home."

"I don't understand," she said.

"Let's hurry home and pack a bag," he told her, "before your mother changes her mind."

Maddie grinned. "A bag?"

"Yeah," he said, "and make sure you include a bathing suit."

On the ride to the most exclusive hotel in the area, Phinn talked Maddie into pretending to be a guest. "When anyone asks for our room number, just tell them we're in 1208," he said, smiling. "And don't hesitate with the answer, or they'll figure out that we're not actually staying there."

Grinning, Maddie shook her head. "Are we actually going to the Intercontinental?"

"Only the best for you, babe," he said.

"Are you sure this is such a great idea?"

He shrugged. "Nine out of ten voices in my head tell me we should do it."

She laughed. "That's my man," she said, "or should I say *men*?"

This time, he laughed.

They parked the car and headed straight to the hotel's massive indoor pool. Quickly changing into their bathing suits, Phinn was already lounging on his towel-draped chair, when a hotel staff member approached. "Excuse me, sir, but are you staying with us?"

"Of course we are."

"Your room number?" the young man asked.

"1208," Phinn quickly replied.

The attendant nodded. "Very good," he said. "Just flag me down if you'd like to order a drink or some food."

"Oh, I will," Phinn said.

Shaking her head, Maddie dove into the pool.

When she came up for air, Phinn was laughing. "Let's hope the folks in 1208 don't get charged for these towels," he told her.

"You're so crazy," she said.

He nodded. "Good thing you love crazy."

She returned the nod. "Good thing."

"And you haven't seen anything yet," he added. "Wait until you see what I order us for lunch."

Laughing, she joined him poolside, collapsing onto her chair. "We can't do that, Phinn," she said, unsure whether or not he was serious.

When the laughter subsided, Phinn asked, "Do you think they have a gift shop?"

"You can't be…" She stopped, nodding toward another hotel staff member who was walking past.

Phinn stood and stepped to the edge of the pool to dip his toe.

"Keep pushing it," Maddie whispered, chuckling.

Looking back over his shoulder, Phinn smiled. "I'd definitely like a new polo shirt," he told her before jumping into the pool.

"Those poor people in 1208," he heard Maddie say just before he hit the water.

An hour passed—a peaceful hour without any diaper changes, or spit up, or the cries of a baby—when a middle-aged couple claimed the lounge chairs beside Phinn and Maddie, threatening their solace.

Friendly nods were exchanged. *Please let them be mute,* Phinn wished.

As if on cue, the man leaned over. "So where are you folks from?" he asked.

"Poughkeepsie," Phinn answered.

Maddie choked on a laugh.

"And where's that?" the grinning stranger inquired.

"Just south of North Poughkeepsie," Phinn said, closing his eyes and hoping for silence.

"Great," the guy said, "that's helpful." With his smile wiped clean, he and his scowling wife headed for the pool.

Stifling a laugh, Maddie whispered, "We'd better get out of here before we get locked up."

Opening one eye, Phinn turned toward her. "As long as there's peace and quiet in the clink," he said, "I'll be happy to take the ride."

Laughing, Maddie reached up to her nose to discover it was bleeding. She hurried off toward the ladies room.

"Are you okay?" Phinn yelled after her.

She raised her hand, signaling that she was fine, just before disappearing behind the fancy bathroom door.

• • •

It seemed only a few more moons had come and gone before the young family was celebrating P.J.'s first birthday. While both families crowded around the kitchen table, Maddie—feeling even more exhausted than usual—helped the boy blow out his single candle.

Everyone applauded.

"Dada," P.J. squealed, clapping along with his laughing family.

"That's my boy," Phinn mumbled.

Maddie caught it. "Go ahead," she said, "keep it up and…"

"I love your Mama so much," Phinn told the baby, "Ma…ma… ma…"

While P.J. laughed, Maddie kissed Phinn's cheek. "Nice recovery," she said.

Chuckling, Phinn helped the baby jam both hands into the cake. While Maddie shook her head, the boy filled his mouth with globs of frosting.

"He's making a mess," Julia muttered.

"No worries," Maddie said, "*Dada* will clean it up."

Everyone laughed.

Phinn leaned into his son's ear. "You can make all the mess you want, buddy," he whispered. "One year ago today, you made my life complete."

"Our lives," Maddie reminded her husband, offering him a weak hug from behind.

"Our lives," Phinn repeated.

P.J. smiled, his face barely recognizable behind the frosting.

As Maddie laughed, she thought, *I really need to start taking a daily vitamin. I shouldn't be feeling so weak and tired all the time.* She shrugged it off. *My immune system must be overtaxed right now.*

CHAPTER 14

While the boy grew, Maddie and Phinn fell deeper and deeper in love with each other.

It was a Saturday, and like most Saturdays, Phinn and Maddie prepared to make the most of the day. After brushing her teeth—the evidence of more bleeding gums circling the sink's drain—Maddie finished dressing P.J. In record time, they headed out the door, destination unknown. As Phinn drove, they talked and laughed, with Maddie's hand laying nestled in his lap the entire ride to Brayton Point Park.

"I don't see Mr. Tetreault," Phinn commented, as he parked the car.

"I'm guessing he doesn't live here, Phinn," Maddie teased.

Phinn chuckled.

As if on cue, Mason approached from the playground's big red slide. "Hey guys," he called out.

"Oh, hi Mason," Phinn said, "don't tell me you've been tackling that giant slide?"

Mason nodded, proudly. "It's only for big kids." His grin slowly dissolved. "I haven't seen you at the park in a while," he said.

"Yeah, we definitely need to get down here more," Phinn replied. "So how have you been?"

"Oh, I'm always good," he said before waving at P.J. "What a cute baby."

Maddie laughed. *What a personality*, she thought. *I hope P.J.'s just like him.*

"What about you?" Mason asked, looking directly at Phinn.

"On top of the world, my friend," Phinn said.

The little boy nodded, clearly pleased to hear it. "Well, I gotta go," he said, flashing his dimples, "I'll see you guys."

As Mason ran off to join the waving silhouette seated on the park bench, Phinn laughed. "I have no idea why, but I really love that kid."

Maddie nodded. *Me too.*

Hand in hand, Maddie and Phinn took a long walk along the river, with P.J. sitting atop his father's shoulders; it was the perfect height for the boy to absorb the wondrous world around him. At one point, Phinn stopped to steal a kiss from his wife. P.J. laughed, rocking his father's shoulders.

"I love you," Maddie said, happy for the rest.

"And I love you, too," Phinn said. "Do you realize that each week that passes, we're getting closer to building our dream home?"

"I know," she said, excitedly, "and more importantly, we haven't had to sacrifice all of our family time."

"I hate to say I told you so," he teased, grinning, "but…"

She kissed him again. "Yes, you did," she said, "and thank you for keeping your promise, smart ass."

On the ride home, they stopped off at the local ice cream shop to treat themselves. "I'll take a large waffle cone of chunky chocolate chip," Maddie told the girl behind the counter.

Phinn lifted two fingers. "Make that two."

While they ate, Maddie counted off the minutes until bedtime.

"Are you feeling okay?" Phinn asked out of nowhere.

"Yes," she instinctively answered, "why?"

"Because you look exhausted."

She smiled. "I'm always exhausted, babe," she admitted before giving P.J. a lick of her ice cream. "And I wonder why?" she asked the baby.

P.J. never answered; he was more interested in stealing another taste of the sweet treat.

As they lay in bed that night, Maddie stroked Phinn's chest and considered their lives together: *When time allows,* she thought, *we still talk for hours on end—about everything and nothing at all. Even when no words are spoken, we're just happy to be in each other's company.* Although the nights of engaging in hours of passionate lovemaking— before falling asleep from total exhaustion—had been put on hold, she thought, *We steal away every moment we can.* It was absolutely magical how they were always rediscovering each other, falling in love again and again and again. *Thank you, God, for bringing such a beautiful man into my life,* she thought, grateful for being blessed with this romance of a lifetime.

● ● ●

"Wake up, beautiful," Phinn whispered, concealing his excitement.

Maddie stirred from her sleep.

"You need to get up, babe," he said.

She started in on a long yawn before her eyes flew open. "Is it the baby?" she asked.

"No," Phinn said, "P.J.'s fine."

"What time is it?" she asked, her eyes struggling to focus.

"It's 5:30," he told her.

"5:30? There's no way P.J. slept all night," she said, trying to make some sense of it.

"He was up a few times, but he's fine. He's been fed, burped, and changed. And he's sleeping right now."

"You were up all night?" she asked.

Phinn half shrugged. "I got a few hours of sleep," he said, kissing her forehead. "But I wanted you to get a full night's sleep. We both know you really needed it. Besides, I wanted you fresh for our date this morning."

"Our date?" she said, looking at him like he was a lunatic.

He nodded. "Come on, get up and throw this on," he said, handing her an old sweatshirt. "I have a surprise for you."

Phinn led his yawning wife out to the back patio, where a full breakfast was waiting on the linen-covered table. Several lilacs were sitting in a small crystal vase.

"What is this?" she asked, fighting off another yawn.

"It's been much too long since I've taken my girl out on a proper date," he explained, placing the baby monitor onto the table.

Maddie lunged toward him for a kiss.

He pulled out her chair. "Mrs. Reed," he said, gesturing that she sit.

"Forever the gentleman," she said.

"Always," he said, smiling. "If I don't practice chivalry, then how can I teach it to my son?"

"He's one lucky boy," she said, "and so is his mama." She scanned the table. "French toast?"

He shrugged again. "I'm trying out a new recipe."

She chuckled.

"Enjoy," he said, pointing to the hair of sunlight just breaking over the dark horizon.

"Oh, my God," she said, realizing her thoughtful husband's intentions. "It's sunrise."

"I love sunsets," he said, nodding, "but sunrises always feel a little more hopeful to me."

"You remembered," she said, overjoyed. She got up to sit in his lap. "After breakfast, what do you think about making love to your wife?"

"Of course," he said, "it was part of the plan, babe."

"That is, if your son can be considerate enough to sleep in for a little while longer," she joked.

Phinn shook his head. "And if he doesn't, then he can cry for a few minutes. It'll be good for his lungs." While the morning sun stretched out of its slumber and the breakfast grew cold, he kissed her passionately.

• • •

Jacob sat beside Maddie the following day, cradling his squirming godchild in his arms.

After explaining Phinn's surprise sunrise date, Maddie said, "I'm still amazed that I have so much love in my life now."

"You deserve every bit of it, sis," Jacob said, making faces at the baby.

"Do I, Jake?" she asked, skeptically.

His head snapped up. "Of course you do, Maddie," he said, "I don't know anyone who deserves it more."

Half shrugging, Maddie's mind drifted off to the detox program that had saved her life.

• • •

Sitting on the edge of her hospital bed, Maddie looked up to find Jacob standing in her doorway. As he stepped into the room, their eyes locked. Maddie immediately felt her face burn red.

"Oh Maddie," he gasped, remaining in her gaze.

Maddie extended her arms, and while her compassionate brother rushed into her hug, she began to cry. "I didn't mean for it to come to this, Jake," she whimpered, "I…I…"

Jacob squeezed hard until the two began to weep together. There were no words needed.

For a while, Maddie sobbed, convulsing in his arms. "I feel so ashamed that I let it get to this," she finally managed when she was able to speak, "but I swear I'm going to…" She stopped, weeping heavily again.

Jacob sat by her side in silence.

Maddie collected herself completely before she spoke again. "But I'm here now, and that's all that counts," she said; this time, the words were more for herself than for her brother. "This is where I'll get the help I need and be able to reclaim my life."

He smiled. "And someday, I have no doubt that you'll look back on this period of your life and give thanks for it."

"My brother, the optimist," she whimpered.

He made a funny face at her.

It was enough to pull a grin through her sobs.

"It's true, Maddie," he said. "I think we both know this is a defining moment for you."

She nodded in agreement. "I just need to make sure I get it right," she whispered, "and I will."

"I know you will," he said, adding a sorrowful shrug. "Maybe

I'm the one who should be apologizing to you."

"What?" she said, taken aback.

"I'm sorry I didn't…" he began, shaking his head. "I should have…"

"Stop, Jake," she said, "this isn't about you. It's about me." She took a deep breath. "I've been pretty messed up for a while now, and I'm not sure how long it's going to take me to get well. But I know I will." She exhaled. "Because I own this."

In silence, the two sat together, holding hands.

"Whatever you need," he said, "I'm here for you."

She searched his eyes one last time. "I know," she said.

"And I'll be by to visit as often as I can," he promised.

"You'd better," she said, tightening her grip.

• • •

Gladly emerging from her past, Maddie looked at her brother. "Everything I have today is by the grace of God," she said. "Nothing more."

"I agree," Jacob said, "but don't forget the incredible strength you needed to muster in order to reclaim your life."

"By the grace of God," Maddie repeated, grinning. "I never had to earn it or pay for it." She nodded. "It's been a gift, all of it."

Jacob nodded. "No argument here."

• • •

It was mid-summer when Phinn received a random phone call from Joshua.

"Where are you?" his childhood friend asked.

"On Martha's Vineyard with Maddie and P.J.," Phinn told him. "We're watching a friend's house for the week."

"Lucky duck," Joshua said, laughing. "Do you mind if Sylvie and I take the ferry over? We're actually on Cape Cod."

Phinn couldn't say yes fast enough.

By his recent account, Joshua had remained a bachelor for many years, while he chased his dreams of being a filmmaker. Drifting from one post-production project to the next, those dreams had eventually evolved from director to film editor. *And he's made his dreams come true*, Phinn thought, feeling a great sense of pride for his friend.

Maddie, Phinn, and P.J. met Joshua and his new wife at the harbor, not far from where Stephen Spielberg had filmed the movie *Jaws*—which Joshua immediately reminded them of. There were no handshakes or polite pleasantries exchanged. Instead, they hugged and then laughed at each other's older—more bloated—appearances. "I knew you'd get chubby," Joshua teased.

"And I never imagined you getting any uglier," Phinn countered, "but here you are."

They both laughed, while the girls shook their heads. Joshua grabbed P.J. and hoisted the toddler onto his broad shoulders. "Little man's with me," he said.

Although the plan was for them to stay one day, that day turned into three—while Maddie captured every moment with her clicking camera. From the very beginning, Phinn realized it was a time he'd cherish forever.

"We love this island," Phinn told the visiting couple, and on the first day, he and Maddie took them for a stroll down Main Street in Vineyard Haven, where shops lined both sides of the narrow street:

art galleries, candy shops, antiques, and collectibles. They visited the mom and pop souvenir shops, each one offering scrimshaw jewelry, seashell wind chimes, and handmade leather bags. They then walked the two blocks to The Black Dog—the historic and legendary tavern whose world-famous four-legged ambassador represented the easy Vineyard way of life—and ate clam cakes and chowder by an empty fireplace. And they talked, Phinn and Joshua catching up on all the time they'd missed in each other's lives. While keeping P.J. happy and quiet, Maddie never stopped smiling.

The following day, they visited Oak Bluffs. After taking a ride on the Flying Horses Carousel, the nation's oldest operating platform carousel, they headed for the gingerbread house colony. With rocking chairs on the front porches, these real-life dollhouses—painted in candy cane stripes of pink, blue, and green—contained miniature gardens behind white picket fences. "So beautiful," the wives marveled in whispers, while Phinn and Joshua laughed.

They passed a fudge shop that had candy apples in the window. "Do you want to snatch a few?" Joshua whispered.

Speechless, Phinn's face burned red.

"Relax," Joshua said, throwing him into a headlock. "I'm just messing with you. It's in the past, but..."

"But?" Phinn asked.

"It's forgiven and forgotten, brother, but I refuse to walk on eggshells around you."

"I don't want that, either."

"Good," Joshua said, "then buy me a candy apple, and we'll call the whole thing square."

"You got it," Phinn said, hurrying into the shop to make the symbolic purchase.

Maddie beamed with joy.

On the third day, with the Atlantic Ocean as a backdrop, they traveled farther inland until they reached Aquinnah, better known as Gayhead. After browsing the Native Wampanoag's wares at clifftop, they headed to the red cliffs and watched the sun set over the turquoise water—marveling in silence.

On the drive back to the ferry, Joshua rambled on. "Someday, I'd really love to film on location in Martha's Vineyard."

Phinn nodded, already writing a new poem in his head.

After several strong hugs, Joshua and Sylvie boarded the last ferry to the mainland, while Phinn, Maddie and P.J. headed back to the house. "Old friends are the best friends," Phinn said aloud, and pondered the cliché. The answer came to him as clear as the stars that shone above: *It's because old friends know you; they really know you. The time and effort needed to cultivate a true friendship has already been put in. You can talk about anything. You can laugh at each other. And most importantly, you can be in each other's company—in complete silence—without feeling awkward or compelled to fill the dead air.* Phinn realized that reconnecting with Joshua was a true blessing. *Old friends are the best friends* was a catchphrase he'd heard for as long as he could remember. But when he was young, it meant nothing to him. Now, that same cliché meant everything.

"Thank you again for reconnecting me and Joshua," Phinn told Maddie, as they snuggled on the couch.

She smiled at him.

He felt a shiver travel the length of his spine. The intensity in her eyes still gave him chills.

Maddie yawned. "Sorry, babe," she said, "I was hoping we could have some adult time tonight, but I'm so tired. I don't know what it is."

"It was a long day," Phinn reminded her. "Get some sleep. I'll ravage you in the morning before P.J. wakes up."

"Sounds like a plan," she said, kissing him. Within seconds, she was snoring lightly, her head buried in his chest.

God, do I love this woman, Phinn thought, realizing that even when they weren't together, he was daydreaming about her. *No matter how much time passes,* he thought, *being with Maddie always feels new to me.* He then considered the future and everything he was looking forward to sharing with her: *Hours of incredible lovemaking. Me reading poetry to her and her begging me to write more. Long showers together. Afternoons of roller-skating and rock concerts. Playing cards and listening to music together. Getaway lunches and late night snacks. Sunrises and sunsets and piggyback rides.* The list was endless. *It'll take us a lifetime to complete,* he realized, the best of it costing more in imagination than money.

Looking down at his snoring wife, he gently kissed her forehead. "I love you so much," he whispered, "it actually makes my heart ache." He could no longer imagine life without her right by his side. *Life's better than good. It's perfect.*

Maddie snorted, nearly waking herself.

He chuckled. "I think it's about time I write you a new poem, babe," he whispered to her, and began to scour his mind. *Sunrises and sunsets and piggyback rides.* He tilted his head sideways. *Now what else did I have in that list?*

• • •

As they prepared for P.J.'s second birthday party, Phinn suggested, "Why don't we get him a puppy? You know, a boy and his dog kind of thing."

"I don't know," Maddie said, feeling the onset of another nosebleed. "We should probably give it some thought before we..."

"I thought you loved animals?" he interrupted.

"I do...especially dogs." She shrugged. "And sometimes more than people." She wadded up some tissues and placed them under her nose.

"Another nosebleed?" he asked.

She nodded.

"You need to go get that checked."

"It's nothing, Phinn," she said, shaking her head. "The air's dry, that's all."

"Then the air's always dry," he said under his breath.

She ignored the comment.

He shrugged it off. "So what's to think about?" he asked, referring back to the dog.

Maddie sighed heavily. "I loved my dog, Raymond, more than I can ever explain. For many years, he was the best companion." After checking the tissues, she took a deep breath. "And then he got old and sick...really sick. I did everything I could to extend his life, but all the money in the world couldn't have saved him. I remember the day the vet told me that the merciful thing to do was to put him down. I spent three days considering my options; they were the worst three days of my life." She replaced the dark red tissues with clean white ones. "But there was no other option. Raymond was in pain, and it was selfish of me to keep him alive." Her eyes glazed over with tears. "On the morning he was put to sleep, he took a piece of my heart with him, leaving behind an incredible feeling of loss. And I swore I'd never own another dog again." She looked up at her husband with swollen eyes. "I don't know if my heart could take it again, Phinn."

"I get it, babe. I do," he said. "I've lost a few dogs too. But the way I see it, the joy they bring when they're with us is well worth the pain of losing them." He shrugged. "And we could say the same about people. Imagine if you'd never fallen in love with me because you feared losing me?"

She slapped his arm with her free hand. "Don't even go there."

He smiled. "So can we get a dog? Can we, Mom?" he teased. "Can we?"

"Fine," she surrendered, checking the red tissues once more, "but I refuse to fall in love with it."

Chuckling, he rolled his eyes. "Sure, babe, we haven't even met the dog yet, and you already love it."

"Did you just roll your eyes at me?" she asked. "Please tell me you didn't just roll your eyes at me."

"Not *at* you," he muttered, like a little boy about to take a time-out.

She laughed.

The following day, the young family toured the local animal shelter. A small, black puppy—a mutt—whined for their attention from the last cage at the end of the Pine Sol-smelling corridor.

"He's the last of his litter," the woman said, opening the cage, "and he's been complaining about it ever since his sister got adopted three days ago."

The puppy made a beeline to Maddie.

She went to her knees and took the mutt's long snout into both of her hands. "Look at you, handsome," she said. "You're a good boy, aren't you?"

He licked her nose.

"Do you want to join our family?"

He gave her another lick.

"Do you promise to look after our son, P.J.? He's a young boy right now, but he'll need you as he grows up."

The puppy barked once in response.

"P.J. has a soft heart," she said, "and he'll..."

The mutt jumped on Maddie, knocking her to the floor and lathering her face in sloppy kisses.

"Okay, okay, you're coming home with us," she said, hugging him tight. "You don't have to get so pushy."

Phinn laughed. "As long as you don't fall in love with him," he teased.

She slapped his arm.

"What do you think about the name, Roscoe?" Phinn asked.

She shook her head and smiled. "Sorry, babe, but he looks like a George to me."

Laughing, Phinn looked down at the dog. "Okay, George," he said, "let's go home. P.J.'s going to love you."

CHAPTER 15

Maddie was drying off from the shower when Phinn walked in. "What's up with your back?" he asked, upset.

"What do you mean?" she asked, turning sideways in front of the mirror.

"It's all black and blue."

From what she could see, there was an extensive bruise starting at her shoulder and running down to the middle of her back. "It must have happened when George wrestled me to the floor a couple days ago," she said, shrugging. "It doesn't hurt."

Phinn looked down at George, whose wagging tail and tongue indicated that he was oblivious to his transgression. "Not a great start for you," Phinn told the mutt.

As if he understood, George barked his defense.

Maddie laughed. "Leave Georgey alone, you big bully," she said in her baby voice, bending to pet the dog. "He was just making sure he got my attention. Isn't that right, Georgey?"

The mutt licked her face.

Phinn shook his head. "It looks like you went three rounds with an MMA fighter and lost."

"It's nothing, hon," she said. "Let's get to bed."

For the next ten minutes, they listened as the mutt whined sorrowfully to join them in bed.

Phinn was firm. "It's not happening, George. You have your own bed on the floor. You're fine right there."

George whined some more.

"It's not happening," Phinn repeated.

"You big bully," Maddie teased, her head comfortably nestled on Phinn's chest. After a few moments, she said, "It's the strangest thing, but I've been thinking…"

"Yeah?"

"I'm really glad you have Mr. Tetreault," she told her husband above the dog's whimpers. "It's so important to have someone in our lives to look after us and who we can go to for advice."

"He's been a blessing for sure," Phinn said, also ignoring George's incessant cries for attention. "Have you ever had someone like that who…"

"My eighth grade teacher, Mrs. Fallow," she quickly answered. "I was having a tough time back then with my dad—and myself. I really think I was on the brink of slipping into a pretty dark place."

George stopped whining, as if he also wanted to hear.

Maddie smiled. "But Mrs. Fallow brought me back. She spent a lot of time with me, really going out of her way to set me straight." She thought about it. "I'm not sure she ever realized that she saved me." As was usual of late, Maddie's mind went back.

• • •

Dressed in a pretty floral dress, Maddie stood before her teacher on the last day of middle school. Once the other students had said their goodbyes, Maddie approached the heavyset woman. They embraced.

"I don't think I could ever thank you enough for everything you've done for me," Maddie told her mentor.

"That's not true," Mrs. Fallow said, smiling. "There are ways."

"Really? How?"

"Leave the world a better place than the way you found it."

"Ummm…I…" Maddie babbled.

"It's simple," the generous woman said. "Just be kind to others." She grabbed Maddie's arm to drive her point home. "There's no better way to thank me than to be kind to others."

"I will," Maddie said.

"You promise?"

"I do."

Mrs. Fallow hugged her again. "I have very high expectations for you, Maddie Renaud."

"And I'll do everything I can to meet each one of them, Mrs. Fallow," Maddie vowed.

"Wonderful!" the middle-aged woman said before searching Maddie's face. "Sweetheart, never let someone else's pain and cruelty decide who you are. Do you understand what I'm saying to you?"

"I do," Maddie said, nodding. *You're talking about my dad.*

"And as you get older, remember that each one of us has a duty to share our blessings." Smiling, the woman winked. "I'm predicting that you'll have more good fortune to share than most."

I hope so, Maddie thought before they parted ways.

• • •

Back in the present—and George's pathetic cries—Phinn said, "It's so awesome when a teacher can have such a positive impact on a student's life."

Maddie shook her head. "Oh, it was a lot more than that, Phinn. Mrs. Fallow taught me that I was worthy…" Her eyes filled. "…a lesson that's helped to mold my life."

"Then you should get in touch with her and let her know. I'm sure she'd appreciate..."

"She died from cancer during my junior year of high school," Maddie interrupted.

"Oh, I'm sorry."

"That's okay. I sometimes talk to her in my prayers."

George's whines suddenly turned to howls.

"No," Phinn barked back, "you have a nicer bed than we do, for Pete's sake! You'll be..."

Maddie slipped out of bed, quickly returning with the mutt in her arms. "He just wants to be with the family, babe," she said. "He just wants to be loved."

"And so do I," Phinn said.

Maddie laughed. "Yeah, but you're not a baby." She kissed the dog's head. "He is."

"Great," Phinn said, "just what I need around here, more competition."

• • •

A few moons passed when Maddie and Phinn tucked P.J. in for the night. The baby plucked the bottle from his mouth and muttered, "Mama. Dada." Smiling, Maddie kissed him and shut off the light. As they stepped out of the room, Maddie stumbled and nearly collapsed to the floor.

Phinn caught her. "Maddie, what's wrong?"

"I...I don't know," she said, feeling groggy. "All of a sudden, I feel so weak."

He helped her downstairs and on to the couch. "Lay down and relax," he insisted. "How long have you felt like this?"

She was ashamed to admit it. "I've been feeling exhausted for a while now," she mumbled. *A long while.*

He looked angry. "A while?" He quickly quieted his tone. "We'll go see the doctor tomorrow, okay?"

Nodding, she lay her head back and shut her eyes, realizing they were in for a long, restless night. Phinn sat beside her, close enough for her to feel his worry. *A doctor's visit is long overdue*, she thought.

• • •

Just as soon as Doctor Catherine Motta, Maddie's primary care physician, entered the exam room, Maddie blurted "I'm so tired all the time, Dr. Motta."

"It's probably just fatigue, Maddie," the doctor predicted at the start of the exam, "with you running around after the baby and all."

"That's what I've been telling my husband," Maddie said.

As Doctor Motta began her exam, she asked, "Are there any other symptoms?"

"I've had some nosebleeds and bleeding gums."

The physician paused to look at her. "Have they been frequent?"

"I guess," Maddie said, considering the term to be subjective. "I also bruise easily now," she added. "Sometimes, I'll be taking a shower and see a new bruise without even remembering that I bumped into something." She breathed deeply, while the doctor conducted her thorough exam. "What causes bruising?" Maddie asked, trying to alleviate the awkwardness.

"Platelets are the blood cells responsible for blood clotting,"

Doctor Motta explained during the prodding. "A shortage of blood platelets can lead to easy bruising or bleeding." She felt Maddie's neck before asking, "Can you lift your arms for me, please?"

Maddie reached for the sky.

"Hmmm," the medicine woman said, "there's some noticeable swelling in your left armpit. Did you know that?"

"Yeah, it's been there for a little while," Maddie admitted, "but it doesn't hurt."

"I see," Doctor Motta said, her tone becoming concerned.

"Should I be worried about any of this?" Maddie asked, nervously.

"Worrying never helps anything," the physician said, being cagey with her response. "To be on the safe side, I'll order a series of tests, okay?"

"O...okay," Maddie stuttered.

"Kay will be in shortly to take some blood and urine," Doctor Motta said, patting her patient's shoulder. "I'll be in touch just as soon as I get the results," she added before leaving the room.

Worrying never helps anything? Maddie repeated, knowing that this nugget of wisdom was sure to inspire even more anxiety.

It seemed like eternity before Nurse Kay entered and began extracting blood.

• • •

Two restless nights passed. Phinn was feeding oatmeal to P.J. in his booster seat when Maddie's cell phone rang. He watched as Maddie hurried to answer it. "Hello?" she said, while his sense of peace immediately turned to fear.

"Yes, this is she…" Maddie said.

Phinn put down the baby's spoon. "Who is it?" he asked, his hackles raised.

She raised her pointer finger for him to wait. "I understand," she muttered into the phone. Her face said it all.

Oh no, he thought, swallowing hard, *this isn't good.*

A terrible moment later, she ended the call and turned to face him. "It was Doctor Motta," she said, reluctantly. "She said the tests came back and …" Maddie stopped.

Phinn stood and approached her. "And what?" he asked, panic filling his heart.

"My blood showed some abnormalities," she said, her voice breaking up. "Doctor Motta wants to see us in her office tomorrow morning."

He grabbed her shoulders. "That's all she said?"

Maddie nodded but couldn't hold back the tears.

Putting on his bravest face, Phinn massaged her shoulders. "It's probably nothing, babe. Let's not worry until we have to." He rested his chin on the top of her head. "And whatever it is, we'll face it together, okay?"

"Okay," she said, falling into his arms for a comforting hug.

• • •

Maddie squirmed terribly in Doctor Motta's office. It seemed like forever before the soft-spoken physician walked in, a manila folder tucked under her arm.

"So what's the verdict?" Maddie asked right away.

Doctor Motta sat on the edge of her desk and opened the folder.

She cleared her throat. "Your blood tests suggest leukemia, but…"

"Oh, my God," Maddie squealed.

Phinn immediately placed his hand on his wife's leg. "Leukemia?" he repeated, momentarily unable to process the word.

The doctor shook her head. "But I can't definitively diagnose without looking at a sample of bone marrow cells," she said, nodding confidently. "We'll conduct some blood chemistry tests that will measure the amounts of certain chemicals in your blood, Maddie, and we'll also run a coagulation test."

"So it might not be leukemia?" Phinn suggested.

"Maddie's symptoms—the bleeding gums, the swollen lymph nodes, the bruising and nosebleeds—collectively, they all point to a blood disease."

"But the lump under my arm doesn't hurt," Maddie said, as if negotiating the diagnosis.

The doctor nodded. "Which is another strong indicator, Maddie."

"Oh God," Maddie repeated.

"But let's do some more testing before we panic," Doctor Motta suggested.

"Yes," Phinn said, locking eyes with his trembling wife, "we need to keep the faith."

Maddie nodded.

"Let's get those tests started today, okay?" the doctor said.

Maddie opened her mouth, but nothing came out.

"Okay," Phinn answered for her.

• • •

On the drive home, Phinn wanted to cry. *But I can't show Maddie my fears,* he decided. *I need to be strong for her.* In the passenger seat, Maddie did enough weeping for the two of them. "We need to keep the faith, babe," he reminded her. "We need to pray on this and hope for the best."

"You're right," she said, but the terror in her eyes told a different story.

They weren't home for a half hour before Maddie's debilitating fatigue won the latest round, knocking her out cold. Tucking the blanket under her chin, Phinn kissed her forehead and made a bee-line for his laptop computer—his tears finally breaking free.

For the next two hours, he frantically researched leukemia, soaking up all the knowledge he could.

Common leukemia signs and symptoms were listed as, *Night sweats, fatigue and weakness that don't go away with rest, unintentional weight loss, bone pain and tenderness.*

While his heart thumped, he told himself, *She's never complained about bone pain and tenderness.* He was desperately searching for any ray of light.

He read on. *Fever or chills; easy bleeding or bruising; recurrent nosebleeds; painless, swollen lymph nodes in the neck or armpits.* He lost his breath, thinking, *Please God, no.*

He willed himself to read on. *Tiny red spots on the skin called petechiae.* He tiptoed into the bedroom and slowly pulled the blanket off his wife's legs, only to discover small red spots peppered across her shins. "Oh God," he gasped, quietly back-pedaling out of the room. While he felt his throat constrict, panic rushed into his bloodstream, making his extremities tingle.

He hurried back to the laptop, forcing himself to continue the research. He typed *Adult Leukemia* into the Google search box and hit *Enter*. His stomach began doing back-flips as hundreds of sites—maybe even thousands—loaded onto the screen.

He read, *About 21,000 new cases of AML are diagnosed annually in the United States. The five-year survival rate for AML is 26.9 percent.* His heart skipped a few beats. *To diagnose AML, a doctor will do blood tests to count the number of white blood cells and to see if they look abnormal under the microscope.* He nodded. *In progress*, he thought before scanning through other potential tests. "Bone marrow aspiration and biopsy; genomic testing; imaging tests; and lumbar puncture, also called a spinal tap," he read aloud. The amount of information was as mind-boggling as it was soul-slaying.

After reviewing the *Tests* section, Phinn moved on to *Staging*. While both his lips and hands quivered, he read, *Once leukemia is diagnosed, it'll be staged. Staging helps your doctor determine your outlook. AML and ALL are stage-based on how cancer cells look under the microscope and the type of cell involved. The presence of immature white blood cells, or myeloblasts, in the blood and bone marrow is also used to stage AML and CML.*

Although Phinn felt dizzy, he understood that knowledge is power and that he needed to forge on to the *Treatments* section. *Leukemia is usually treated by a hematologist-oncologist,* he read. *These are doctors who specialize in blood disorders and cancer. The treatment depends on the type and stage of the cancer. Chemotherapy uses drugs to kill leukemia cells. Depending on the type of leukemia, you may take either a single drug or a combination of different drugs. Chemotherapy is given by intravenous (IV) treatment. Induction usually lasts four weeks, with a week of chemotherapy and then several weeks for bone marrow recovery. Radiation therapy uses high-energy radiation to damage leukemia cells and inhibit their growth. Radiation can be applied to a specific area or to the entire body. Stem cell transplantation replaces diseased bone marrow with healthy bone marrow, either the patient's own or from a donor. This procedure is also called a bone marrow transplant.*

Phinn had just enough strength to internalize one final page. *In general,* he read, *about eighty percent of adults will have complete remissions at some point during these treatments.* He inhaled deeply, considering this to be a positive piece of information. *This means leukemia cells can no longer be seen in their bone marrow. Unfortunately, about half of these patients relapse, so the overall cure rate is around forty percent.*

As he stood up from the laptop, he felt his knees buckle, nearly pulling him to the floor. *Forty percent,* he repeated in his spinning head, before running to the bathroom to vomit.

CHAPTER 16

The longest, most tormenting week passed before Maddie and Phinn were summoned back to Doctor Motta's dreaded office.

While the physician painfully stalled, Maddie squirmed terribly, looking left to see her worried husband doing the same. "Just tell us, please," she blurted, her nerves frayed.

With the most sorrowful expression, the doctor looked up and broke the devastating news. "You have leukemia, Maddie—Acute Myelogenous Leukemia, or AML."

While Phinn leapt to his feet, Maddie felt ready to faint.

"But it can be treated, right?" her husband asked, his voice quivering.

Doctor Motta shook her head. "Phinn, right now, there is no cure," she said, sadly, "but..."

As if he'd been violently shoved, Phinn collapsed back into his seat. He rubbed his head over and over. "Oh, dear God..." he moaned. "Oh, dear God."

"Although AML is the most common form of leukemia, it's still a mysterious disease," the doctor explained. "When you have leukemia, the bone marrow starts to produce abnormal white blood cells—leukemia cells—that don't do the work of normal white cells. For whatever reason, they begin multiplying, growing faster than normal cells, and they start killing off the red cells. Over time, leukemia cells can crowd out the normal blood cells and..."

"But there's no cure?" Maddie interrupted in a whimper.

"Well..."

"I just read that most patients with leukemia are treated with chemotherapy," Phinn jumped in. "Some patients even have radiation therapy or a bone marrow transplant."

"Sure," Doctor Motta said, "but..."

"But?" Maddie asked, terror paralyzing her core.

The doctor looked directly at her. "Unfortunately, you're already at stage four, Maddie. It's the most aggressive and..."

"Oh God!" Phinn blurted, cutting her off.

"I should have reported my symptoms earlier," Maddie muttered, piling guilt onto the heap of sorrow. "I've been so tired and weak," she babbled, "the bruises and bloody noses and..."

"There's nothing you could have done," Doctor Motta interrupted, trying to ease her patient's mind, "as there's no known way to prevent leukemia." The doctor shook her head. "It's often hereditary, but in this case..." She stopped.

Maddie and Phinn were both crushed; definitions obviously weren't going to help.

"The disease often goes into remission for long periods of time," the doctor added, softly. "Some people live for years after being diagnosed."

Maddie began crying uncontrollably.

Phinn sat up straight, trying to be strong.

Terrified, Maddie suddenly felt like a little girl and not the tough, confident woman she'd spent years becoming. Phinn wrapped his arms around her trembling body. "Phinn, what am I..." she stuttered, "what are we..." She stopped, convulsing with each sob.

"Together," Phinn said, "we'll face this thing together." He leaned in to her face to make eye contact. "I'm right here with you, Maddie," he promised, inhaling deeply. But his own whimpers stopped him from going on. It didn't matter. No words existed to ease the pain or stop the horror. They were about to face an unmerciful monster, and they both knew it.

Doctor Motta shook her head. She was obviously disgusted to be the bearer of such heinous news—with nothing more she could do for the distraught couple.

Phinn and Maddie returned home to face the nightmare.

• • •

While Phinn silently wept, he stroked Maddie's hair until she fell asleep—with George by her side. After kissing her forehead, he checked in on P.J. The baby was sleeping peacefully in his crib, so Phinn headed for the front door.

He moped solemnly along the Taunton River until finally dropping to his knees on the muddy bank. Clasping his hands together, he looked toward the sky and began his negotiations with God. "Dear Lord," he pleaded, "please don't take Maddie away from me… from *us*." He sobbed fiercely. "I'll do anything, God, just don't let her die." With his head hung in desperation, he knelt in silence for a long while before looking back toward the sky. "Show me a sign, Father," he begged. "I need to know that everything's going to be…"

He felt a tap on his shoulder and jumped.

"Sorry to startle you, Phinn," Mr. Tetreault said, standing over him. "It looked like there was something wrong."

"Maddie has leukemia," Phinn blurted, weeping.

"Oh," Mr. Tetreault said, taken aback. "There are treatments, Phinn—chemo, radiation, bone…"

"It's too aggressive," Phinn said, cutting him off. "Stage four."

Taking a seat on the ground, Mr. Tetreault placed his strong hand on Phinn's shoulder. Phinn waited for his mentor's wise words, but the man said nothing. Instead, he stared out onto the dark horizon. And while Phinn's whimpers turned to uncontrollable sobs, Mr. Tetreault never removed his hand from Phinn's shoulder. When Phinn finally came up for air, he turned to his old friend. "I didn't ask for this," he whimpered. "This was not part of the plan."

"Some people live an entire lifetime in one moment, Phinn," Mr. Tetreault whispered. "It's what you make of it." He looked hard into Phinn's eyes. "Don't waste another moment."

• • •

Phinn's eyes opened, as another squeal traveled from across the hall. "Mama. Dada," P.J. called out from his crib.

P.J.'s up, Phinn's fuzzy mind finally registered, *and I need to do the same.* Slipping out of bed, he stumbled to his son. Scooping him up, he whispered, "We have to be quiet, big guy. Mama needs to rest so she can get better." He carried the boy to the kitchen to prepare a warm bottle.

As P.J. settled back into his crib with his pre-dawn breakfast, Phinn took a seat in the rocking chair in the corner and wondered, *How can this be happening? There's no way. Not to us. We just got started…our whole lives are ahead of us. It doesn't make sense.* He began to cry again. *It's just a bad dream, that's all this is. We're all going to wake up and Maddie's going to…*

P.J. burped loudly, breaking Phinn out of his wishful daydream. *Oh, it's a nightmare, all right*, he remembered, *and we're living it.*

P.J. began to wail from his crib.

Instinctively, Phinn took a break from his grieving and got up to tend to his baby boy.

• • •

The months that ticked off Maddie's illness were the cruelest imaginable. As the seasons changed—along with Maddie and Phinn's reality—the Reed and Renaud families came together to support the young couple. And as Maddie's health deteriorated by the day, Phinn took primary care of their son.

Phinn held P.J. upright until the toddler could gain his own balance. Finally letting the boy go, P.J. took three quick steps before falling into Maddie's arms. They were overjoyed. While Phinn applauded, Maddie kissed the boy. "Phinn, please take him," she said, clearly feeling ill.

Phinn placed P.J. into his playpen.

Maddie sighed. "I'm so grateful I was here to see his first steps."

"Grateful?" Phinn repeated. "You're not fighting this thing hard enough, Maddie," he barked; the desperation was eating him alive. "It's like you're giving up."

"There's nothing to fight, Phinn," she replied, gently, "and I'm not giving up. I've just placed it all into the hands of God."

"But He's not listening, is He!" Phinn screeched, storming out of the room.

• • •

Alone with her thoughts, tears rolled down Maddie's face, salty droplets shed for her husband's pain and for all she was going to miss in P.J.'s life. She thought about her boy's first day of school and the anxious look on his face when he stepped onto the big, yellow bus. *All the report cards I'll never read,* she pondered, *the new clothes he'll pick for his first date and the daffy smirk he'll wear after that first kiss.* She cried from her soul. *I won't be there for his high school graduation, or to offer my support through his college years.* Her heart ached as she pictured him standing alone at his wedding when it was time for them to dance. *And not playing Grandma for his children.* The inconsolable pain caused her entire body to shake. "We're all being cheated," she said aloud, weeping harder than she'd ever wept.

• • •

Phinn ended up on Brayton Point Park where the realization of Maddie's impending death brought him to his knees once again. He was through negotiating with God and had reached anger long before. Feeling betrayed, he looked toward heaven and screamed, "I've made my mistakes, we both know I have, but I've done everything in my power to change my ways. I've worshipped you. I've worked hard. And I've been good to people, treating them as I want to be treated." He was enraged. "And this is what I get for it? I've waited my whole life to find someone to love, and when I finally find her, you're going to take her from me?" Shaking his head, his roar was reduced to a wounded grovel. "You took my mother from me way too soon, and now you want my wife?"

Weeping uncontrollably, he reached his hands toward heaven. "I feel so alone. Why have you left me?" he screeched again. "Why?"

Mr. Tetreault appeared on the dark horizon, walking along the river toward him. As he approached, Phinn looked up, his face awash in tears. The man gestured toward the grassy hill. Phinn nodded. Mr. Tetreault took a seat beside him. After a moment of shared silence, Phinn said, "I don't know what to do, Mr. Tetreault."

There was a long pause. "Then do nothing," the man whispered. "Just be."

"*Be* what?" Phinn lashed out, getting to his feet. "Be happy that my wife's being eaten alive by cancer right in front of my eyes, with nothing I can do about it?"

Mr. Tetreault didn't respond, remaining seated.

"I didn't choose for this to happen," Phinn sobbed, "for Maddie to get sick."

"Maybe it wasn't your choice to make?" Mr. Tetreault suggested.

As much as it hurt, for whatever reason those words made sense. Phinn looked at Mr. Tetreault and, for the first time, pondered the idea of acceptance. He reclaimed his seat beside the man.

The two sat together in silence.

"It's not about you, Phinn," Mr. Tetreault added softly. "It's about Maddie." With a nod, he continued looking straight ahead. "Sometimes acceptance is the only path to peace, my friend," he whispered, "and the most loving thing we can do for someone we care about is to let them go."

Oh God, Phinn thought, sobbing from his soul. "I…I don't know if I can…"

• • •

Maddie's life had become a pendulum of pain, swinging between a physical torment she'd never imagined possible and a deep worry for her family that never relented. The combination made her feel delirious. *We need help, Father*, she prayed, *we need a miracle*. From sheer exhaustion, she finally fell asleep.

• • •

Standing in a thick bank of fog, Maddie opened her eyes. She struggled to recognize her location. *A cloud*, she thought, *I'm in the middle of a cloud.*

"You're all a part of me," God said, "as I am in you."

Maddie cleared her throat, straining to say something. "Well, some people think…"

"…in some great collision," God said, finishing her thought. "Sorry about that. Finishing people's sentences has always been a bad habit." He shrugged. "It's the downside of knowing all things."

"Well, according to science…"

"I love science," God said, chuckling. "I created it."

Maddie struggled to derail from this random and delusional train of thought and focus on the answers she so desperately needed. "Why?" she finally managed.

"Why?" God repeated, grinning.

"Why did I have to get sick? Why do I have to die now?"

God nodded. "My child, it's not…"

• • •

Maddie awoke in even more pain and without one single answer. *Please Lord,* she prayed, *please help us.*

• • •

As though she refused to linger and cause her family any more pain than she needed to, Maddie took a quick turn for the worse. "I just thank God I was able to experience motherhood," she told Mr. Tetreault in mid-conversation.

"Ahhh, the miracle of birth," he said, sitting at the side of her hospital bed and holding her hand. "But why is death any less a miracle," he asked, "returning from where you came?"

Maddie took a deep breath, but never answered.

"You weren't afraid to come into this world," he said, "so you shouldn't be scared to go home."

"I'm not," Maddie whispered.

Mr. Tetreault smiled. "Good," he whispered, "because you, my dear, have nothing to be afraid of."

"But Phinn and P.J..."

"Be at peace, Maddie," he said. "They'll be fine. I promise."

• • •

Julia entered Maddie's hospital room, holding a large container of hot soup. "All they had was..." She stopped when she noticed a stranger standing by her daughter's bedside. "Oh hi," Julia muttered to the man. She looked at Maddie and shrugged. "I'm sorry. I didn't know you had company."

"That's all right," Mr. Tetreault said. "I was just leaving." He grabbed Maddie's hand and winked. "And I'll see you soon," he whispered.

Through the incredible pain, Maddie smiled brightly.

Mr. Tetreault grabbed the doorknob and tipped his hat to Julia. "Mrs. Renaud," he said, bidding his farewell.

Julia stood baffled. "Nice to meet you," she managed, watching as he disappeared behind the door. She turned to Maddie. "Who was that?"

"An old friend who came by to ease my mind about Phinn."

Still confused, Julia dismissed it with a nod. "Speaking of Phinn, he's on his way here right now with the baby," she remembered aloud.

Maddie looked ready for tears. "Oh Mom, he's not handling this well at all."

"I know, sweetheart. It's because he loves you so much." The emotions began taking over and she hurried to finish. "We all do."

"And it's a mutual love that'll never change," Maddie confirmed. "That can't change." She smiled. "It's been promised."

Again, Julia looked surprised. "Promised?"

Just then, Phinn and P.J. came through the door.

Maddie dismissed Julia's question and turned on her smile. "And here are my handsome boys now," she chirped, extending her arms. "Where are my kisses?"

Phinn carried P.J. to his mom. Big sloppy kisses were exchanged. After spending a moment with her son, Maddie turned to Julia. "Mom, how about taking P.J. outside for a walk?"

Julia took the baby from her. "Come on, Grandma's angel," she told the toddler. "Let's go pick some pretty flowers for Mommy, okay?"

P.J.'s innocent laughter stayed in the room a few seconds after they were gone.

• • •

Phinn sat quietly by Maddie's side, holding her hand.

"When did the contractor say he could start framing the house?" she asked, breaking the silence.

He looked at her, surprised that she would bring up such a trivial topic. "The house?" he asked.

She peered back at him but didn't respond.

"He didn't," Phinn answered, "and I couldn't care less if he ever starts."

"But I do," Maddie declared, with as much conviction in her voice as she could muster.

He remained confused. "Maddie, please."

"No, Phinn, promise me," she begged, staring hard into his eyes. "Promise me that you'll finish our dream home."

By now, he was all choked up. "But…"

"No matter what happens, babe, promise that you'll do it for P.J.," she added, "for all of us."

Crying, Phinn placed his face into her shoulder. "I promise," he sobbed.

• • •

A few nights passed—maybe more, it was hard to recognize anything beyond the nauseating pain—when Maddie awoke. As if some masochistic tether had finally snapped, she floated out of the broken vessel that restrained her. The pain was gone, a distant nightmare. Instantly, the past, present, and future converged into one: and one brief moment was like a billion years. All of the secrets of the universe were revealed, and there was no want for anything. Better still, there was but one feeling fluttering in her heart; it was love. Peace and serenity replaced fear and torment. She felt so young, so energetic—*so alive.*

Weightless in both mind and body, she was now fearless, limitless, completely worry-less. *I was right,* she thought, *I've always been a spirit having a human experience.*

She bathed in the strong scent of lilacs that surrounded her. Blinking once and then again, she tried to focus. *It's a rainbow,* she realized. *I'm standing in the middle of a rainbow, hovering just above a...*

But Phinn and P.J., her mind suddenly registered, *my boys.*

At once, the darkness closed in all around her until the beautiful soft light became a tiny pinpoint and then disappeared completely. The intense pain—the voracious disease that was devouring her insides like a pool of ravenous piranha—pulsated through every cell in her body. As she fought to hold on and say a proper goodbye, wave after tormenting wave smashed into her.

Please, dear God, she begged, *have mercy.*

• • •

"There's nothing more we can do," the doctor told Phinn. "We'll keep Maddie as comfortable as we can, but she doesn't have much time."

"Thank you," Phinn whimpered, finding the words odd.

Both families were contacted and rushed to be with Maddie.

• • •

Julia sat at her daughter's bedside. Without needing to use words, they said goodbye. Julia was a wreck. Maddie, however, appeared to be at peace. Julia kissed her little girl. "You should rest now," she said, sorrowfully. "I'll be here when you get up and..." The last few words drifted on emotion. Julia couldn't help it; she was losing it.

Maddie smiled, compassionately. "Okay, Mom," she managed through the pain. "Please tell Jake I need to talk to him."

Before drumming up the courage to leave, Julia grabbed Maddie's face and kissed it. "I'll send him in," she whispered, "and don't you ever forget how much I love you."

Maddie nodded. *It would be impossible,* she thought. "I love you, too, Mama," she groaned.

• • •

Overwhelmed with grief, Jacob took a seat at his suffering sister's bedside.

Trying to smile, Maddie produced two folded sheets of yellow, lined paper. "I know this will be tough for you, Jake," she moaned, "but it's very important to me."

"Name it, Maddie...anything."

She handed him the first paper. "When they lay me to rest, please read this to those I love." There was a compassionate pause. "Read it at my funeral, okay?"

"Oh, Maddie..." Jacob whimpered. As if it were too much to take, he shook his head several times before forcing himself to read Maddie's final message. Once done, he wiped his eyes and hugged his dying sister. Folding the paper, he placed it into his pocket. "Okay," he said, "I'll do it."

"Thank you," she managed, handing him the second paper. "I've written Phinn a letter and put together a scrapbook for P.J. Please make sure they get them." She struggled to take in air. "The instructions are right here."

"Consider it done," Jacob whispered, fighting to be strong.

• • •

Distraught, Phinn and the Renaud and Reed families were gathered in the hallway, trying to support each other; the overwhelming grief was inconsolable.

Jacob came out of the room and gestured toward Phinn. "She wants to see you—alone," he said.

While the rest of the family tightened their huddle, Phinn wiped his eyes and stepped into the room.

• • •

Maddie—his beloved wife—was in such pain that Phinn would have given anything to switch places and suffer it for her. *It's time to say goodbye*, he realized, feeling like he was the one about to die. He knelt by her bed. "I'm here, babe," he sobbed, kissing her hand. "You're not alone."

She reached for his hand. "I know, Phinn," she whispered, "and..." She moaned in pain. "...and I never have been. None of us have."

Phinn was moved by her amazing faith. *It's like she really knows,* he thought.

She smiled faintly. "And I need you to know that my life is complete."

Phinn bowed his head and started to cry.

She gently continued. "Phinn, listen to me. We created a beautiful son together, and I will cherish your love for all eternity. But..." She moaned again. "But I need to go home."

Home? Phinn thought. "I...I can't say goodbye, Maddie," he stuttered.

Her smile turned into a painful grimace. "You don't need to," she whispered, moaning. "Just read to me, my love. I need your voice to soothe me now."

Phinn fumbled in his pocket for a poem that he'd written her. In a quivering voice, he read:

"You're the light that filters through the clouds
when days are dark and bleak;
an ancient wish upon a star,
the answer that I seek.

"The song of doves and passing winds,
the music in my heart;
the calm before a rainstorm,
the hope where dreams can start.

"The purest snow upon the hills,
the sparkle in my tears;
the bank upon the river,
a refuge from my fears.

"The setting sun and smiling moon,
the one who steals my breath;
the woman who I vow to love
beyond that place called death."

He emerged from the poem to find Maddie's eyes closed. A faint smile had replaced her pained expression from before. She was gone. "Oh God, no!" he screamed out, and began crying uncontrollably.

As family members came rushing through the door, he stroked his wife's dark hair and mourned the loss of a lifetime; it was an excruciating and somewhat familiar pain that throbbed from his soul.

CHAPTER 17

Maddie's entire life flashed before her eyes; not so much in individual memories, but a culmination of all she'd experienced—all the love she felt for others and what they felt for her rolled up into one single moment of poignant clarity. *I'm connected to everything*, she realized, feeling the truth of it in the marrow of her once aching bones.

Without her eyelids ever flinching, Maddie awoke. Instantly, she knew death was a liberation. Physically, she recognized the absence of pain, feeling infinitely better than her very best day on earth. She felt light now; this wasn't so much body weight as it was being free from guilt, shame, worry, fear, regret, embarrassment—all of it gone, distant memories from a dream that once played out as reality.

She'd always figured that death would feel like waking from anesthesia—groggy and confused. *I couldn't have been any more mistaken.* From the millisecond she left her broken body, she'd never been more aware or cognizant of her true self, her rightful place in the universe, and how she was directly connected to all living things. Until now, she felt as if she'd been asleep, her senses dulled. Now, in a heightened state of being, she innately understood the fabric of life. She could feel the rhythm and the flow, the river that all beings traveled along during their experiences on earth, as well as into the afterlife. *No fear. No pain. No worry or wonder*, she understood. *Just freedom from the rusty chains of every dark thought and emotion.*

There was so much light that shadows could not exist, any hint of darkness no more. As if she'd always belonged, she entered the brilliant glow of God's presence. Although there was no comparison, she was reminded of the warmth she'd felt as a baby falling asleep on the rise and fall of her mother's chest. Joy overflowed. Suddenly, she understood her worth and power, of being a piece of the whole—the real family.

The silver chord connecting Maddie's body to her spirit had been severed; she was now free to travel to the places she'd only seen in her most magnificent dreams. She could finally breathe again, released from the rotting shell she'd occupied on earth. Plucked from a world of smoke and mirrors, of the illusions that existed on earth, she now understood that life could never fail to exist. *We are never separated from God,* she thought, *or each other.* There was no superiority perceived here, the winners dominating the losers. *That's reserved for earth or the hell we created for ourselves there.* But even that made sense now. *It was the ideal testing ground to earn one's degree in compassion for his fellow man.*

She smelled wet, musty dog hair. Unsure whether she'd traveled for a wink or a thousand years, she turned to see Raymond—her beloved dog—sitting there, wagging his tail. *This beautiful mutt's been waiting for me to come home,* she realized. *I never lost him after all.*

Time—a mere measuring stick—was suddenly just one eternal moment of now. In earthly terms, Maddie wasn't really sure how long she'd been back in heaven. *What I do know,* she thought, *is that there's no need to fight for what we think we need. There's one truth shared by all, with no manipulation. We are one with nature again and not at war with it like on earth. All things are equal, understood and created to serve the whole in unison. The illusion of insufficiency no longer exists. Death is fiction.* She smiled at the truth of it. *Life is eternal.*

Maddie looked around. There were no words to describe all that she saw. None existed—even though she now knew everything. *If life is like looking through a tiny crack in a wall, straining to see all we can and then making sense of it all with the limited information available, then death is like knocking the whole wall down.* Suddenly, she could take it all in and understand. *It finally makes sense why I felt homesick my entire life.* All the hunches she'd had, the times of intuition that she'd ignored were actually hints of knowledge from this higher plane. Those random and infrequent moments of clarity Maddie had once experienced were now magnified by infinity.

Bathed in light, Maddie watched as the silhouettes of others approached. The more people that gathered, the brighter the light glowed. Babies began laughing and kept laughing until Maddie couldn't help it and joined them. As she giggled, she couldn't feel a hint of physical pain—*no more mental or emotional anguish.* She'd finally been freed from such burdens. *Heaven is reality,* she realized, *the rest was imagined.*

One by one, deceased family members and friends stepped into the light to greet her. *Relationships don't end,* she now knew, as she started to make out faces, *they just change form.*

Her dad approached first, beaming with love. "It's about time," he teased in a whisper, grabbing Maddie's hand. "I've been waiting."

Her dad looked different, younger than she remembered him. *And he's happy now.* Without asking, she could see every truth in his smiling eyes. There was no more pain to cloud the love he'd always felt for her, no more scar tissue to block the love she felt for him in return.

He was glowing—literally—and though he spoke not another word, it didn't matter. She could read his every thought, feel his every feeling.

For a heavenly moment—a second, and forever—they embraced.

This life is better, she decided. There was no need to ask any more questions. There was only love and complete understanding.

God, how I love you so, her dad thought.

I know, she replied in thought.

Though it was unnecessary, he asked for her forgiveness without uttering a word.

It's already forgiven, she thought, *all of it*. And then it came back to her: *Long before I was ever born, I asked that you play the harsh role of my earthly father, and you reluctantly agreed.*

He nodded in confirmation. *It was the toughest thing I've ever done, but it was my job to guide you to where you needed to go. By causing you to suffer, I taught you compassion,* he thought: and Maddie read his mind as clearly as she could read her own.

She grabbed for her dad and hugged him again. *The purpose of your miserable life was nothing more than a favor to me*, she thought. *Thank you.*

Another spirit stepped forward.

Maddie saw her face, while a second glance revealed fuzzy slippers on her feet. *It's Nana!* Maddie squealed like a child at Christmas. "I knew I'd see you again," she said, her heart gushing with joy.

Madelyn! Maddie's grandmother thought, hurrying to her. They jumped into each other's arms, swaying back and forth like they had when Maddie was a child.

You still smell like roses, Nana, Maddie thought. *I hope you can still make your famous French toast?*

Her grandmother's spirit glowed brighter.

Yes! Maddie thought.

It suddenly made absolute sense why Maddie had chosen the life she did. *Why I chose the family I did,* she thought. *They were meant to teach me the lessons I needed, so that my soul could grow and my spirit could evolve into a higher being.*

Maddie's life on earth had been a dream come true. As clear as the light upon her face, she now remembered that she'd dreamt it long before she'd been sent into the world—*long before I'd spent each worldly moment creating my own reality.*

In that instant, she also realized that not only did she retain all of her memories from earth, but that she could experience them again— with every vivid detail and feeling as the first time they'd happened. *I haven't lost a moment*, she thought. She could smell her mother's scent, a mix of Ivory soap and the lavender body lotion the loving woman always used. She could hear her father's baritone voice, fol-lowed by his heavy footsteps up the stairs toward his bedroom—like the pounding of hail on a tin roof. She was back in middle school, sitting in her assigned seat in the front row, and could see every letter and number Mrs. Fallow scratched on the faded chalkboard. The taste of her Nana's French toast lingered in her mouth, the grittiness of the cinnamon and sugar crunching between her teeth. The distinct smell of a campfire at a Girl Scout outing. Her first kiss; the butter-flies in her stomach and the touch of his dry lips on hers; although she was young, she somehow knew they hadn't gotten it right. She saw herself crying on her bed, thinking that her life was about to end—not realizing that it was yet to even begin. She could still feel the thrills of each Halloween and the excitement that made her mind buzz every Christmas morning, a small mountain of wrapped pres-ents flowing out from the base of a twinkling pine tree. She could feel the biting wind on her face while ice skating with her neighborhood friends, and the cold on her backside each time she fell. The school dances; the visits to the beach each summer, licking the salt on her lips. The wild rides in Becca's Jeep, the music blaring and their hair whipping around in the summer wind. She remembered the day she met Phinn; she could still feel the excitement she'd felt as she approached him in front of the Italian restaurant. The excruciating and glorious pain of childbirth, and the first time she saw P.J.'s tiny face and fell in love all over again.

Miranda, Maddie's niece, appeared next. She was surrounded by angels, all of them dancing and laughing.

I've missed you, my love, Maddie thought, *and so have your parents.*

I know, the little girl replied, *I'm with them every day.* Giggling, she faded off with her winged entourage.

Gail, Maddie's childhood friend—who'd taken her own life by walking out into traffic—stepped up next. Her body was whole again, her spirit intact. She was smiling, the colorful rings of energy that surrounded her revealing nothing but happiness, joy, and love.

I've prayed for you for a very long time, Maddie thought, and she had—every night from the moment of Gail's death.

I know, Gail said, her thoughts and feelings completely transparent. *and I could never thank you enough.* She paused. *Besides being a broken contract, suicide is a terrible loss of faith*, she explained. *No sooner did I step off that curb, when I asked myself, How can I quit on my own life when my sweetest breath may be the next one I take?*

Maddie nodded that she understood.

Mrs. Fallow, Maddie's eighth grade teacher, stepped up next. *Thank you for keeping your promise to me*, she said, *and leaving the world a better place than how you found it.*

I couldn't have done it without you, Maddie said.

The wise spirit nodded. *None of us can accomplish anything alone.*

Suddenly, Victor—her uncle who'd been gay in life and had

passed on much too early—was standing by Maddie's side. He winked at her, and she laughed—really laughed. *You made it, too,* she thought, thrilled to see him. As Maddie had been unable to completely shed her childhood prejudices, for years she'd prayed hard that her uncle would be forgiven.

Thank you, he offered, recognizing her prayers, *but don't look so surprised to see me.* He laughed.

Good for you, Maddie thought.

The spirit has no gender, Maddie, he reminded her. *Those who have hate in their heart are quick to judge, and it was my life's purpose to reveal that to many of those poor souls.* He nodded. *It was also my destiny to die the way I did,* he explained. *I was taking care of some bad karma.*

The spirit has no gender, she repeated. *I remember now.*

What about Mr. Tetreault? she wondered.

As quickly as the question arose, the answer came from within her. *Mr. Tetreault is an angel—earning his wings, so to speak. It is the same for Mason Sterne. They are both looking after Phinn.*

Maddie then met the one face she'd never seen before, but had always known in her heart. She was the real *teacher.* Her name was Lola, Maddie's Guardian Angel, and she was prepared to explain everything: *Only by separating from God in the illusion called life can we understand our true worth,* she began. *We are perfect creations made by His very hand; therefore, we do not have to do anything to become perfect. The purpose of life lessons is to bring an awareness of oneness. You see, as each moment dies before us on earth, we recreate ourselves anew— again and again and again. Depending upon growth and spiritual evolution, souls reach different levels of understanding. And upon passing from that dimension into this one, our energy merely changes form.*

She smiled, and Maddie could feel it warm her soul. *The key to life is found in giving,* Lola explained in thought. *Success is found there, empowering others, helping others to succeed. By giving others what we want, we too receive the same—as we are but one entity. You did very well in your life, Madelyn.*

I hope doing well was enough, Maddie thought, lifting the ledger she held.

Lola smiled.

What about... Suddenly, Maddie could see and feel everything that others had experienced because of her words and actions on earth. The ledger vanished.

True pain is feeling distance from God, Lola confirmed, *which is also the essence of who you are.*

Maddie could feel Lola's spirit unite with her own until they were one. *Whatever you resisted, persisted,* the angel explained. *Whatever you gave, you became. God is life and has and always will exist, and we are all a part of that life. Life and everything in it is a process of creation, not a process of discovery. Those who truly know who they are, love who they are, and love God within themselves, understand that we create our own realities. It is these souls who are capable of altering other lives, other worlds. Love is there, always there. It's just a matter of realizing the outcomes of our choices.*

Maddie wondered about the time on earth she didn't get.

You took all the time you needed, Lola explained. *There could have been less or more, but it was always up to you—through your actions, words, and thoughts. Before the soul can leave the body, it must prepare. Once you learned, or remembered what you needed, you were ready to come home.*

But P.J.? Maddie thought.

You can watch and be right by his side, but you mustn't interfere. His soul is evolving at the pace he chooses. Trust me, he's fine. In less than a heartbeat, you'll be together again—laughing. Lola radiated with love. *Now can you see the whole picture?*

Maddie nodded. *I think so.*

Lola waved her hand all around. *Those who have passed over, those on earth, and those in the process of being born—when all put together, that is God.* She peered into Maddie's eyes. *God is life, and life is a reflection of God, broken into individual pieces. When the puzzle is complete, though, only God in His supreme light remains. And only in heaven can the picture be complete. Remember, Madelyn, no different from the life you knew on earth, heaven is anything you want it to be. Your choices, your thoughts, your actions create the reality you wish to experience.*

Anything I want it to be?

Lola's smile glowed. *If you so chose, you could have created heaven on earth.*

With no more than a simple thought, Maddie watched as a bank of billowy clouds gathered in the distance, rolling in like a stampede of wild mustangs. A dark silhouetted tree line against a steel gray sky set the awe-inspired background for Mother Nature's welcome home gift. The air temperature dropped, and Maddie watched as a pair of tiny snowflakes danced in the pink light, swirling and drifting—until landing on the tip of her nose and making her giggle. *Oh,* she thought, her heart filling with unbridled joy. *They're even cold,* she thought, while countless snowflakes fell from above, covering heaven in a baby blanket of white. The entire experience brought a sigh of relief. *I don't have to miss a thing,* she realized, looking at her guardian angel again.

Lola nodded. *You can travel by thought or take an actual ride if you wish—on a snowflake, a trade wind, an ocean current, a zebra's mane, a loved one's whisper.*

Giggling, Maddie changed her mind, watching as the clouds dispersed, only to be replaced by the sound of chirping birds on a warm summer breeze. Everything was green and plush again.

I tried to make the most of the gifts God gave me, Maddie told Lola. *I tried to make Him proud.*

Smiling, the angel pointed.

Maddie turned to find God smiling at her. *Oh Father,* she thought, crying from the overwhelming joy that consumed her.

God spread His arms wide.

She hurried into His embrace.

"Welcome home, Madelyn! How was your journey?" He asked excitedly, like she'd just disembarked from her first roller coaster ride.

"Inexplicably wonderful," she answered. "It seemed like it only lasted a moment, though."

God nodded. "Every life on earth—whether one year or a hundred—is over in the blink of an eye." There was a blissful moment of silence. "You asked to experience love," He said. "Did you?"

"Oh yes!"

"Family? Friends? The miracle of motherhood?"

"Yes, all of it," she answered, solemnly.

"Having children gives you some insight into my love...the aching, the worry." He winked. "But only a tiny glimpse."

As if on cue, Jesus appeared, His light shining bright.

"My son, Jesus," God announced, proudly.

Jesus approached Maddie and hugged her. "Welcome home," He said.

Maddie felt enveloped in pure, unconditional love.

Wearing a smile as wide as the grand canyon, God shrugged. "What can I say, a parent's love is a parent's love, right?"

Maddie nodded that she understood.

Studying her face, God grabbed Maddie by the shoulders. "Tell me what troubles your heart then?"

"I'm going to miss *my* son's life," she explained.

"Oh no," God said, smiling, "you'll be there for P.J.'s first day of school and it's your presence he'll feel when he steps onto the big, yellow bus. You'll be the first to see his report cards, the outfit he'll pick for his first date, and the daffy smirk he'll wear after his first kiss. You'll have better than a front row seat for his high school graduation, and it's your support that will help him get through his college studies."

Maddie realized these were her thoughts—*verbatim*. She suddenly smelled rain; it was the scent of her own tears.

"I promise that your son will know you're with him on the day of his wedding. And as far as your grandchildren," God added, "you'll meet them long before P.J. ever does."

Maddie let her tears fall to the clouds beneath her feet.

God searched her eyes. Without uttering a word, He asked her to go on.

"I never got to kiss P.J. goodbye," she explained.

God shook His beautiful head. "There's no such thing as *goodbye,* my Madelyn. You're connected to those you love forever."

"I know that," she vowed. "I do. And I'm eternally grateful. But I need to kiss my son once more."

Peering into her face, He hugged her again. "Go then," He whispered, gesturing that she could leave, "but don't be too long. You no longer belong in that world."

CHAPTER 18

Phinn dropped his mug of coffee, just missing George, who lay at his feet. Before the cup ever hit the floor, Phinn could feel his life shatter into a hundred jagged pieces, each ceramic shard splintering straight into his heart. As the scalding liquid ran under his feet and George scrambled for safety, he read:

Madelyn Ann (Renaud) Reed, 32, of Swansea, died Thursday evening at Mass. General Hospital following a brief illness. She was the wife of Phinneas Reed. Born in Stamford, CT, the daughter of Julia (Dube) Renaud and the late Henry Renaud, she lived in Swansea the past few years. Besides her husband, she leaves one son, Phinneas Reed, Jr. She was also the sister of Jacob Renaud. The funeral will be held Monday at 8:45 a.m. at Rosini & Rosini Funeral Home, 14 Forge Rd., Swansea, with a Mass of Christian Burial at 10:00 am in Saint Thomas More Church, Swansea. Burial will be in Maple Grove Cemetery.

Although Phinn had lived with the paralyzing grief for days, reality was taking its sadistic time sinking in. *I'll never feel her head on my chest again,* he thought, *or hear her beautiful voice get after me when I roll my eyes or say something stupid.* He collapsed onto the kitchen chair and wept. George hurried to him, resting his cold snout in Phinn's lap. It was the most profound and devastating news Phinn had ever read. Between the violent sobs, the truth hit him: *The newspaper barely reveals a fraction of my amazing wife.* The world would never know the colorful characters Maddie had met along her journey, the woman's experiences, or any of the seemingly trivial parts that made up the whole of her blessed life. Phinn considered this an added tragedy.

In that one brief moment of inspiration, Phinn vowed, *But her son will know her.* With gritted teeth, he nodded. *P.J. will know every detail about his amazing mother.* He put down the newspaper and sobbed. *I will remind him of his mother's love every step of the way.*

· · ·

It was just after dawn when Maddie's shadow appeared on P.J.'s nursery wall. Seeing her, the baby reached out with both hands. "Mama, Mama," he said, excitedly.

The silhouette leaned in and kissed the toddler's forehead.

Dressed in his dark funeral suit, Phinn hurried into the room. Maddie's shadow remained motionless. Without noticing it, Phinn lifted his son out of the crib to comfort him. "It's okay, buddy," he promised, "Daddy's here now."

"Mama, Mama," P.J. repeated.

Phinn's tone turned to a whisper. "I know you miss your mama. I do too. But she's up in heaven now." Whimpers were threatening to turn to sobs. "She's with the angels, where she doesn't have to feel any more pain." He held P.J. firmly in his arms, gazing into his boy's chestnut eyes.

Smiling, the toddler touched his father's face. "Dada, Mama," he said.

"But we still have each other, right?" Phinn managed between dreadful sobs. "Yes sir, it's just the two of us now. And do you want to know a secret, P.J.?"

The boy cooed.

"As much as you need me," he wept, "I need you more."

Giggling, P.J. squirmed in his father's arms, stretching desperately to touch his mother. "Mama," he called out again.

Phinn started out of the room with the baby in his arms. Just as they reached the door, P.J. looked over his dad's shoulder and waved. "Bye, bye, Mama."

On the wall, Maddie's shadow blew her son a kiss.

George scampered in on all fours and whimpered. As he glared at the shadow on the wall, his head tilted sideways. Maddie's shadow placed an index finger to puckered lips for the dog to keep quiet. George lay down and whimpered one last time, promising to keep his late master's secret.

• • •

At the funeral parlor, Maddie's translucent image glided gracefully, her feet never touching the floor. Suspended above reality in a dimension to which she no longer belonged, she peered down at her frozen shell. Friends knelt by the shiny mahogany casket, mumbling their brief prayers. "She looks good," they whispered to each other.

These comments alone were proof that Maddie was dead because not one of them could hear her playful snickering. She floated closer, took a look at her hardened remains, and cringed. But a second look made her smile. "I always did look good in yellow," she muttered.

She also took note of how Phinn had honored her last wishes. A crucifix hung above her head in the casket's lid. Beside it, a photo of them and P.J. had been carefully placed. She kissed her index finger and placed it to P.J.'s smiling face. A purple blanket of lilacs covered the bottom half of the coffin. *Thanks, babe*, she thought.

Moving past several more mourners—who never noticed her presence—she proceeded over to the extravagant flower arrangements. She bent and read each card.

Her cherished husband stood with her mom and other family members in the receiving line. *He looks so alone*, she thought. Rivers of tears flowed straight from his splintered heart. She could feel his pain, and without thinking, hurried to him. "Don't cry for me, Phinn," she pled. "My heart is filled with all of your love. I finally know peace and…" She stopped. Grabbing his face, she kissed him before whispering into ears that would never hear her. "My love, it's not your time yet."

The man just kept staring, the tears pouring freely from the open wound in his heart.

"You still have more to do," she said, "but trust me, we'll be together again soon. I promise."

He stared straight ahead, his eyes locked on the woman who was once his wife.

Maddie approached her family next. After kissing each one of them, she turned and scanned the growing crowd. The funeral director was pacing the floor, worrying whether the Reed family would satisfy the outstanding debt owed him. *In a few hours, after the pall bearers grab the last flower arrangement,* she thought, *this twisted man will be bending my fingers back and stealing my rings.* She could already see it. *Too bad the dead tell no tales because those who rob them are rarely discovered.*

One well-dressed person after another entered the dark parlor. Most signed their names into a guestbook that would never be read. Some dropped off envelopes containing donations to the American

Cancer Society. All proceeded to the coffin to pay their last respects. With keen eyes, she escorted each one.

Neighbors, co-workers, and friends she'd met along the way blessed themselves before her decomposing body and spoke to God. Some even spoke to her in their thoughts: *I hope you have no more pain, Maddie; I'll miss you Maddie Reed. I'll miss you something awful.* Though no one realized it, she responded to each one of them.

With Maddie as their escort, the mourners then proceeded to Phinn. She stood right beside her loving husband, as the heartfelt sympathies began. "I am so sorry for your loss," they said. "My deepest condolences."

Maddie eavesdropped on several of the overlapping conversations. Mrs. Tuggle, an elderly and seemingly sweet soul, spoke in hushed tones to her friend. "Maddie Reed was a spoiled brat," she whispered. "She never once wanted for anything." Her tone went even lower. "I don't know why anyone's crying for her."

Her friend, the town librarian, agreed. "I know. If only we could have all been so lucky." The librarian looked at Phinn. "She had everything," the witch complained. "It's so unfair."

These old hags must bathe in pickling juice, Maddie thought, grinning, *because something's keeping them alive.*

Both gossipmongers shook their heads in disgust. Maddie bent down between them. "And I thought you were both nice!" she screamed into their deaf ears.

Maddie bounced to a different grouping. Corliss Frazer, her comical hairdresser, told funny stories of her and Maddie's time together. Robert Fazzina, her mailman, joined Corliss in praising their fallen friend. "I can't remember ever being in Maddie's company and not leaving with a smile on my face."

This kind of talk shocked Maddie as much as the old hens who gossiped about her. It was the same throughout the room. People either praised her or tore her to bits.

Mr. Tetreault, seated in the back row, smiled at Maddie. He was the only one in the room who could see her. She returned the smile.

The pastor finally arrived, carrying the pallbearers in his wake. "Don't tell me Phinn chose Karl Wilson as one of my pallbearers," Maddie groaned, playfully.

Karl looked right through her with the same goofy smile he'd worn since she'd met him. She laughed.

As the ceremony commenced, Maddie took a seat right above her family to watch.

The young priest quieted the small audience with Maddie's favorite prayer. The chorus of mourners recited, "Our Father, who art in heaven, hallowed be Thy name. Thy kingdom come, Thy will be done on earth as it is in heaven. Give us this day, our daily bread and forgive us of our trespasses, as we forgive those who trespass against us. And lead us not into temptation but deliver us from evil. For thine is the kingdom, the power, and the glory—now and forever. Amen."

At the conclusion of the prayer, the priest sighed. "To lose a loved one so young…"

His voice was drowned out by sniffles and sobs. Phinn only lifted his head when Jacob was called to deliver the eulogy.

Jacob stood and prepared to speak. Maddie floated closer to him. *That's my brother*, she thought, proudly. She adored him.

"Madelyn Ann Reed is my sister," he began.

Seats squeaked with squirming behinds. Jacob was speaking in the present tense. Maddie was the most surprised.

With a quivering voice, he went on. "To the world, Maddie's life might have seemed insignificant."

The squeaking became louder. Maddie cringed.

"But I am living proof that her life was anything *but* insignificant." He took a deep breath and explained, "My sister had the heart of a lion, yet she was unashamed to cry. She was always quick with the truth but never harsh or condescending. She was one to voice her opinions but never pass judgment. Capable of opening her gentle soul, she gracefully forgave the mistakes of others…" He stopped briefly to regain his composure. "Maddie has encouraged and inspired me," he said, "yet taken credit for neither. She was a woman who reached and dreamed but never left anyone behind. Not sparing with her mercy, compassion, or love, she often accepted less from others. And that's only what she meant to me." Jacob pulled a folded piece of paper from his pocket. "Maddie asked me to read this today. Although the author is unknown, she said it was one of her favorite poems." He cleared his throat. "It is titled, *In The End.*"

Phinn was startled from his paralyzing grief. He looked up at Jacob, then quickly over at the casket. The tears poured freely. As he shook his head, a smirk forced its way into the corner of his mouth. He looked back at the casket. *Author unknown, huh?* he thought. *You always could keep a secret, babe.*

Jacob's quivering voice read:
"Standing on the threshold of death,
a lifetime of memories sweeps me away.
My weary mind rewinds every second
and my heart is filled with peace.
I can't seem to recall the material objects

which I once believed had brought me joy.
The cars, the houses, the money—
like grains of blowing sand,
they have sifted through my fingers.
As vivid as the moments we shared,
I only see the faces of those I loved.
I hear the laughter, even cherish the tears.
Like counting sheep, the beautiful smiles
of family and friends appear before me,
but I am tired and it is time to rest.
Awakening above my own wretched body,
my spirit hovers in complete bliss.
There is a sad echo of those who mourn,
but still I must smile—
for the only thing that ever mattered was love.
As a blessing, I have known that love,
both in giving and receiving
and my life's work is done.
Now it is time to go to my Father,
but looking back one last time,
I will take all of that love to Him.
As it was in the beginning, in the end…
there is only love."

Your work is inspired by a higher source, Phinn, Maddie thought,
and you hit this one out of the park.

The funeral parlor was drowning in heavy sobs.

"I now know why my sister wanted to share this beautiful poem
with everyone she loved," Jacob said. "It is impossible for a woman

like my sister to die. Although she will be missed in the physical sense, just by looking around this room it's clear to me that from here on, her spirit will simply live in the hearts of others."

Gesturing toward Phinn, Jacob struggled to finish his eulogy of love. "When Maddie's son P.J., and his children's children go forth into the world and brush against the lives of others..." He paused to wipe away his tears. "...it is my sister's touch that the world will feel." By now, he was sobbing heavily. "Madelyn Ann Reed is my sister. And I, for one, have been blessed." Jacob looked back at the casket. "*In The End*, Maddie's chosen poem, is just a reminder for us that someday we'll all be together again."

Maddie glided to Jacob and tried to tussle her little brother's hair. It never moved. "Thanks Jake," she said. "I owe you one. And this is from Miranda." She kissed her brother's cheek. Jacob never felt it. "Oh Jake, if you could only see her. Miranda dances with angels now, and she is so happy that she radiates." She kissed him again. "And you'll be together sooner than you think."

Jacob never heard a word. Realizing this, Maddie approached her grieving husband.

Phinn stared at his beloved wife's corpse. Through the tears, he smiled. *Thank you for the poem*, he secretly told her. *Thank you, my love.*

Maddie could hear his thoughts and beamed. Placing her invisible lips onto his rolling teardrop, she kissed him again.

This time, Phinn felt it. As he touched his cheek, his forearms turned to goose flesh. *I'd never miss that kiss anywhere*, he thought, *in life or death. It's Maddie's sweet kiss.* He just knew it.

She read his mind, as though he were speaking the words to her. Nothing was hidden now.

I love you, babe, he thought.

Maddie smiled. "I know, Phinn," she whispered, "I can feel everything you feel. And until death do we part is a crock, babe. You're not getting rid of me that easy."

He continued to stare at the empty body in the casket.

"Don't look there, my love," Maddie told him, "I'm not there anymore." She placed her hand on his chest. "Jacob's right. Look in here, inside your heart. It's the only place we don't ever have to leave." After a long pause, she promised, "The pain you feel now is only the intensity of the love that bonds us forever." She kissed him one last time. "You gotta take the bad with the good, right? That's the design, babe."

Meet me in my dreams tonight, Maddie, he thought. *I'll be waiting for you.*

I'll be there, she thought, turning to begin her journey home. There was a whole new dimension to explore—with colors, tastes, and smells she could have never fathomed on earth. *Besides, I need to get home,* she told herself, *my husband's going to be along in the blink of an eye.*

Moving toward the light in the ceiling, she glanced back to see Mr. Tetreault watching her from the back row. He was still smiling. She mouthed the words, "Thank you for everything."

Nodding, Mr. Tetreault shot her a wink.

Maddie returned the gesture. *It really was an amazing life,* she thought, and was gone forever.

• • •

It was eternal dawn when Maddie returned to the cloud—to God.

It all came back to her again, her spirit flooding with the truth. Beyond the stars, though Maddie's mind's eye had struggled to remember, this was the place from where her soul had come. *In this glorious existence, there is no need for material objects,* she immediately understood. *Any substance needed to flourish comes from unconditional love. It is where time holds no captives and dark shadows do not exist. All that is beautiful and kind and righteous dwells here, sent into the world we know if only to experience and appreciate all that was created. Our spirits, merely parts of the whole, spend the gift of life stumbling around in search of answers. But the truth is not meant to be discovered,* she now understood, *but simply remembered—each of us remembering who we are, the love that sent us to illuminate the world and the home that awaits our return.*

Waiting patiently for her to emerge from this understanding, God hugged her.

"Thank you for allowing me to kiss my boy," she whispered.

God nodded. "No more worries, okay? Not one of my children is ever alone," He promised.

Maddie suddenly realized they were standing together on the front porch of a full-dormered Cape; it was a big, wrap-around porch. She felt a bolt of excitement shoot through her, as she looked out to see a small residential neighborhood, the rolling land covered with perfectly manicured emerald green lawns. The mulched, kidney-shaped flowerbeds sprouted wildflowers of honeysuckle and lilac, while black-eyed Susans and tiger lilies shared space with columbine, clover, and Oriental poppy. There were a couple of small Japanese cedars shading hydrangeas, pansies, and impatiens, with green and red ornamental grasses mixing beautifully with silver mound, Russian sage, and juniper. *The colors are breathtaking,* she thought.

"You are connected—always," God told her, draping His arm over her shoulder, "but you cannot interfere." He pointed toward Phinn—who was shrouded in terrible grief—and whispered, "Just watch."

"Okay," Maddie said.

As she looked down from heaven, God smiled as brightly as the sun. "Hey, do you want to meet your granddaughter?" He asked.

"Are you kidding?" She was beyond excited.

"I never joke," He said, laughing hard.

"Of course I want to meet her," Maddie said, overjoyed. "What's her name?"

"Madelyn," God said, "after her grandmother."

Maddie's spirit radiated. "Hey, I know someone with that name," she joked.

"Small world," God said, grinning. "Well, let's go meet her then," He said. "I don't have all day."

Maddie looked at him, unsure whether she was being teased.

"I'm just kidding," God said. "Take all the time you need, kid. We have eternity."

Maddie looked back down at Phinn and beamed with joy. "Good to know," she whispered.

CHAPTER 19

Jacob returned home with his brokenhearted brother-in-law. He took a seat near Phinn on the porch. "Maddie's funeral was very beautiful," he said.

Phinn snickered at the idea of such a foolish notion, refusing to reply or even make eye contact.

Jacob wrapped his arm around Phinn, who remained unmoved. *And why not,* Jacob thought, *he's been cheated the love of his life.* Jacob smiled at him.

Phinn never batted an eye.

"I'm here if you want to talk about it," Jacob said.

"What's there to talk about, Jake?" Phinn asked, more disheartened than angry. "My life's basically over."

"Over?" Jacob snapped back, removing his arm. "Oh no, brother, you just need to have some faith."

"Faith?" Phinn repeated, the word obviously stinging in his ears. "Where was God when my wife was taken from me?"

Right there with you, Jacob thought, placing his hand on Phinn's shoulder. "Trust me, faith is the answer."

"How could God have taken Maddie from me?" Phinn screeched. "I never wanted to be a single dad."

Shaking his head, Jacob revealed a tattered envelope and a photo album. He handed both to Phinn. "But He didn't take her, Phinn," he whispered, "at least not all of her."

Phinn looked up, confused.

"Have a closer look and you'll see." Jacob handed Phinn the sealed envelope and photo album. "The letter's for you," he explained, "and Maddie put together a scrapbook for P.J. to read as he gets older." Jacob stood. "You've got a lot of people in your corner, brother," he said, squeezing Phinn's shoulder. "Your family's right here with you. I'm right here with you." With a final pat, he left Phinn to be alone with his wife.

• • •

Wiping his eyes, Phinn opened the envelope.

I love you, Phinn, he read, *and have since the moment I saw you. I would apologize for getting sick, but I know that would just make you roll your eyes.*

Through the first sobs, he laughed.

I know you didn't ask for this, Phinn, being left alone with a toddler. But you're an amazing dad, and you're going to do an incredible job raising our boy. I know that more than I've ever known anything.

He stopped again, trying to take in oxygen.

Although you won't be able to see me, I'll be right there with you the whole way. I promise. You're not alone, my love. You never have been. You never will be.

Please go on with your life, babe, and make sure that you fill it with joy. We both know you'll never forget me, my love. My fear is that you may forget yourself. Please don't do that. Life is precious, so it's important you make the most of every day you're given. There's nothing more valuable than that. God blessed us with a beautiful boy. Please show him everything the world has to offer. Teach him to be the good man that you are and enjoy every minute of it.

We'll be together again, Phinn, but in the meantime, please live your life to the fullest. I could never ask for anything more.

Promise me.

All my Love, Always—Maddie xoxo

Through a waterfall of tears, Phinn read the letter twice more before nodding. "Okay, babe," he said aloud, "I promise." He sighed heavily. "But I'm going to need some time before I get there."

Carefully, he placed the letter down, knowing full well that it needed to last the rest of his life. He grabbed the scrapbook. It was nothing fancy from the cover, burgundy with a gold embossed title, *For P.J..* He smiled. *It kind of looks like a menu,* he thought, his heart flooded with the warmth of a hundred priceless memories.

He opened the front cover to see a photo of Maddie, him, and the baby; all three had been laughing when the picture was taken. *Oh Maddie,* he thought, a new wave of tears breaking free and racing down his cheeks. Through blurred vision, he studied the picture for a long while before flipping the page.

Next was a letter from Maddie to their son, the page's border stickered with red and pink hearts. Knowing he'd need the oxygen, Phinn sucked in a few deep breaths and began to read.

P.J., when you came into the world covered in your own poop, I knew you'd have a great sense of humor. I also fell head over heels in love that day!

Each day that I've watched you grow into a kind and sensitive little boy, I have been filled with more pride than I could ever explain. My life has never been the same since you came into it, and I thank God for that every day.

From your very first bre ath, I needed to be the best mom I could be for you. And because of that, you made me a better person. Thank you for that, P.J.

As you continue to grow and become the good man I know you'll be, there are things that I really need you to know.

Phinn turned the thick page.

Above all else—LOVE; this message was located in the middle, while the rest of the page was decorated in Maddie's pencil drawings and photos of their family. Phinn gasped at the sight of it.

Finally drumming up the strength, he turned the page.

It's one life—YOUR life, P.J.—so make it a great one. There were more stickers and doodles, and his wife's personal photos.

While a cascade of tears impaired his vision, Phinn turned the page.

Never be afraid to fail. Sometimes, you'll have to fail many times before you succeed, Maddie wrote to their son.

Each page had a single quote surrounded by photos of Maddie, Phinn and P.J., each memory with a caption beneath it explaining the experience. "Thanks for taking all of these pictures," he whispered, imagining her telling him, *I told you so.* He smiled at the thought of it.

Phinn flipped through the beautiful scrapbook.

Please have the courage to follow the dreams that you keep in your heart. Even if that path is a scary one, trust me—it'll be worth it.

Don't worry so much. Have faith that everything will turn out okay, because it will.

You're never alone—ever. Phinn read that one a half dozen more times, adopting it as his new mantra.

You are perfect, exactly the way God made you, so never try to be someone that you're not.

Be polite and kind to all people, P.J. These traits will define your character.

Say your prayers. Faith will help you through the tough times. The sun won't shine every day, but the rain doesn't last forever either.

Enjoy the little things in life that make you smile and laugh because those will be the things you remember.

Give your very best in everything you do, P.J. No one—including you—could ever ask for more than that.

Flipping past dozens of pages, Phinn finally arrived at the last page.

And know, always, that your mom loves you. Actually, the word love may be an understatement. I adore you, P.J.—always have, always will.

Wiping his eyes, Phinn closed the cover for a moment. "Maddie's still here with us," he realized aloud. "I don't have to raise P.J. alone." He opened the book again and started from the beginning. *Thank you, babe.*

• • •

Weeks went by before Julia insisted that P.J. and George sleep over her house. "Phinn, it'll be good for you to have some time to yourself," she suggested.

The very idea terrified Phinn, reminding him of his life before Maddie. Still, he agreed.

After dropping off the toddler and his dog, Phinn had no clue where to go or what to do. *I guess I'll just head back to an empty house,* he decided, dreading the long night ahead of him.

As he pulled into his driveway, he spotted Jacob sitting on his stoop. *So this whole thing was a set up,* he thought, his heart starting to drum in his chest.

"Hey Phinn," Jacob said, standing to greet him, "I was hoping we could talk."

"Wow, I wonder how you knew I'd be alone and available to talk?" Phinn asked, his words dripping with contempt.

Jacob shook his head. "Don't be upset, brother," he said. "We're all worried about you and…"

"I don't need the games, Jake," Phinn interrupted. "I understand that everyone wants to help and I appreciate it, but I can't take…"

"I get it," Jacob said, "I get it." He reclaimed his seat on the stoop. "So can we talk?"

With a heavy sigh, Phinn took a seat beside him.

After a long silence, Jacob said, "It's best to get it out, Phinn. It helped me heal."

Phinn stared straight ahead. "So you came here to tell me that time will heal this pain in my heart, right?" he asked, his tone bitter.

Jacob shook his head. "No, not time," he said, placing his hand on Phinn's shoulder, "love."

Pure rage made Phinn's head snap sideways. "Wasn't it *love* that caused this pain in the first place?" he roared.

"True," Jacob admitted in his even voice, "but it's that same love that will reunite you and Maddie someday. You have to believe that."

Phinn glared into his brother-in-law's eyes. "I do, huh?" he hissed.

"It's like the poem said," Jacob answered. "In the end, there's only love."

Jacob had hit a nerve. *Oh man…* "So you honestly think you'll be with Miranda again someday?" Phinn inquired, cynically.

"To be honest, brother, when Miranda first died I seriously considered taking my own life so I could be with her…so that she didn't have to be alone."

Phinn's heart skipped a beat. *Jake could be a mind reader,* he thought.

"But something deep inside my soul told me that suicide was the worst thing I could do, that my life wasn't mine to take, and that Miranda would never be alone..." He nodded. "...that nothing is more impossible."

Phinn matched the nod. *I agree,* he thought, *if Maddie taught me anything...*

"So to answer your question—no, I don't *think* that I'll be with my daughter again. I *know* I will," Jacob said. "Haven't you ever felt someone enter a room before you saw them? We're more than just bones and blood, brother." He peered hard into Phinn's eyes and went for broke. "Look, the most brilliant minds to walk this earth claimed that we're energy and in our purest form, we would be light. The good news is, energy can't die, Phinn. It can only be transformed. So the only question left is—where do you believe it goes?"

Phinn threw his face into his hands and started to cry. "So what do I do in the meantime?" he whimpered. "What do I do without Maddie by my side for the rest of my days here?"

"Just take good care of the beautiful gift she gave you."

Through the tears, Phinn looked at Jacob—and finally nodded.

Jacob hugged him. "Open your heart again, my brother. You're surrounded by love."

• • •

Some impossible weeks passed, with one day—sometimes even a single hour—taken at a time. Phinn sat on the weathered park bench, while P.J. played in the massive sand box with two other children. *I hope there aren't any cats living around here,* he thought. Although the thought grossed him out, he couldn't bring himself to pull the boy out and wipe the giant smile from his face.

Over and over, P.J. filled his blue plastic bucket and emptied it—like it was his job. *And P.J. loves his work.*

Phinn laughed to himself. *I buy the kid a battery-operated car he can drive around in, and he'd rather play with a two-dollar bucket.*

One of P.J.'s playmates reached for the blue pail. "My turn," he wailed.

"No," P.J. barked back, continuing to scoop and dump.

Phinn stood and approached the massive litter box, with George leading the way. "P.J.," he said, using his stern voice, "you need to share, buddy."

"But Dad."

"No buts! Give your friend a turn."

George barked twice, offering his two cents.

"But he's not my friend, Dad," P.J. said, honestly.

Phinn beat back a smile. "And you won't have any friends unless you can learn how to share, right?"

Although his face was filled with contempt, P.J. reluctantly handed over the bucket.

"Good boy," Phinn said, nodding.

The other kid filled the pail halfway, dumped it out and then lost interest—abandoning the task for his next impulse.

Smiling, P.J. resumed his landscaping project.

Laughing to himself, Phinn whistled for George; the two returned to the bench to see a woman sitting there.

"I'm sorry," she said. "Did I steal your bench?"

Phinn shook his head. "It's not my bench."

She patted the seat beside her. "Good thing there's room for the both of us," she said, flashing two rows of straight white teeth. She was attractive, maybe his age, with a smile that made her eyes look like they were on fire. "I've seen you here before," she said, "but I never had the guts to say hi."

Sitting on his haunches, George released a low growl.

Phinn nodded, remaining focused on P.J.'s construction site.

"Hi," she said.

He looked at her and smiled. "Hi."

"I'm Amanda."

"Phinn." He shook her hand.

George growled again.

There was silence for an awkward moment or two.

"It's not easy being a single parent, is it?" Amanda said, almost as if she were talking to herself.

So she's on a fishing expedition, Phinn realized. *Ugh.* He shook his head. "It's definitely not something I'd planned," he said, surprising himself.

"How long have you been divorced?" she asked, sliding closer.

Phinn turned to look her in the eye. "My wife passed away last year," he said.

"Oh, I'm so sorry."

"Thank you," Phinn said.

"I'm divorced," she said. "It's been two years."

George whimpered, as though he'd heard enough.

Phinn nodded. *And you've been lonely ever since, right?* he asked her in his head. *How strange,* he thought, softening his gaze, *that I lost my spouse to death but may actually be in a better place than Amanda.*

There was silence again, something Amanda clearly couldn't

accept. "Hopefully, someday we'll both find someone," she said.

Phinn smiled, kindly. *Thank God I don't need someone other than my son to complete me,* he thought, and stood. George followed suit. "Maybe someday," he said. "In the meantime, you take good care of yourself." With a quick wave, he headed over to the sandbox.

"Come on, P.J., we need to get going."

"But I don't want to go yet," the boy said, still excavating his heart out.

George barked again, supporting his master.

"Now," Phinn said, reverting to the stern tone.

"Can't you just talk to your friend some more?" P.J. asked.

"My friend?"

P.J. pointed toward Amanda.

"She's not my friend, buddy," Phinn said, honestly. "Now let's go!"

They were a half dozen steps from the car when Mason Sterne approached.

"Hi Phinn," the taller boy said, wearing his usual grin. "How have you been?" He waved at P.J., who returned the gesture.

"I'm okay, I guess," Phinn said. "How about you, Mason?"

"Oh, I'm always good." he answered, honestly.

Phinn nodded, thinking, *I wish I knew your secret, kid.*

Mason's smile turned mischievous, like he wanted to share the secret but was sworn to keep it.

• • •

That night Phinn's cell phone rang. He looked at the caller ID. *It's Micah,* he thought, and quickly answered it.

"I'm not sure if it's still a really bad time, Phinn," the teenager said, "but I was hoping I could see you."

"Of course," Phinn said, pushing George onto his side of the bed, "I'm sorry I haven't been…"

"No worries," Micah said, "I'm not calling because I need something."

"You're not?"

"No," the kid said. "You've done so much for me, Phinn, and I was thinking that maybe it's my turn." He paused. "I'd like to make you feel better." He coughed, clearing his throat. "Or at least try."

"That sounds great," Phinn said. "I really appreciate that."

"So when can we get together and shoot some hoops?" Micah asked.

"How does tomorrow sound?"

"Sounds good to me," he said.

"I've missed you," Phinn said, honestly.

While his master was distracted, George inched back until they were touching.

There was a long pause on the other end of the phone. "Me, too," Micah whispered, "and I can't wait to whoop your butt again on the court."

Phinn chuckled. *I think spending time with Micah is exactly what the doctor ordered,* he thought, wondering whether their paths crossed so that he could help the teenager—*and not the other way around.*

With P.J. in one arm, Phinn hugged Micah with the other. "How are you?" he asked the teenager.

"Oh, I'm okay," Micah said. "The real question is—how are you?"

Phinn looked at P.J. and grinned. "One day at a time, my friend," he said, putting the toddler down. "But we'll be okay, thanks."

"Good to hear it," Micah said.

"So are you ready to shoot some hoops?"

Looking down at the little boy, Micah shrugged. "If it's cool with you, I'd rather play with P.J.?"

Phinn nodded, his eyes filling as he watched P.J. and Micah walk off to play on the parquet floor. *My boy has grown*, he thought, and he wasn't referring to his son.

CHAPTER 20

Impossible weeks ground their way into difficult months.

It was dawn. With P.J. and George at Julia's for their weekly pajama party, Phinn instinctively headed to Brayton Point Park. *I still feel so lost,* he thought, as the morning light struggled to wipe away the darkness. As he started walking, he noticed Mr. Tetreault's silhouette lingering in the distance. He hurried to him.

As if he expected Phinn's visit, the man nodded his usual greeting. "How are you, my friend?"

"The truth?" Phinn shrugged. "I feel like I'm standing in quicksand...like I'll never find my way out. I wish I could just close my eyes and sleep forever."

"That sounds like a permanent solution to a temporary problem."

"I wasn't talking about suicide," Phinn clarified.

"Good," Mr. Tetreault said, "but either way, you wouldn't be there for P.J., would you? And he needs you."

Phinn nodded, but didn't respond.

"I had a niece, Gail, from Connecticut who was born with a birth defect that affected her sight," Mr. Tetreault began to explain. "By the time she was seven, the doctors fitted her with a glass eye." He shook his head. "As you know, kids can be cruel—but probably no more unkind than Gail was to herself."

Phinn struggled to pay attention.

"So one day," Mr. Tetreault continued, "Gail decided she'd taken enough. She was walking on the sidewalk of a busy street when, without warning, she stepped out into traffic, right in front of a pickup truck."

"Oh my God," Phinn blurted, suddenly alert. "Maddie knew your niece. She told me about Gail. They were childhood friends."

Mr. Tetreault nodded. "Small world," he commented. "They said Gail died instantly." He shook his head. "Do you know that I felt so bad for the driver of that pickup that I spent the next two years travelling back and forth to Stamford, doing everything I could to keep him from taking his own life? Now how crazy is that?"

Phinn nodded.

"From then on," Mr. Tetreault said, "I dedicated my life to helping others." He stopped to peer into Phinn's eyes. "So you see, we all have a story to tell. We all carry some heavy cross and experience our fair share of pain in this world. But it's what you do with that pain that defines your life, Phinn. It's bizarre, but my life was nothing until my niece died. I was drifting along in a state of oblivion. But since the greatest tragedy I could have ever imagined, I've helped many people in her name." He smiled. "Phinn, you just need to decide what you're going to do with your tragedy." He inhaled deeply. "And you'd better be careful what you ask for," he added, his tone firm.

Phinn's head flew up. "I wasn't talking about suicide," he reminded him.

"Maybe not, but you did mention wishing to close your eyes and sleep forever." He shook his head.

"You're a very religious man, aren't you?" Phinn asked.

Mr. Tetreault grinned. "Not at all. I rely on *faith*. I suppose you could say that I have an understanding that we're just spirits having a human experience."

That's the same thing Maddie used to say, Phinn recalled.

Mr. Tetreault forged on. "Stop seeing the world through your eyes, Phinn. That's true *faith,*" he said, adding a subtle shrug. "The good Lord doesn't take without giving in return."

Nothing could ever replace Maddie, Phinn thought, holding his tongue.

Mr. Tetreault also kept his silence, waiting for Phinn to speak.

"You once told me that I could have whatever I wished," Phinn said. "We ask and God delivers, remember?" He didn't await an answer. "From the moment we learned that Maddie was sick, I begged for her to get well. Night after night, I pleaded with God." He shook his head. "But my prayers obviously fell on deaf ears."

"Sure, God will deliver," the wise man said, "whatever you wish for *your* life, not someone else's."

Phinn pondered this.

"From where you stand right now, Phinn, what is it that you want most?" he asked, every one of his words deliberate.

"To be at peace...to be happy again."

"Then *be* happy again."

Phinn looked at his mentor in disbelief.

"We don't *do* happy," the man explained. "We simply decide to *be* that way and then we are. Phinn, we can't always choose what happens to us, but we can choose how we think or feel about it. And whatever attitude we adopt, that's exactly what will dictate the life we live."

It made sense, making Phinn feel better; it was a sign that he was finally getting his feet under him. "You make it sound so easy," he muttered.

"Because it is," Mr. Tetreault said. "Life *is* simple. We're the ones who make it difficult." He offered a wink to drive the point home. "Believe me, when you get to the end of your road and look back, you're going to see that it was the small things, the moments that seemed inconsequential at the time, where your journey took place."

Phinn found it peculiar that the man was suggesting that he look back on a life yet to be lived. "What about just being a good dad?" Phinn asked. "Would that be enough?"

"Are you kidding?" Mr. Tetreault said, grinning. "That would be everything." Phinn was taking it all in when Mr. Tetreault grabbed his shoulders, peered into his eyes, and went for the kill. "Phinn, every morning for the rest of your life, ask yourself, *Is this who I want to be today?*" He shrugged. "When you're that aware of the responsibility you have for your own life, every decision you make will take you one step closer to whatever it is that you want. Perseverance will take care of the rest. But the catch is…" He dove even deeper into Phinn's eyes. "These choices can only apply to *your* life."

A slight grin worked its way into Phinn's granite face. "You would have made a great preacher."

"No," Mr. Tetreault said, "people don't listen to preachers. They listen to friends."

Phinn extended his hand. "Thank you for everything, my friend."

"That's what I'm here for," Mr. Tetreault said. "You're going to be fine." He nodded, knowingly. "The both of you."

Phinn's eyes filled. For the first time, they were tears of relief.

"I know I've said it before," Mr. Tetreault began, "but…"

"But?"

"Don't be so serious, Phinn," the man said, smirking. "It's only life."

Phinn's skin tingled from deja vu. He returned the smile to his teacher, watching as Mr. Tetreault walked off into the distance until he became a silhouette that grew smaller until it completely disappeared.

When I was young, Phinn thought, *I used to think that to be family you had to share a last name, the same blood.* He thought about Mr. Tetreault and smirked. *How crazy is that?*

Phinn sat alone on his grassy hill on the Taunton River. Wiping his eyes, he adjusted his gaze to the heavens above. "Maddie," he whispered, "I love you with all my heart, I do. But you're right. I have to go on with my life now. For P.J.'s sake...for my own sake."

"It's about time, my love," Maddie whispered on the wind.

Deaf to the afterlife, Phinn stood and headed home to his son.

● ● ●

That night—with P.J. and George safely tucked in until morning—Phinn fell asleep.

In the dark abyss, he could hear the faint sound of a heart monitor flatlining. *Oh no*, he thought.

● ● ●

Phinn opened one eye to see Death standing before him, shaking his disappointed head. "It's not looking all that promising for you now, is it?" he said, laughing.

Phinn felt desperate. "I've...I've had many friends in my life," he vowed, opening the other eye, "I swear I have."

"Really? I suppose that would depend on your definition of friendship. People who feel bad for you or are nice to you only because they need something from you can hardly be considered friends." He laughed again. "You really haven't learned a whole lot during your time here on earth, have you?" Before Phinn could answer, Death checked his watch. "Okay, enough foolishness. We both know that there's no one who will go with you." He turned to start their journey. "We need to ride. I've got a lot of..."

God suddenly appeared. "I'll take it from here," He said.

"But boss," Death said, "we were just..."

"I've changed my mind. It's not Phinn's time yet." He smiled. "Besides, Maddie's been singing his praises upstairs." Although God was still speaking to Death, He looked Phinn square in the eye. "Phinn still has much work to do before he comes home."

"Thank God," Phinn said.

"Oh, and you should do just that," Death quipped before placing his icy hand on Phinn's shoulder. "Make the most of the time you have left, kid. You never know when I'll be back for you." He vanished into thin air.

Phinn turned to God. "I'm going to honor Maddie's memory by making many beautiful memories with our son," he promised. "And I'll live each day to the fullest, with unbridled kindness for my fellow man and for myself."

"That's a good start," God said. "I like where you're heading. We have to move ourselves before we can move the hearts of others." He laughed. "As a poet, you should understand that more than most."

Right then, Phinn decided to capture his own life—his past memories, present experiences, and future dreams—in a collection of verse. "Maddie loved my poetry," he said aloud.

"She still does," God told him.

"That's how I'll touch other souls," Phinn announced excitedly. *And as a bonus*, he thought, *I'll pass this gift onto P.J. to teach him everything I've learned along the way.*

"Priceless bonus, if you ask me," God said, letting Phinn know He could read his every thought. "The secret to a successful life is not found in answering life's great questions, my son," God explained, "but in asking." He nodded. "Allow the journey to inspire the poetry within, Phinn, not the idea of actually finishing the trip."

• • •

Phinn awoke from his dream and shot up in bed—with God's wisdom still echoing in his pounding head.

That's it! I'm going to put together a collection of my poems for P.J., he thought, determined to unify his verse and prose into a work of love. *I'll draw inspiration from family, friends, and the kindness of strangers*, he further decided, nodding, *and capture our lives through poetry.*

He looked toward the ceiling. "I'll make you proud of me, Maddie," he whispered, "If it's the last thing I do, I'll make you proud of me, babe."

• • •

P.J. was nearly three years old when Maddie and Phinn's dream home, a full-dormered Cape, was built on the side of Brayton Point Park. Two Adirondack chairs—one large and one small—sat on a big, wrap-around porch that faced the river. Skylights, located above the bedrooms, glistened in the sun. *So I can look up at Maddie each night before I fall asleep*, Phinn thought. *And I'll start the landscape next season, though there's not much to design there.* He smiled. *Maddie was very detailed about what she wanted.*

Phinn was putting the finishing touches on a sandcastle he'd built for his son when the boy ran over and fell on it, crushing most of it. Phinn shook his head and laughed. He picked up the boy and tossed him into the air a few times. As P.J. reached hysterics, Phinn whistled for George. The dog approached with a red tattered leash hanging from his salivating jowls.

While Phinn used his free hand to hold George's leash, he and P.J. walked along the river. A couple hundred yards into their stroll, they ran into Mr. Tetreault.

"Hi P.J.," the man said, taking a knee and fist bumping the little boy.

"Hi, Mr. T.," P.J. said.

Mr. Tetreault looked up at Phinn. "I've just gotten an opportunity to help some folks down in the Carolinas, so I'll be out of town for a while."

"Really? How long?"

Standing, the older man shrugged. "Until they don't need me anymore, I suppose."

"An angel that travels," Phinn joked.

"Thanks for the compliment," Mr. Tetreault said, chuckling, "though I doubt my ex-wife would agree with you."

Phinn laughed.

"Are you good?" the sage asked, peering into Phinn's eyes.

"I'm good," Phinn answered, nodding.

"Good."

"Thank you," Phinn said, and meant it.

"You're welcome, Phinn." He looked down at P.J. "Take care of your dad for me, okay?"

"I will," the boy said, and meant it.

Both men smiled before exchanging a hug. "You have my number," Mr. Tetreault said. "Let's not wait another twenty years before we speak again."

"I plan to stay in touch," Phinn said, "I promise."

"Good," Mr. Tetreault said and then turned his body toward a new journey filled with joy—and its fair share of pain.

As his mentor faded into the distance, Phinn looked down at P.J. "So you're going to take care of me, huh?" he asked, smiling.

P.J. nodded, his face serious. "Yup, I am."

Shielding his eyes from the sun's glare, Phinn peered into the sky. "Thank you, Maddie," he whispered. "Thank you for this amazing boy."

As he unleashed George and let him run free, he and P.J. continued down the river bank—hand in hand—toward the sunset. With peace in his heart, he glanced down at his smiling son once more before reciting his newest poem in his head.

Are We There Yet?

Holding to a steady pace,
from the back seat came a voice.
In belief that life was one long race
and fate, a simple choice.

"Are we there yet?" was his main concern,
as he twisted in his seat.
And I felt the sorrow he would learn
for the trials he had to meet.

"A few more miles…a little while,"
though I knew the trip was long.
But in the mirror, beamed a smile,
for my word could not be wrong.

So we talked and laughed, we shared the ride
and in time he took the wheel.
Through the years, we traveled side by side,
to think, to hope and feel.

Then I turned to him—my tired voice,
"Are we there yet?" was my plea.
He grinned and said, "That's God's own choice!"
For at last, my boy could see.

• • •

The clock continued to tick, while one sheet after the next was torn from the calendar. Feeling inspired, Phinn commissioned a finish carpenter from Maine to build a box for P.J., a wooden box worthy of holding a priceless treasure—Maddie's scrapbook. It was constructed of oak with a strip of zebra wood running the length of the lid, the entire thing satin finished, with burgundy-colored felt—a tinge somewhere between wine and blood—lining the interior. A brass plaque, with the inscription, *P.J., Enjoy the Journey, Love Dad,* was fastened to the front.

A framed photo of Maddie was the first item placed into the box. P.J.'s scrapbook went next, followed by a stack of early photos held together by a rubber band.

Phinn prepared to drop in his first collection of poetry. Entitled *In Layman Terms,* it remained unpublished. *Who cares,* he thought, *as long as P.J. reads it someday.* The collection included everything he'd learned and composed since his boy's birth, poems such as *Lost & Found, Once, Ten Lifetimes More, Unity, Dream Chaser, More than Our Share,* and *Are We There Yet?*

In that moment, he felt overwhelmed with gratitude for all the people and experiences that made up the whole of his life. *Every one of us is just trying to make the most of the time we're given,* he'd learned along the way, *and in the end, have our time on earth make a difference.*

When he'd lost Maddie, Phinn believed that she'd taken a piece of him with her. What he now realized was that she'd left many pieces of herself behind, and that he was one of those pieces. The poetry book was a tribute to that love, as it was an homage for the dreams he had for P.J. and the gratitude he felt for his own life. *We were all connected long before we came into this world,* he finally believed, *have been blessed to share our journeys together, and will remain connected long after we all leave this place.*

As he started to place the book into the box, he was surprised to discover that offering his son this gift didn't have the same effect he'd once hoped. He now understood that he wasn't going to spare the young lad even the smallest amount of pain. Like him and his father before him, Phinneas Reed, Jr. was destined to travel his own roads and learn his own lessons. *The most I can hope for is that P.J. knows he'll be loved forever.* He smiled. *I'm the one who's learned through the poetry,* he realized. *But as P.J. faces his own set of trials and tribulations, at least he'll know that his father's done the same and is right there with him—always. He'll know that he's not alone.*

Phinn flipped the poetry manuscript to the first page and wrote, *P.J., my son, take responsibility for your life. Whether it's happiness or misery, it's your choice. All My Love, Always—Dad.* As he completed the inscription, he thought about his beautiful boy and nodded. Alas, the circle was complete. He had no idea what the future held for either of them, but he was fairly certain that P.J. was destined to do great things and make a positive difference in this world. *I just know it.* He placed the book into the box.

• • •

More months passed at their usual pace. P.J. was playing with one of his toys, when he took notice of his mother's photo and smiled.

"That's your mom," Phinn explained, watching the small boy. "She loves you very much." He collected himself with a few deep breaths. "She got sick and had to go to heaven…"

"I know," P.J. said.

"You know?"

"I know Mommy," P.J. said. "She loves me a lot. I remember her from heaven."

"You remember heaven?" Phinn asked, shocked.

The boy smiled wider. "Yeah, it's beautiful there, Dad. Everything's gold, even the grass. People can fly, if they want to." He returned to playing, as though he hadn't uttered a word.

"And you remember Mommy?" Phinn asked, his eyes misting over.

The boy nodded, his attention still on his toy. "Yeah, I was thrown into a trash can before you and Mommy came to get me out."

Oh, my God, Phinn thought, unable to stifle a gasp—and suddenly feeling the distinct touch of his wife's hand on his shoulder. *Oh, Maddie,* he thought, while both his heart and eyes filled.

P.J. looked up at his father. "That's okay, Dad. I knew you loved me."

Phinn couldn't speak for a long while. "And Mommy?"

"She loves me too," he said. "Don't worry. We'll all be together again."

"We will?"

"Of course, Dad," the boy said, matter-of-factly. "We're family." He smiled again.

While Phinn tried to process this divine insight, P.J. returned to playing. "Dad, what's the first poem you ever wrote for me?" he asked.

Phinn thought about it for a moment. *There have been so many already.* And then it came to him, the memory smacking him in the forehead like a sledgehammer. "It was called *Unborn Child,*" he told the grinning boy.

"Can you read it to me?" P.J. asked.

Phinn's brow creased. "I may need a little time to remember it," he said, "I wrote it a long time ago, buddy…long before you ever came into the world."

"That's okay," P.J. said, his grin intact, "we've got time."

Phinn searched his mind. "Unborn child, my future friend," he recited from memory, "into the womb, this vow I send—upon your birth, I'll take your hand and carry you until you stand."

Putting down his toy, P.J. reached for his father's hand.

Phinn held the boy tight, as he continued on. "Unborn child, I've seen your face, within my dreams, a kinder place…"

• • •

It was eternal dawn. Two silhouettes stood in a cloud. Maddie clasped both of her hands on her chest in a display of love.

God looked at her. "Now do you see that there's a perfect plan for everyone?" He asked, smiling.

She nodded. "I do," she said, "and I'm so very grateful, but…"

"But?"

"Did I fulfill my life's purpose, Father?" she asked, hopefully.

God wrapped His great arms around her. "Madelyn, my child, you asked that your life would make a difference." A giant smile illuminated His face. "You made all the difference in the world," He said, pointing down at Phinn and P.J. "You introduced soul mates."

EPILOGUE

Golden finches, blue jays, and humming birds met at Maddie's feeders, while pairs of turtle-doves chased each other at play. Ground cover of ivy and moss blanketed the stone wall in her backyard, and beyond it, there was a vast, sweet-smelling pine grove with ranks of soft-needle trees. Rows of box hedge met a giant weeping willow tree, a tire swing hanging from its massive limb. Every detail was exactly how she imagined it.

Out front, there were two wine barrels cut in half, used as planters. Daisies, crocuses, daffodils, and mums complemented the red and pink roses that climbed Maddie's white lattice trellises. Out back, a stack of split cordwood separated her yard from the neighbor's barking dog. A square of vegetable garden produced fresh tomatoes and cucumbers. And she'd finally perfected Nana's French toast recipe.

Like two white dandelions that floated on air, enjoying a gentle breeze, it was the ideal place for Maddie and Raymond to waste the lazy days away.

When she wasn't home, Maddie spent much of her time—if that's what you call it—traveling. She and Raymond would often visit the Taunton River for a taste of salt air or western Massachusetts for a peek at the starry sky. She also discovered that St. Lucia was Raymond's favorite sunset too.

And even though Phinn and P.J. never knew it, Maddie had learned to be anywhere they were—at the speed of thought.

IN BEFORE THE DARK
by P.J. Reed

I begged and pleaded, "Let me go. I swear, I won't go far."
He said, "It hurts to watch you grow…
be in before the dark."

I headed out, this stubborn child, a world away from home.
He held my hand through every mile,
not once I walked alone.

I laughed and loved and worked and played,
ignoring every clock,
but heard those words each time I prayed…
"be in before the dark."

I braved the winds and blinding snow, but also felt the sun.
For sixty years of joy and pain,
I stayed out on the run.

Then on it came, the first street light—yet still came as a shock.
As Father called me from the night…
"be in before the dark."

ABOUT THE AUTHOR

Steven Manchester is the author of the #1 bestsellers *Twelve Months, The Rockin' Chair, Pressed Pennies* and *Gooseberry Island;* the national bestsellers, *Ashes, The Changing Season* and *Three Shoeboxes;* the multi-award winning novel, *Goodnight Brian;* and the beloved holiday podcast drama, *The Thursday Night Club*. His work has appeared on NBC's Today Show, CBS's The Early Show, CNN's American Morning and BET's Nightly News. Three of Steven's short stories were selected "101 Best" for Chicken Soup for the Soul series. He is a multi-produced playwright, as well as the winner of the 2017 Los Angeles Book Festival and the 2018 New York Book Festival. When not spending time with his beautiful wife, Paula, or their children, this Massachusetts author is promoting his works or writing. Visit: www.StevenManchester.com

Made in USA - Kendallville, IN
1226554_9780984184255
02.22.2021 1653